Blood and Bone

Blood and Bone: The Redspot Chronicles

Nora Ashe

To request permissions, contact the publisher at contact@boundtobrew.com

Library of Congress Cataloging-in-Publication Data has been applied for.

ISBN 978-1-953500-00-7

First Edition

Edited by Team LLC

Printed by Steuben Press in USA

Team Publishing
9457 S University Blvd. 819 Highlands Ranch, CO 80126

Boundtobrew.com

Acknowledgements

They say it takes a village to raise a child. Well, apparently, it also takes one to write a book. In light of that, I'd like to thank the following people:

To my parents, Mike and Susan, for always supporting me and to my partner, Alex, for being my rock.

To all my friends who listened to me talk for hours on end about strange medical procedures, and especially to Brendan, Alex J, Sheila, and Carlos for reading all my attempts to pen them.

To the team at Bound to Brew for all their hard work in helping me make my dream come true.

And, of course, you, dear reader, for taking the time to read the book!

Thank you all. It's been quite a journey.

CONTENTS

CHAPTER ONE
The Nest

Shafts of early morning sunlight reflected off the dead cars that lined the street. Most still had windows, although many were boarded up with wood and scraps, transforming the cars into makeshift shelters. Gasoline had long been funnelled out of them, and into cars that had escaped Toronto four years ago, at the start of the second wave of Redspot.

The sky was a deep, cloudless blue. It offered no reprieve from the hot September sun. I glanced up, blinking away the sweat that threatened to drip into my eyes. Overhead, a red-tailed hawk circled lazily.

Shielding my eyes, I quickly scanned the high-rises that reached for the sky. In the decaying ruins of Toronto, Rotters and Bleeders alike were hidden in the skyscrapers. The soulless buildings seemed to stare back at me, as I wondered how many infected lay within their walls.

I was roused from my thoughts when our newest squad member, a baby-faced recruit named Brad Jameson, leaned on the wall beside me, fanning himself. "Hey-a,

Clara." He scrunched his face and corrected himself, "I mean 'Belford.'" He was nineteen years old, like me, and still new enough to make a lot of minor mistakes. He glanced over to the Squad's Sergeant, Piper Longboat, who stood next to Mona Rossi, in the alleyway. Both women had their masks slung around their necks, just like I did. Mona was an Italian American from Brooklyn. She liked to joke that she owned the streets both before and after the pandemic, but her attitude out in open Rotter territory showed she was dead serious. She led Fireteam Alpha, which consisted of myself, Brad, and the team medic, Evan Reihman. Piper oversaw both Fireteam Alpha and Bravo, which formed Squad 13. Her high cheekbones and dark eyes made me think she was from the Iroquois Nation.

Piper's short grey hair shone like silver in the September sun, whereas Mona's charcoal hair seemed to absorb it. Stamped on their backs was the Facility's emblem: a snake twisted around a rod with a fish in its mouth. It marked them as being part of the security faction at Runar's Institute of Virology and Infectious Disease Research Facility.

We paused in the alcove of an alleyway before moving to the main street. Piper pulled out her radio and buzzed back to Strategy for an update on any biological attacks or hot zones in the Old City.

This scouting trip was our last mission in the downtown area before we suited up for tonight's patrol in the Clarington Colony. There were rumours of an attack underway, either on the powerplant in Clarington or in the Old City, on the Facility itself. Piper, as usual, had one last thing she wanted us to check out. I gave Brad a sidelong glance. She probably squeezed in a scouting trip, so the new guy's first mission wasn't at Darlington. The nuclear power plant was intimidating, even when everything was ok.

I glanced back at the Facility. Pristine, it shimmered amidst the ruins of other skyscrapers. Once one of the top cancer research hospitals in the world, after the pandemic hit, the building was retrofitted with Biosafety Level 2 and Level 4 laboratories to research both deadly mutations of the virus: Wave Two and Wave Three.

Brad's face was already ruddy with sweat, just like mine. "Holy hell, is all this gear hot."

I was glad that the scarf I wore over my face hid the smirk that fell on my lips. "Just wait 'til after the scouting's finished, and we actually have to suit up. Those CBRN suits are no joke." I laughed, but it sounded a little hysterical to my ears. Chemical, Biological, Radiological, and Nuclear suits were heavy, hot, and only meant to be worn in places where we might be exposed to things that were both lethal and invisible.

Evan joined us in the shadows. He tapped his Medi-kit repeatedly, like he was afraid it was going to fall off his pack. Evan was a mousey-haired guy with ropey muscles who was way too tightly wound up. In fact, the only time he ever looked relaxed was when he was covered in blood, giving first aid. He waved but didn't say anything.

Brad faced me and asked, "So, where are your bites? I heard your infection was messy." He leaned towards me and whispered inquisitively, "Is it somewhere I'm not allowed to see?"

I laughed, despite myself. *Maybe my nerves have gotten to me.* "A bit messy, yeah. I had to get a blood transfusion. Wanna see 'em?" I tugged off my gloves and rolled my sleeve up to my forearm, showing off the bite on my wrist. Brad squinted as he looked down at it. The patch was impeccably done. The two shades of pink were almost seamless as the skin transitioned to the graft.

"That's it?" He pulled off his own glove and ran his fingers along the patch of foreign skin. "Looks like a birthmark. You had to get hospitalized for that?"

I stepped away from the wall to shrug off my rifle sling,

then pulled aside the collar of my undershirt to show off my other mark. "Actually, this guy is why I needed the blood transfusion."

Brad's eyes widened as he took in the smooth, chocolate-coloured mark that ran from my upper bicep to the edge of my collar bone. The dark flesh ended abruptly like a large freckle. "Jesus. Did it try to eat your shoulder off?" he said.

Mona wandered up next to us and examined my shoulder with Brad. "No, she used to be into body mods."

He tilted his head as his eyes flitted to the other bits of my visible skin, "Are you serious? You were a mercenary?"

I snorted, "Do I strike you as a Leuko?"

Mona's eyes glinted wickedly as she waited for Command to give us the all-clear. She made sure her radio was off before she said, "I wouldn't be surprised if you ran with those assholes before the Facility picked you up." She laughed when my mouth dropped open in mock outrage and added, "I'm just saying you're a good shot, Belford. That's all." I chuckled and shook my head at her, feigning disappointment.

Evan leaned in closer to my shoulder. "Exquisite patch, though. Mine are always lumpy." I took a moment to look over my smooth skin with pride. The patch was done by the founder of the Facility himself, Dr. Runar. After the hospital had all but been abandoned during the economic collapse, Dr. Runar used his military connections and scientific prestige in the virology community to start the Facility. He was one of the first infected with the necrotizing strain of the virus, a mutation that turned people into Rotters, where the flesh rotted off their bones while they lived. That was two years ago. Now, instead of rotting, he was spearheading the cure effort. To date, he was the only person to have lived longer than two years after infection. Most of us lasted about six months to a year.

I traced my fingers along the edge of my patch as I thought about Dr. Runar. A smile came to my lips as I recalled the first time we met.

***

It was four months ago, in his office. Inside, wall-to-wall bookshelves made of gilded wood were filled with medical textbooks that ranged from shiny, barely touched paperbacks, to old leather-bound hardcovers.

In the middle of the room was an ornate, beautifully carved desk. A plaque with large gold letters reading 'Dr. Braeden Runar MD MSPH' sat alongside various piles of paper. The high-back chair behind the desk had been empty; its occupant across the room, looking out a large window. I paused in the doorway, unsure of what to do.

He must have sensed me because he turned from the window, and my breath caught. In front of me was one of the most handsome men I had ever seen.

His eyes beamed with intelligence, framed by a thick fringe of black eyelashes. They studied me with intensity. His lips formed a perfect cupid's bow, promising a dazzling smile. At the time, though, his face had been solemn and worn.

A dark five o'clock shadow dusted his jawline, and I got the impression that even if he just shaved, dark stubble would still be visible. No hair grew in the middle of his chin because of a shiny white scar.

"Hey, you're awake," he said. His pale skin was nearly translucent, the bruises beneath his black eyes revealed he hadn't slept properly in months. Yet, as tired as he was, his smile was warm. "How are you feeling?"

His midnight eyes swept over me appraisingly. I realized belatedly how ridiculous I must've looked— standing there in my sweat-stained hospital gown, with mussed hair, holding onto my IV drip. His deep voice was soft as he added, "How is your shoulder?"

"Oh," I was taken aback. I involuntarily touched my right shoulder where the new flesh sat hidden beneath the fabric.

"Yeah, it's fine."

He moved from behind the desk and inclined his head towards me in a small bow. "Dr. Braeden Runar. I'm afraid we've only met while you were either hallucinating or unconscious, Miss Belford." Stopping a short distance away, his eyes were intense as he offered me his hand.

"Just call me Clara," My tongue tripped as I slipped my hand into his to shake it.

"All right, Clara." He said my name as though he were tasting it. "Then please call me Braeden."

***

Piper's voice snapped me out of my memory. She announced, "Good news, team. Reports say the area is clear of Wave Two, so we're at MOPP 0 today." It was a military term from the Old States that stood for 'Mission Oriented Protective Posture,' and it designated the level of protective gear we were supposed to wear on missions. I breathed a sigh of relief. Being at MOPP 0 meant the area was low risk for inhaling the strain two mutation, so my hot rubber mask was going to remain around my neck for most of today. The rubber already chafed against my skin. I gulped down air and shut my eyes. Even as early as it was, I could tell today was going to be hot.

With the all-clear, Piper gave us a two-fingered signal to move out. We treaded back along the narrow alley towards the main street. Grass reclaimed the pavement. Tire tracks cut rivets through the path from the Facility to the main street. The farther we wandered from the Facility, the more nature encroached.

The five of us entered a main intersection. The once bustling streets were now silent. Huge looming skyscrapers were reclaimed by nature. Vines crawled up the sides of the buildings and moss covered the stones. Our team kept quiet. We needed to stay alert in open Rotter territory.

In the distance, a crow cawed. Another replied to it.

As I approached the edge of a building, a low groan bellowed from around the corner to my left. Silently, I pulled out my dagger and gestured for my team to halt, signalling to Piper that I could hear only one. She directed me to engage with two fingers and a subtle nod.

I crept closer to the edge of the concrete building. The debris scraped beneath my boot, and the faint shuffling stopped.

I held my breath, counting. My eyes shut briefly as I strained to hear around the other side. Confident only one Rotter awaited me, I opened my eyes. Its shuffle was distinctive, with a rattling breath just out of sight. It was investigating.

Pale, rotted fingers curled around the edge of the building. Time slowed as I slid into my quiet place.

I shifted my blade into my left hand and unholstered my pistol in my right. I stabbed my blade into the back of its hand, holding it in place, trapping the Rotter. A gurgled shriek tore from its throat as I turned around the corner and shot a bullet into its chest.

The Rotter flew back from the impact of the bullet and my blade sliced free of its decayed hand. It lay still where it landed, blood dripping out of its wounds. I holstered my pistol and wiped the blade clean on the twitching pantleg of the dead Rotter. I sheathed it, straightened, and cradled my M4.

Scanning the street ahead of me showed no movement, other than the growing puddle of blood from the Rotter on the ground. Piper confirmed it was clear and signalled for the unit to press forward. According to our briefing, the engineering department noticed an abnormal amount of electricity being used in the Old City, just ahead on the nearly dead grid. That is what Piper wanted to check out before the patrol tonight, even though all other signs pointed to the attack happening at Darlington. She liked to be thorough.

I stepped around the Rotter's body and picked my way through the bits of rubble scattered on the street. Piper must have given a signal behind because the others fanned out into a line on either side of me. We walked apart in the centre of the street. The blown-out windows opened to decrepit department stores and little restaurants; some still had toppled tables and chairs within. Rusty escalators ran into puddles of water from the recent rainfall. Half of the street was partially flooded. The storm drains were buried beneath debris and plant matter.

In the distance, a large Roman Catholic cathedral with a high spire and ornate windows stood proud amongst the skyscrapers: St. Michael's Cathedral Basilica. Scenes of the bible decorated the stained-glass windows, and heavy doors with peeling red paint guarded the entrance. Beyond the wrought iron gates, hundreds of fake and dirtied flowers strewed the cobblestone courtyard. They had become little more than litter on the ground.

"I remember this place," Brad whispered as we approached.

Everyone did.

***

A year and a half ago, the cathedral housed the dead after the Burlington Bay Bridge Massacre, just at the peak of the third wave. Most of the supply lines to the Southern Horseshoe Colonies had been choked off by the Old States. The colonists had been desperate for that fortnight's ration and supply drop from the Facility. Hundreds of famished people in desperate need of supplies came from all over the southern shores of Lake Ontario to the Burlington Bay Bridge.

Rotters were camped on both sides, where the bridge met land. When the supply drop came, they swarmed from the north and south, trapping almost all the uninfected in an ambush. The only people who escaped were the ones that managed to get into the water and swim before the first blood was spilled. Over four hundred were reported dead, many more infected. At the time, the morgues, hospitals, and even the hockey rinks were already filled with Bleeders. They were taken to the cathedral as a last resort.

A plaque gleamed in the autumn sunlight. It was all that remained of the dead. After the incinerators stopped running, their ashes were spread over the lake.

***

Though it was only a year and a half ago, it felt much longer. Piper paused briefly at the brass memorial; her sister had been among the victims.

"Sarge, you're positive the engineers said it was the memorial cathedral?" Brad asked.

Piper raked her hands through her hair, a surefire sign she was agitated. Her teeth were clenched as she replied, "Yeah, Jameson, the engineers pinned this exact spot for the power usage." She turned away from the plaque, her hands gripped her rifle tighter than they had a moment ago. "Remember, the bastards don't hold anything sacred. Let's check it out."

I felt a stab of anger. "I know they say all's fair in love and war, but the way they trapped all those people... I can't believe anyone could be so evil." I said, thinking about the terror and pain.

Brad shrugged, "I can't believe that's what it turned into. It should have always been humanity against the virus. I dunno how we lost sight of that."

"We didn't lose sight of that. They did." I replied with a snarl, tapping the trigger guard with my pointer finger. "They made it into war when they weaponized the infected." I got the feeling Brad wanted to say more, but he kept his mouth shut.

We walked up the concrete steps towards the looming building. After a cursory check from the outside, the chapel appeared empty. The muscles in Brad's shoulders bunched as he pressed both hands against the heavy oak doors. They groaned in protest as he threw them open.

I let out a soft "ooh" as we entered the cavernous, old building. The cathedral's arched ceiling and great stone columns crawled with moss and vines. The windows were dirty but still glistened like jewels as the sun broke through in long, multicoloured beams.

Though the floors were dusty, it was easy to see that beneath the dirt was shining polished stone, laid in a symmetrical pattern down the aisle. At the fluttering of wings, I looked up to see several pigeons flying above.

The team began investigating the church while I proceeded down the main aisle of the nave. The old pews were rotted and overturned. They removed the pews before storing the dead. Even after they started running the incinerators, the stains of rot remained where the infected began to pile up.

Ahead of me was a sanctuary where blue velvet chairs, covered in mould, sat behind a large white altar.

As though it had been left in the middle of Mass, a Bible sat open on the decayed white cloth. The pages were yellowed and worn. Gilded edges of the book flashed brightly, but the ink had almost completely faded. I didn't dare touch the fragile book, convinced it would crumble in my hands. Large candles made of thick beeswax filled the stands around the altar. The holders were made of heavy brass, which shone dully in the sunlight. I moved across the dais towards the old throne. Nothing hid within the chairs flanking the Bishop's cathedra, but something caught my eye to the right.

Partially obscured by spoiled wood piled in the corner was a trapdoor. I stepped over shards of glass and shoved the wood out of the way. The handle was rusted, and the hinges gave a sharp squeal as I lifted it up. Steps led to darkness in front of me. "Guys," I called to Mona and Brad,

"I found something."

Brad grabbed one of the candles off its stand and looked around for something on the altar. "Does anyone have something to light it? A lighter, match, anything?" Brad asked. Mona glared at him.

"Hey, Jameson, how about we don't die in a fiery inferno, and you just stick with the scope lights?" she said as she pointedly clicked hers on. He sheepishly placed the candle back on the stand. I raised my eyebrows at Mona but didn't say anything. It was Jameson's first time outside the Facility since his fever broke. She was usually nicer than that to the new soldiers. Mona rolled her eyes.

Clicking on the light mounted to my gun, I made my way down the steps. It took a few moments for my eyes to adjust in the darkness. As we twisted downwards, the air became cooler, but with the coolness came a stench. "Smells like decay," I whispered into my mic.

"All units, this is Reihman. Masks on." Evan ordered us over the radio. The smell was vaguely sweet at first, but it disappeared once my mask was in place over my face.

The air was brisk as we reached the door to the chapel crypt. Mona pushed it open and my heart stilled as our beams hit rows of pews. Every seat was filled. My light swivelled around the room as I strained to hear any noises. As my eyes darted between each body, I noticed heavy signs of rot, but very little fresh blood. *Good. Probably not hybrids.* We recently learned that someone could be infected with both deadly strains simultaneously. *One was enough, thanks.*

In the corner of the crypt was a pile of bones, some human, some animal. Above the bones, marked in spray paint, was a familiar flourished 'R' with a phoenix flying out of it. My heart thundered in my chest as soon as I saw it.

"All units, we have a nest in the chapel crypt," I said quietly.

11

"Hold until we get there." Sergeant Longboat's voice replied. "Any sign of hostiles?"

"No, but they left their calling sign." I couldn't stop staring at the splattered red paint under the phoenix. *It was supposed to look like fire.*

I tried to tear my eyes away from the stupid symbol, but even when I did, memories played like a clip show inside my head. The first time I saw the phoenix was four months ago, when I still lived in the Oakville Colony.

It was the night I got infected. Unlike this one, that phoenix's red splatter had come from my mom's blood.

***

It was May. The three of us, mom, my brother Leo, and I, were all relaxing in the living room. I was having an especially lazy day. I struck a bargain with my neighbour that we would alternate supply runs for our families. It was my turn to stay home while he braved the trek to collect this fortnight's rations from the drop.

I was cleaning my gun while mom and Leo worked on a puzzle. Looking over at them, it was easy to see that they were cut from the same cloth. They shared the same olive skin and green eyes. Leo wore his hair longer than mom's, so from behind, as their lithe frames both leaned over the puzzle, it almost looked like they were twins. In contrast to them, I had blue eyes, like my dad, and kept my auburn hair short and spiky. The only thing Leo got from his dad was his height; he was 6'4".

Aside from the cosmetic differences between us, Leo and I both had mom's fine bone structure. It was easy to tell that we were related, even if we were half-siblings. *Mom had strong genes, I suppose.*

Leo excused himself to go to the basement. *I couldn't even remember what he was going to go do. What I did remember was it was the last time I ever saw him.* I left my guns unloaded because the neighbourhood kids had been

12

over earlier. *Idiot. I never left my gun unloaded.*

Leo screamed. Not his usual manly yell—he *screamed.* Mom sprinted into the basement after him, gun in hand. I only had my knife on me. I swore and reassembled my gun as quickly as possible. My fingers fumbled as I loaded it. My heart was racing as I heard blasts from my mom's rifle downstairs.

Once it was loaded, I rushed down the stairs to the basement. What I saw was a horror scene. Mom's lifeless eyes looking up at the ceiling while a horde of hungry Rotters tore strips from her body.

Not real. I noticed on the wall, above my mom, the sinister 'R' with the phoenix coming out of the flourish. That was when I learned about the Resistance.

***

To my surprise, my knife was unsheathed in my hand when I snapped myself out of it. My jaw set as I blinked away the moisture from my eyes. Slipping it back into the sheathe, I diverted my scope light to the rot oozing from the bodies in front of me. I took in a few deep breaths and ran through my exercises. I inhaled, focusing on the feel of the gun in my hands. *I was in the chapel crypt, getting even with the Resistance scum.* I exhaled slowly.

As the other two soldiers joined us, their lights created weird shadows in the crypt, making the silhouettes look eerily alive. Plastic sheeting covered the floors and pews. There was an odd trail of dried-up blood on the plastic, but for the number of Rotters, everything was surprisingly clean. If it weren't for them being propped up, I would have thought they were dead.

The lenses of my mask fogged. I wiped at them when I heard the door click shut behind me. Evan shut the door against the warmth, keeping in the cool air. He shrugged and said, "The warm air might rouse them."

Brad was silent next to me. His clothing and hair

blended into the shadows, making his pale skin float in the darkness. I frowned, watching for the rise and fall of the Rotter's chest closest to me.

"Sarge, did Medical request any specimens to be brought back?" Mona whispered.

"I'm gonna guess they'd want them alive," I said as I nudged one with my boot. The lifeless body flopped onto the one next to it. A black outline stained the seat where it had been. The Rotter groaned.

"Oh shit!" I started.

Trying to push itself upright, its skeletal arms with large sores shook with effort. I aimed my pistol, but waited, repeating Mona's question.

Piper responded, "Any signs of fresh bleeding from them? I want to get some of these guys back to Medical if it looks like there's any sign of Wave Two present."

I swept everything again to double-check. "Nope, run-of-the-mill Wave Three Rotters," I said.

"Yeah, Medical has enough of those," Piper replied. Her beam swept along the ceiling of the crypt. "All right, seal it and gas it," she said as she tossed a duffle bag into the centre of the group.

We pulled out plastic, duct tape, and canisters of gas and busied ourselves sealing up the doorways and vents throughout the room.

As Brad and I sealed the door near Piper, I overheard her radio to Command come to life with a burst of static. "Falcon Alpha One Three, this is Striker. Rendezvous at the Grotto, immediately. Over." I paused, my heart racing. The Grotto is where all the squads meet to gear up before raids. *They were calling us back early. The other scouts must have found something.*

Piper pulled the radio up and gestured for us to keep working. "Finish prepping the room for extermination and decontamination." She talked into the radio, "Striker, this is

Falcon Alpha One Three. We've just commenced a D and E. Over."

The crinkling plastic drowned out the sound of Piper's conversation. I kept my focus on the task at hand, and we finished sealing every doorway into the crypt. Its recently renovated doors were modern aluminum with glass, easy enough to seal.

Once we finished, Piper called out to the room, "Everyone, set the canisters, and let's move. Darlington is under attack."

My beam of light landed on the phoenix one last time as the gas canisters erupted with white fog. I had a good feeling about tonight.

CHAPTER TWO
Going Nuclear

The Grotto was massive inside. It was larger than any of the other rooms in the Facility's tunnel network. The lockers lining the walls were colour coded light blue and navy to indicate either Extraction or Harvest Platoon. The soldiers of Harvest Platoon wore heavily camouflaged gear without any identifying symbols, unlike Extraction's light blue suits boasting the Aegis Shield emblem on the back. They stood apart, packing weapons, including several varieties of gas canisters.

I strode over to the equipment lockers filled with specialty gear. The soldiers looked like aliens with their pointed respirators and gas masks. A hulking man named Chase was sitting behind a display made of thick glass. Guns lined the walls behind him, while swords were displayed inside a case. Rows and rows of sterilized gear were labelled and ready to be doled out. Chase and another armoury worker were handing out sealed bags to squad members.

Chase's big voice boomed out to greet me. "Clara, you made it! Let's see what I've got for you today." The smile on his face faltered as he scanned his list. "Do you have an updated medical sign-off for me?" He asked.

My heart dropped. *He noticed.*

"I was out with my team just an hour ago," I said. I hated the note of a plea in my voice. "Come on, man, what's the difference?"

He sighed and sat back in his chair as the line of impatient soldiers grew longer behind me. "Look, a temporary sign-off from anyone other than your primary physician is only valid for two weeks," he rattled off the line from memory. "I can't give you your gear without an up-to-date form. It's the rules."

I stared at the sheet as he slid it across the display case. My primary physician, Dr. Missy O'Donnell, was a foreboding redhead who happened to be one of the Facility's most in-demand surgeons and Braeden's right-hand woman. Even on the best of days, she wouldn't see me with less than three hours' notice. I glanced down at my old form, which held the swooping signature of Dr. Jade Inkerman, another top researcher and surgeon in the Facility. Jade, unlike Missy, almost always had a moment to spare for little ol' me, despite being extremely busy herself.

I'll definitely remember to make an appointment with Missy after this one last time. I grabbed the form from the top of the display case and cut across the room towards the tunnels. At this hour, Jade was probably wrapping up her labs, which meant she would be in BSL-4 on level 2. After meandering through the confusing maze of concrete tunnels, I arrived at the Facility's subbasement elevators and hit the number '2.'

The rumbling of the air filtration system on the third and fourth floors grew louder as the elevator crawled higher. On level two, the doors opened to a long hallway with small circular windows. The hallway was clinical and grey, and the windows revealed numerous laboratories with adjoining showers. Scientists in the labs wore light blue plastic suits with big clear head coverings that made them look a bit like astronauts. We dubbed the BSL-4 scientists as 'spacesuits.' Coiled, yellow hoses hung from the ceiling, plugging into the suits. I scanned the clear headcovers for Jade's recognizable platinum hair.

Through one window, two scientists wheeled something that looked like a metal hatbox into the centre of the lab. They popped the lid off the cylinder, and white fog rolled out from the top, down the sides, and onto the floor. One spacesuit rifled through the little freezer. The vapour swirled in eddies around his arm as he removed a small vial containing a light brown powder. The other scientists crowded around him, like ducks hoping for bread. I moved along after they obscured my view.

I wandered past the chemical showers, suit room, body showers, and the lockers.

Through another window, unconscious on the table was an elderly man, bare from head to toe and covered in velvety pustules: a hallmark of Wave Two Redspot. Red filled his gums and eyes, as the Bleeder stared vacantly at the ceiling. Brain scans were glowing from the monitors surrounding the room. Jade's hair was visible as she leaned over the man to take a blood sample. After she extracted the needle, a dark bruise blossomed down his vein, meaning he was infected with Wave Three as well. *I didn't know she was working with hybrids.*

As if she could feel my gaze, Jade turned towards the window I was staring through. The right side of her face was a ruin of knotted, shining white scars where an eye used to be. Her remaining eye was as sharp as ever and it landed on me immediately.

She gave me a merry little wave, jotted a few notes down on a label, and placed the blood vial in a small holding tray. I waved back before I gave her an elaborate pantomimed request for medical clearance.

Jade looked exasperated and shook her head at the ceiling. She pointed to the door of the labs and held up her finger as if to say, "*One minute.*" The massive latch spun open, and she exited the lab.

I made my way around to the adjoining door and entered the locker room, just outside the decontamination showers. Locked bins filled the room floor to ceiling. Jade was visible through the window of the decon room—her spacesuit was dripping wet from the disinfectant showers beyond. She unzipped the suit to reveal plain blue scrubs and socks taped up to her knees. Jade grinned and pulled off her latex gloves as she approached the glass. She tossed them into a nearby biohazard bin and rolled up her sleeves. Her right arm was marked with bite-sized messes of pearly white scars.

Jade called through the glass, "Just give me one second to finish decon." A few moments later, she emerged in jeans and a t-shirt; wet hair dripped onto her collar. "You're lucky I finished my labs already, Clara. What's up?"

I flashed her a hopeful smile and held up the form.

"Let me guess. Since the raid siren just went off, and you probably haven't even bothered to ask Missy, you want me to give you clearance."

I smiled even wider.

Jade levelled her gaze at me. She was a few inches shorter than I was. The left side of her face showed a pretty woman in her late thirties, with high cheekbones and a shimmering amber eye. Her one good eye did a quick, thorough sweep over my body, and I watched her small facial twitches mentally catalogue the marks on my shoulder and forearm.

"All right, come with me." She gestured towards her examination room down the hallway. "You're lucky I like you." She called over her shoulder. I thanked my lucky stars and followed her.

The medical clearance was completed in no time. Jade snapped off her gloves and gave me another look. "You know, you really should be going to your primary physician for clearance, Clara." Her voice was reproving, but a small smile tugged at her lips. "I know Dr. O'Donnell can be a bit trying at times, but I can't keep clearing you without her approval."

I shrugged, meeting Jade's eye unflinchingly. "You know how busy she is."

Jade raised an eyebrow. "You pulled me out of BSL-4 for this. Do you have any idea how much of a pain it is going to be for me to set up my labs again?"

"You said you were finished." I shot back. "Plus, I know you wouldn't leave your labs for anything, especially me."

Jade shrugged. "That doesn't mean they're not going to be a pain to set up tomorrow, though." She grinned.

I laughed and hopped off the table, the ink from Jade's signature still wet on my form. "Thanks again."

"This is the last time, Clara." She called after me as I rushed back to the tunnels.

Back in the Grotto, I noticed that the rows of combat-ready clothing became mostly hangers and empty shelves, as the squads had already suited up.

Chase grinned when he saw me jogging across the floor to him. "Well done. I never thought O'Donnell would clear you." His grin dropped when he saw Jade's initials instead of Missy's. "Ah, I take it she was too busy to see you again, hm?" He shook his head as he scanned his list for my name and selected four bags. "MOPP Level 4." A thrill of fear shot through me.

The first bag held my chemical protective undergarments and overgarments; the next bag contained my mask and hood, footwear covers, and 25-mil gloves. Chase held the gloves for a moment longer and said, "You weren't cleared for anything special yet, right?" I shook my head no. He nodded and pushed the gloves into my chest. "Yup, these'll do nicely then. Not great for surgery, but easy enough to shoot a gun with. Go to your squad to get your field gear."

A little dazed, I gathered up the plastic bundles and moved over to Extraction Squad 13's designated area. Mona gave me a twitchy wave as I approached the group. Beside her was Feliks Kowalski, the leader of Fireteam Bravo. Kowalski had the face of a retired boxer and spoke with a thick Polish accent, despite immigrating to Canada decades ago. He snapped his fingers to bring Mona's attention back to the map he was holding.

The thick grey material of my undershirt and pants were stiff as I pulled them on. The overgarment suit settled weightily onto my shoulders. It zipped up to my chin and my own body heat was reflected by it, making my temperature rise. Sweat started to bead on my forehead and on the back of my neck.

"Whew," I said, fanning myself futilely.

"At least the bastards are attacking at night, right?" Brad laughed as he tugged at his collar and sweat poured down his temples. He said it just in time for Sergeant Longboat to overhear him.

Piper rolled her eyes. "Keep the suits off until we get closer to Darlington, or you'll get heat exhaustion. Rossi, get us up to speed."

Mona pulled out a blueprint of the nuclear plant. "Squad 13 is doing an extraction of any civilians within reactor three. The reactor was shut down earlier today for maintenance. We have intel that at least four people are trapped. Our mission is to clear out and quarantine the uninfected. The Resistance may be using Wave Two particles," she explained to us as I undid the front of my overgarment and my undershirt.

Kowalski and I memorized the map as Evan pulled out a roll of black tape. "What's that?" I asked, afraid of the answer.

21

"M9 Detection Tape." My pulse began to thunder in my ears. From the Aegis Shield training manual, I knew that the presence of nerve gas or blistering agents, like mustard gas, would turn the black tape a reddish colour. He wrapped the tape around my left wrist and right bicep.

"Oh." My voice sounded distant as he worked on my left shin. My heart rate began to explode in my chest as I stared at the innocuous little piece of tape on my wrist.

"We don't believe they're using liquid agents at this time, but this is protocol for MOPP 4. If they're using biowarfare, we're not ruling gas out," Evan said as he straightened himself up. "If it turns red, pink, purple, or brown, just make sure you keep your gear on, and you'll be fine." He patted my back. I swallowed and gave him a small smile.

"Gee, I thought I only had to worry about being shot," I said sarcastically, pulling the mask onto my neck. It rubbed against my chin.

Viruses, fallout, and gas. Great.

Evan wheeled over a massive cylinder made up of glass tubes. "What kind of weapon is that?" I asked nervously. I couldn't recall seeing that inside the manual.

He patted it affectionately. "UVC light for the medical tent. Thirty minutes under this baby makes decontamination a breeze." he said in response to the group's curious glances.

As Bravo and Alpha finished suiting up, a hush fell over the squads like a wave. Curious, I strained my neck to see what had caused it. Making his way to a stage in the front of the room was a short, squat man with tiny glasses perched on the edge of his rather bulbous nose. Not the sort of man who physically drew attention to himself, he was followed by silence due purely to his reputation. His name was Commander Hakim Dekkar, and he had the most brilliant mind for strategy of anyone I ever met.

Hakim stood on the raised platform at the far end of the massive room. Attention was turned expectantly to him. His voice echoed throughout as he divided the evacuation teams into red for offensive and white for defensive. Most of the squads were protecting the powerplant because it had priority. We couldn't afford to lose Darlington after Niagara Falls fell to the Old States. The nuclear plant powered the Horseshoe Colonies that ringed Lake Ontario. Still, several squads were staying behind as defence for the Facility, just in case.

He said, "Falcon Reds, rendezvous with the Leuko forces on the Northeast of Darlington by the medical zone." The announcement was met with murmurs from the squads.

"They hired mercenaries?" Evan's voice was shocked. "The last time we needed Leukos, we were outnumbered fifteen to one." Muttering to himself, he unclipped his Medi-kit to recount the patches.

Hakim looked at each of the squads meaningfully and continued, "Hawk Platoon, remember your training and use minimal force. Double check your gas canisters and be aware of the location and ventilation in the areas you deploy. We don't want a Nord-Ost siege on our hands." My eyes found Brad's. He shrugged as I raised my eyebrows in question. "Avoid the turbine hall, that's Extraction's prerogative. Move out!"

Light blue military passenger trucks awaited us in the adjoining garage. Mona helped Evan wheel the massive UVC light into the idling truck. I filed in after them.

We were jostled as the trucks drove down the cracked and barren streets of Toronto. It was dark, but through the window that led to the truck's cabin, I made out the shining outline of dead buildings ahead. We pulled onto an old boulevard where people once walked along the waterfront. A few boats were stationed in the black water of Lake Ontario, waiting for us.

The engines cut, and we unloaded from the trucks. Boarding the boats was strangely quiet. The only sounds were from the gentle lapping of the water, and the occasional squeaks as the rubber chafed on our biosafety suits.

Once aboard, the motors puttered to life. We cut across the inky waters. The wind, damp with mist from the lake, whistled against my ears. Mona wandered over unsteadily as the boat skipped across the water. She plonked down next to me on the bench and gave me an impish smile. I knew that smile. *She wasn't going to let what she saw this morning drop.* I shifted in my seat a bit and decided to be very interested in the trigger mechanism of my M4. "So, you and Dr. Runar were looking cozy this morning," she said, referring to when Braeden was asking about my life before the Facility.

***

We were curled on the couch in the Memorial Hall on the fourteenth floor. Glittering on the wall were thousands of names of those who were lost, written in gold on black. He hugged me close to him. "Do you ever miss Oakville? Do you ever want to go back?" he whispered against my temple.

I shook my head, shifting closer to him on the couch. "No." The answer came surprisingly easily to my lips, "I don't have any reason to go back after my family…" My throat closed, and I couldn't finish the sentence.

He wrapped both his arms around me and held me close for a long while. I didn't cry anymore; I just felt the aching loneliness. His eyes met mine, and I noticed the laugh lines that usually made my heart skip a beat as he gave me a sad smile. Without thinking, I bit my lip. His hand slipped into mine. His fingers were warm and callused. I slid my palm along his. His breath picked up, and his mouth parted.

***

Like this morning, Mona's voice pulled my mind

abruptly away from the image of Braeden's lips. She continued, "Hey, I don't mean to be nosy. Braeden's been a complete cold fish to everyone he meets. It's refreshing to see him act like a red-blooded male for once. The guy might even be a looker if he wasn't such a prick." I smiled to myself as Mona chatted on. She didn't seem to mean any offence by it. She was just relaying this as a harmless comment rather than a scathing character review.

Anyways, he wasn't a prick. He just didn't show affection the same way other people did. After Oakville, he set up a task force to find my father. It was last rumoured that my dad was in the Old States or the Western Provinces. So I knew Braeden was trying in his own way. Maybe it was because, aside from his twin brother, he had lost almost all his family too. Bonding over our families was what brought us together in the first place. *He was the one to tell me the news about my own family after all.*

Not wanting to get into it, I shrugged at Mona's comments. "I just kind of react to him," I said vaguely.

"If he was getting all hot and heavy with me, I'd probably react too." She stared at the dark horizon over the water thoughtfully, then added, "Though, between the two brothers, I'd rather have Kaye. Same good looks, but with a sense of humour." There was no denying that Kaye was the more light-hearted one. Of course, he didn't carry the burden of leading the cure effort.

I smiled and excused myself to go check on Brad, partially to get away from the conversation, but mostly because Brad looked a little green as the boat hopped towards Darlington. He opened his mouth as if to speak, but then closed it and just shook his head, too nervous to say anything.

"You'll be fine, man," I said, hoping to comfort him. He gave me a weak smile.

"I've just… I've never shot at a human before."

Evan chuckled. "What do you think Rotters are?" Brad looked stricken at the thought, so I hastily added, "In all seriousness, it's us or them. We're lucky these idiots keep sending wave after wave of donors for us. I dunno what we'd do otherwise."

Brad's brow furrowed. "What do you mean?"

Mona snorted and joined the conversation. "Basically, Jameson, just think of the Resistance as organ donors for a good cause."

I grinned. "Exactly. They're doing more for the benefit of humanity stripped down to their parts, given to the people who are actually trying to find a cure." I spat in the water. "Alive, they're just dogs." Sweat trickled down my back, and my breathing picked up. I closed my eyes and forced myself to take a few slow, deep breaths. There was no point in getting too worked up before the fight even started.

The nuclear power plant rose in the distance and lit up along the shore, like a carousel. The massive building had four distinct sections – one for each nuclear reactor. Our civilians were inside reactor three.

I recounted the mission briefing.

Most of the squads were focused on securing Unit Zero – the control room and the evacuated turbine hall. Our squad was going into the heart of one of the reactors. Fireteam Alpha would collect the civilians, while Fireteam Bravo would act as security detail.

The boats docked outside a high fence that surrounded the plant. It was made of jagged stones that looked like they were pulled from the Canadian Shield itself, with thick coils of barbed wire around the top. The wall was lined periodically with mounted turrets. Large gates opened to welcome the boats. Inside the walls, a medical tent was partially constructed. I stumbled as we disembarked.

I looked over to the people milling on the dock, scanning for the mercs. Sure enough, I easily spotted a Leuko body mod: the man had a dark stripe of flesh over his eyes while the rest of his face was pale. I rolled my transplanted shoulder joint. Most Facility members tried to shade match their skin patches so they wouldn't draw attention to themselves. These guys liked to modify themselves for fun.

A man with thick dreads and a mask slung around his neck walked up to Piper. Even where I stood, I could smell the reek of peppermint he wore to cover his scent. *Uninfected.* Without a word, the squad masked themselves before the man got too close. Hanging from his neck was a cross, which glinted through his mask. He was a security officer, here to guide us through, into the reactor. He looked over each of us with a discerning eye as we exchanged terse greetings. He gave a quick overview of where we were going in the plant before it was time to get into the fray.

In the distance, the fight had already begun. The Leuko's were holding the line in front of the building that housed the Turbine Hall.

Once in formation, Piper corralled the squad towards the gunfire. She waited until we hit concrete before ordering us to zip up our suits. Our boots sounded heavy as we marched along the wall.

Several of the squads had already joined the ranks of the Leukos. The Resistance had mobilized the Rotters to thin out our numbers and our ammunition.

A solid line of Facility soldiers mowed down row after row as they swarmed from all directions. Harvest deployed gas canisters that drowned the area with smoke. Flares and gunfire lit up the gas clouds like a thunderstorm.

The line hadn't been breached yet. Piper screamed instructions over the gunfire, ushering our team as we sprinted with the security officer towards the plant's main entrance. The squads assigned to the entryway herded us through quickly, issuing cover as we entered the nuclear plant.

Once inside the large doors, we came across the first security screening point. The officer placed his hand into a machine that scanned his palm and measured his bones. The doors admitted us.

The interior hallway could have belonged to any office building. Standing on the boring grey carpet, surrounded by white walls, I felt like I ought to be wearing a business suit instead of my rubber CBRN one. We weaved through a few passageways, and the sound of gunfire became more distant.

Once we entered the Turbine Hall, the scenery changed from an office building into an industrial plant. The other side of the impressive hall faded into blackness, too far away for me to see.

On the floors of the factory were four distinctly coloured lines. Our squad traced a green line painted along the floor leading to reactor three. After numerous tunnels and across a few corridors with complex equipment and computers, our guide eventually stopped in front of a huge door with a spinning latch.

A dark grey vault stood before us. Mona and Brad pressed to either side of the door, clutching their guns. The plastic of their suits rubbed loudly against the concrete walls. Our guide cranked the massive latch and revealed a dark, tubular room. We emerged at the top of the reactor room from the other side of the vault.

Metal walkways crisscrossed the room, down to the ground floor below. Pipes and tubing ran throughout, mostly in uniform grey, but occasionally painted bright yellow. In the centre of the room sat a huge cylinder, comprised of rods. The security officer shouted something. Unable to hear it through the gear, Mona handed him a mic to speak into. His voice screamed over the microphone, making the unit jump. "That's the calandria evaporator! The engineers are hiding behind there." He pointed to the cylinder.

Huddled behind the machinery sat several nuclear scientists. They wore flimsy, white suits shielding their bodies from radioactive particles. With sweat pouring down my back, I eyed the light suits with envy. The scientists recognized the Aegis emblem on our gear and waved us over. As we crossed the room, I was impressed by how dwarfed we were next to the reactor.

Mona passed me a quivering, paper-shrouded woman. I handed her a plastic isolation suit and said, "Hey, I've got you now. We're gonna get you out of here safe, okay?" I tried to make my eyes crinkle so she could see that I was smiling through my gas mask. Her look of terror told me my attempt to soothe her didn't work. I was sure she'd feel more comfortable if I didn't have my mask on, but it was just as much for my protection as it was for hers.

She tugged the isolation suit over the white paper. Placing a mask over her face, I manoeuvred her back up to the vault to await the rest of the squad. The rest of Fireteam Alpha prepped their civilians and brought them up to the vault door. Fireteam Bravo formed a perimeter while Mona guided the way through the mess of corridors in the plant. Tubes and ducts ran along the walls and ceilings into various control boards and computers.

We entered the Turbine Hall, a long room with several monitors and system panels. We had nearly crossed to the other side of it when brownish dust floated into the room through an air vent.

"Particles!" Mona's voice crackled through the earpiece. "Check your civilians' masks!"

The engineer buried the mouthpiece of her mask in her hands and shut her eyes. I rubbed her back, "Hey, you still with me? Is something wrong with your mask?" I waved the spare mask from my pack in front of her face. She shook her head frantically. Her bloodshot eyes were wide and terrified.

The Leukos and squads had lost ground. Several

29

Rotters slipped through and shuffled around the darkness of the Turbine Hall. The door on the far end of the hallway broke open and more Rotters tumbled in. Mona swore. The first Rotter swiped at Kowalski before he had a chance to react. The blast from Mona's gun sent it flying back. We focused on the Rotters as they poured in. "Fireteam Bravo, neutralize them and find their handler!" Piper's voice came into the mic. "Fireteam Alpha, move!"

Holding my civilian firmly and guiding her, we marched single file out of the contamination zone. Pops of gunfire filled the air as Fireteam Bravo picked off the Rotters drawn to the smell of the uninfected. There was a firefight in the distance. Sirens and alarms were already wailing. We exited the nuclear plant as fast as we could.

Even after our feet were on the grass nearby, our suits remained zipped up. In the distance, the medical tent gleamed in the darkness. I guided the civilian past the barricade, towards the plastic tent.

Inside, spread through the area, were four ultraviolet lights. The white spacesuits of the field medics were brilliant underneath the UVC. Like aliens in the purplish glow, the civilians sat around the room. Medics moved through the room like astronauts, dispensing decontamination kits to each person.

I helped the engineer struggle out of her protective plastic and demonstrated how to rub black decon powder all over her skin. "See?" I said. "Don't leave anything uncovered. The black makes it easier to see where you've missed a spot." Shaking, she began to rub the powder onto her skin.

A spacesuit collected the panicking woman from me, and I followed Mona outside. We doused ourselves in disinfectant showers and unzipped the swelteringly hot suits. As soon as the cool air touched my burning skin, I let out a groan of relief.

Regrouped and preparing to head back into the turbine

hall, I was surprised to see Piper holding her boots. She gestured for me to follow her away from the group.

We walked around the corner of the medical tent, out of eyesight and earshot. Piper stopped abruptly before me, forcing me to a halt. She crossed her arms as she towered over me. "Apparently, a message was sent out with another squad after we deployed. Squad 13 has been called back." She shifted, glanced around, and leaned closer. "Specifically, Dr. Runar has called *you* back."

"He can't be serious," I said, aghast. "He knows being part of the Aegis Shield is the reason I stayed at the Facility."

"Well, apparently, he's forgotten. Or he knows you've got nowhere else to go."

I felt an annoying claustrophobia that I always got whenever anyone mentioned how tied we all were to the Facility's treatments. "I dunno," I snapped a little too defensively. "I just know that I made it very clear why I was staying there." I groaned, "I'll just sort it out with him when we get back from patrol."

"Do you have any idea why he would call you back?" Piper pressed.

Blood rushed to my face as I was simultaneously furious and humiliated. *How dare he do this?* I stared resolutely at my rubber boots. "He never wanted me to go on the raids," I admitted. Shaking from rage, I tried to swallow down my anger and think rationally. "He's protective and doesn't want me to get hurt, I guess." I knew that Braeden had lost most of his family to the virus. The only living family he had left was his brother.

That didn't give him the right to control me like this, though.

Piper was dumbstruck for a moment. She flailed her arms. "What?" She cried. I braced myself for what was to come next. I expected her to tear strips off me for not telling her. Instead, her next words made me smile. "What kind of sexist bullshit is that?"

She combed her fingers through her short grey hair and paced around the hillside. "All right. I'll sort it out later, but for now, we need to go back to the Facility. The order came straight from High Command."

We came around the side of the tent to see the rest of the squad milling about, awaiting orders. Piper stood before the tent, bathed in the fluorescent light from inside. She gestured for the group to gather around her. The team was hyped up.

Kowalski ripped his mask off. "What's wrong?" he demanded, stepping forward from the semi-circle. Piper gave him a cold stare before turning to the rest of the squad. He slowly stepped back into line with the others.

Piper's voice was strong. "We've been called back as reinforcements for the Facility. We have reason to believe an ambush is underway." I frowned but didn't say anything. *Ambush?* Piper continued, "Reactor three has been cleared, the other squads have this under control for now."

My emotions were in turmoil as we trundled our way back to the awaiting boat. Before I could board, Piper grabbed me by the upper arm and leaned in close. "We'll talk later. This is only temporary."

I clambered into the boat and felt a little lighter, happy that Piper was in my corner.

CHAPTER THREE
Invasion

The boat docked slightly farther west than where we originally disembarked—one lone truck sat by the water, awaiting us. The back of the truck was immeasurably more comfortable without the heavy CBRN suit on.

It revved to life and sped down the desolate streets. Within moments we would be arriving at the great gates to the underground garage. In the silence, Piper's voice from the front seat gave me chills, "Something's not right."

I sat up and peered through the little window into the front cabin. Through the front windshield, I saw smoke rising from the skyscrapers. The Facility was dark, emergency lights flashed through its windows.

Piper swore. She yelled into the back, "Everyone, get your gear ready! We've got a Code Red." She punched the front dashboard in frustration before wriggling her own CBRN suit back on.

Piper directed the driver to go through an ancillary entrance, as she frantically radioed ahead.

Her voice carried easily into the back of the truck. "All

units, this is Falcon Red One Three. Does anyone have eyes on the situation? Over." She yelled into the mic. "All units, does anybody copy? Over." The only response was a burst of static. Piper swore through clenched teeth before trying one more time. "All units, this is Falcon Red One Three. Do we have eyes on the situation? I say again: do we have eyes on the situation? Over." There was still silence from the radio as we drove underground. It was dark, yet a dizzying array of lights strobed across my vision.

We rushed out of the van, and Piper held her radio close.

Finally, a voice came through. "Falcon Red One Three, this is Hawk White Four. Hostiles inbound for Papa Romeo One and Four. Over." The conversation faded into white noise as I processed what I just heard. *Papa Romeo One… PR-1, that's Braeden's panic room.*

Another voice crackled onto the radio. "Breaker. Breaker. All units, this is Eagle White Six. Hostiles have breached Lima Two. Urgent assistance! Over." *The second-floor labs.*

"… responding priority. Out." Piper turned to us. "You heard him; we need to help secure the second-floor biosafety lab. Masks on! Move out!"

I was roused from my thoughts as Piper snapped her fingers in front of my face. "Belford, you're sitting this one out."

"What?"

"Look, I believe the reason you gave, but my hands are tied until I can sort this out with the higher-ups. You're not allowed with either of my fireteams tonight. Give me your earpiece." I grumbled and placed my tiny comm device into her open palm.

Brad punched my shoulder sympathetically. "Next time, Belford." His voice was muffled by his face mask. His eyes brimmed with excitement. They jogged towards the Biosafety Level Four labs.

After my squad disappeared, I counted to ten, then took off into the tunnels after them.

The shriek of the sirens was soon joined by the cacophonous sounds of gunfire and people shouting as I drew closer to the main basement. I exhaled, clicked the safety off my rifle, and prepared myself. The noises grew louder in the main basement and several bodies lined the floor. I didn't look at them too closely. *Those were just those murderous bastards... or Rotters, just like every day.* I ducked when the sound of gunfire came from behind me. Not bothering to find out who they were aiming for, I took off down the side path leading to Braeden's panic room.

I stepped over a body in the side tunnels and made the mistake of looking down at it. The face that gaped back at me looked robust, healthy, and very human.

And very much dead.

His glassy stare gazed at the ceiling. A faint tremor ran through me. People dressed in Facility gear charged past me. I flinched as a bullet whizzed past. Ducking into an alcove, I clutched my gun close to my body as I tried to control my heart rate. The image of the blood-spattered 'R' floated through my mind. Gritting my teeth, I pushed forward to Braeden's panic room.

More bodies littered the floor as I drew closer. Further ahead, a woman wearing a white coat with flaming red hair was being held up between two Facility soldiers. *Missy.*

I ran towards them while frantically scanning the hallway, hoping to see any sign of Braeden or Kaye. My heart sank as I saw the door marked PR-1 yawning open, empty.

Dr. Missy O'Donnell was hysterical and could barely walk. She cried, "He's upstairs. He went after his brother. He's upstairs!" Her wide blue eyes looked imploringly at everyone around her. "Please!"

"Where upstairs?" I demanded.

"I don't know!" She wailed, not recognizing me with my mask on. She started sobbing, becoming unintelligible. With no time to waste, I sprinted back the way I came.

At the base of the stairs, someone in Facility gear was directing people deeper into the tunnels. I jogged over to him.

"Have you seen Dr. Runar?" I shouted. The man gave me a worried look.

"No, but I've been here for five minutes at most!" He shouted back. I pushed past him up the stairs. Though my gear was heavy, the additional adrenaline flooding my system let me take the stairs two at a time. I moved towards Jade's office on the second floor.

I opened the door with a bright yellow '2' painted on it, and the floor was chaotic. I crouched, ducking down, as bullets sprayed the wall to my left.

My heart pounded. I swallowed thickly and peered out from behind the door. Everything moved in slow motion, with reality further away than it was a moment ago. The Facility scientists and soldiers alike were holed up in the lab, while the Resistance shot at them from the hallway. Their shots echoed in my head.

Flinching as another bullet whizzed past, I pulled back behind the wall. Reality crashed over me once again.

I held my rifle tightly to myself and counted down from five. My heart rate slowed marginally, and my panic subsided. I breathed out one more time. *The way to Jade's office was the opposite direction of the fight. If I was quick and hugged the walls, the two groups would probably be too preoccupied with each other to notice me.*

I was painfully aware of how close the constant stream of gunfire was.

I bounced on my heels a few times before leaping to my feet and tearing down the hallway.

I stayed close to the wall, recoiling with every shot I

heard. No bullets came my way. I slowly peeked around the corner; the hallway was empty. Jade's office door was still missing the glass panel that had broken during the last attack. Relieved, I was about to sprint straight up to her door until I saw the barrel of a gun poking out through the absent window.

I froze and weighed my odds. *If I shouted and it wasn't her, I would give myself away.* A mirror slid through the door, angled towards me. I could make out an amber eye in the reflection.

"You're not getting into my office!" Jade yelled loudly through the door.

"Jade! It's Clara!" I shouted so loudly my throat hurt. I ripped off my gas mask—the Resistance wouldn't release particles with their own units inside. The mirror retracted, and the gun barrel withdrew. The door opened, and a pale hand ushered me inside quickly.

Jade gave me a big hug when I got into her office. "Jesus-tap-dancing-Christ, I thought you were one of them."

"What are you doing in here?"

"I came here after they raided two other offices," Jade breathed heavily.

"Have you seen Braeden or Kaye?" I demanded.

Jade went back to peering out the door, her rifled rested on the open window. "I think Braeden went to his office. He was with me on the first floor when we realized the offices were being ransacked. No clue about Kaye."

"I gotta go find Braeden."

Jade looked grimly at me and squeezed my upper arm. She gave me a once-over before saying, "All right, Clara, you look after yourself out there."

Impulsively, I gave her a quick hug. My heart hammered almost painfully against my ribs as I let go. "I will, Jade. Stay safe."

She saluted me with two fingers as I grasped the doorknob.

I slipped out and approached the balcony overlooking the atrium. Gunfire flashed from the ground floor. Staying as close to the wall as possible, I ran up the stairs. I was halfway to the third floor when I noticed blood slicked the steps.

I slowed. The blood led up to a looming mass on the third-floor landing. Getting low on the steps, I took aim with my rifle. In the strobing light, I made out a person.

I trained my crosshairs on their head; they were not wearing Facility gear.

Only when they rolled over did I recognize Braeden's strong jawline and dark features. In a panic, I raised my gun and scrambled up the steps towards him. I slipped on the blood that covered the glossy tiles, and my knee sank into a step. My hand caught me while sliding through a blood-slicked puddle of glass, shredding my palm to ribbons. Ignoring my injury, I clambered up the last few steps to Braeden.

My panic rose at how heavily he was bleeding. I couldn't make out the location of the injury in the dim lighting. His clothing was damp and coated in blood. Despite being cool to the touch, he was sweating profusely. His face was pale.

Braeden's eyes fluttered open, and he looked around as if in a daze. "Where am I?"

I choked out a half-sob-half-laugh, relieved that he was still alive. "Where were you hit?"

He vaguely gestured over his stomach. I tentatively rolled up his shirt. A huge hole was ripped into his abdomen, and the smell was overwhelming. I covered the wound back up with his shirt. Placing my rifle at my back, I used both hands to prop Braeden upright. He rolled and grumbled but allowed me to move him. Hauling him by the armpits, I dragged him away from the stairs and into the shadows of the third floor.

Braeden's lips opened in a soft moan. With a faint voice,

he asked for his brother. I could barely hear him over the sirens.

Stroking back his damp hair, I assured him that we were going to find his brother as soon as I got him to a medic. He calmed. I adjusted when my right hand began to sting from sweat mingling with my cuts.

"Why do I need a medic?" he asked groggily as his head lolled. Blood sluggishly oozed down his front. I murmured to him softly, soothing him with nonsense. Tears formed in my eyes, and my throat constricted. I tried my best to swallow them down.

It will do neither of us any good if I break down right now.

Instead, I opened the door to a dark room nearby and dragged him in. I propped him underneath a desk, hiding him as best as I could.

Braeden's eyes were feverish as he held my hand tightly. I kissed his cracked lips before I stood to leave him. "Stay here and stay safe, okay?" My voice broke halfway through. He mumbled something that I couldn't hear over the sirens.

My finger remained on the trigger as I made my way through the deserted third floor. Next to the emergency stairs laid the slumped form of a guard. I approached cautiously, looking around for whatever had attacked him. The guard was a young man who was presumably watching the stairwell. I kneeled beside him to check his pulse. I muttered a small "thanks" that he was still alive.

The only problem was now I had no idea who was on the other side of the door or how trigger happy they might be.

I rapped my knuckles on the door. Nothing. I announced loudly, "Soldier, this is Belford from Extraction Thirteen. I need assistance!" After no response, I pushed it open to be met with the barrel of a gun in my face. The guard dropped it when he saw my uniform.

"I need a medic! Two injured!" I cried.

"Lady, we're kind of busy right now!" The guard shouted back. I gritted my teeth.

"It's Dr. Runar! He's hurt!" I screamed.

The guard looked at me quizzically. "I know he's hurt. We've already got him in the emergency care unit."

I glanced back at the closed door of the third floor. *What?* My confusion was quickly replaced with understanding, then panic. *Kaye.* "You've got his brother! Dr. Runar is injured on the third floor. Right now!"

The guard looked at me with disbelief. I could feel my frustration spike. "Goddammit, if Braeden Runar dies because of you, I'm going to shoot you myself. I need a medic now!" He gave me a doubtful glance but radioed for a medic before flagging down two soldiers to give me assistance. I took them with me to where I left Braeden.

He still lay partially propped up under the desk. His hand glistened from the wound on his stomach. One of the guards dropped down to perform a quick analysis.

"No spinal issues, but we need to get him a patch immediately before I feel comfortable moving him." As if on cue, the medic ran past the open doorway. "Oy! We're in here!" He slid to a stop and scrambled around. Once he was through the door, he dropped to his knees with a painful crack against the tiles. Seemingly unfazed, he opened his kit and carefully selected the proper specimen.

Braeden feebly spoke, "Let me… see … the list." His breathing was laboured. I looked questioningly between the two men. The medic seemed to know what he was asking for, as he produced a piece of paper. I used my scope light to illuminate the page for Braeden.

Braeden blinked and refocused on the paper a few times. "Number five, please." He murmured before shutting his eyes.

I watched in fascination as they trimmed the decaying flesh from the wound, gently applying the fleshy patch. They wrapped clean bandages around his midsection. "It won't stop the internal issues, but it should stem the necrosis and halt some of the bleeding. We need to get him into an O.R. stat for his gut," the medic announced to no one in particular, as he assembled a stretcher.

With Braeden safely strapped to the stretcher, we moved out.

When we entered the emergency stairwell, the guard's eyes widened with shock as we carried Braeden past him. I resisted the urge to give him an "I told you so."

An entourage of other Facility soldiers escorted us down into the tunnels to ensure the Good Doctor's safety.

CHAPTER FOUR
Sick Bay

A makeshift sick bay had been set up for the evacuation inside the tunnels. The large room was set up with hundreds of small cots, forming rows. Nurses and doctors moved quickly between the injured, applying patches and making lists of what was needed for surgery.

Guards were trying to keep the crowd at bay. A nurse who was scurrying past stopped when her eyes landed on Dr. Runar's unconscious form. She let out a strange squeal before clearing her throat and calling out, "Dr. Cottier, Dr. Cooper, I've got Dr. Runar here!" Both doctors turned towards her, wearing similar masks of confusion. The two doctors looked like clones of the same middle-aged man with a neat white beard; however, Dr. Cottier was tall and lean, while Dr. Cooper was short and round.

"Are you sure?" Dr. Cottier began, cutting himself off as he saw me. Heat flushed up my cheeks. Though Braeden and I had tried to be discrete, they knew who I was. Word of Dr. Runar's arrival rippled throughout the room.

Dr. O'Donnell cut through the commotion of the crowd.

The doctors wheeled the stretcher towards her. Her heart-shaped face went blotchy when she saw Braeden. The skin patches on her cheek and throat turned a deep red.

"Place him beside his brother." She pointed towards the corner where Kaye must've been. I moved to follow, but she stepped before me and put her hands out to stop me from going any further. Her white latex gloves were smeared with blood. With puffy eyes, she no longer looked distraught, but determined.

"Clara, go back," she said forcefully. Then she swallowed and added, "Trust me, you don't want to see this."

A lump formed in my throat. Pushing her aside, I forced my way through the crowd to Kaye's bed. His black hair was slicked to his forehead with sweat. His skin was frighteningly pale, almost purplish. The veins on his cheeks and throat were raised, like wounds.

"They made the same mistake we did. They thought he was the doctor," Missy said miserably behind me. I heard snaps as she took off her gloves. "I didn't realize it wasn't him until we cleaned the blood from his face."

Silent tears poured hot and heavy down my cheeks. I reached out to touch him, but Missy's hand grabbed my wrist.

"Infection," she said simply. I pulled my hand back. Both brothers were moved next to each other. Medical staff started to work feverishly to save them both. She then looked at my hand, sliced by broken glass and dried blood flaked away from my already blackened flesh. She held the injury up to her eyes and said, "You'll live. I've got other people to tend to. You should go down the hallway over there with the other evacuees. See me afterwards."

She turned her attention back to the brothers, shouting orders with impressive authority for such a petite woman.

I headed in the direction she pointed. Sitting in an underground room with the other evacuees, I felt like I was in limbo: waiting to hear that the Facility had been cleared and if Braeden and Kaye were going to make it. I was trying hard not to cry in front of the others.

God, please, don't let them die.

Without thinking, I reached for the scar just above my heart. I had spent hours on the fourth floor of the Facility, sitting in the soft armchairs of the chemo clinic. The drugs had been mainlined straight into my heart by a port on my chest. My fingers traced back and forth over the small purple scar.

***

Braeden's eyes were framed with impossibly long and thick eyelashes as he languidly examined the chamber. His shining hair fell across his forehead and curled behind his ears. Barely visible through the hair was a long, thin, white scar.

He noticed where my eyes were trained and lightly tapped the scar. "Medulloblastoma. Malignant." I stared at him blankly. "A brain tumor. Getting treated for it was partly why I wanted to become a doctor." I felt an unexpected warm rush towards him. *So we were both cancer survivors.* I stared at the scar for a moment longer.

"I used to cry in a closet before my radiation therapy." I laughed as I shared that with him. "I dunno if it was because I was just a kid, but I was terrified." I glanced at him.

He was watching me, enraptured. "Go on," he said quietly.

"I guess I still get terrified." I smirked as we gazed out over the skyline of Toronto. The tops of several buildings had windows blown out where flames had once licked their charred edges. "Do you ever get overwhelmed?"

"I do. A lot. Something I learned working in medicine is that you need to be able to hold onto hope, wherever you can find some," he said. "Two years ago, the Facility nearly died out, in part because the winter was so harsh that year.

Between the power outages and the cold snaps, a lot of our members succumbed to frostbite after getting caught outside on scouting missions. Some while trying to keep the supply lines going through the city. I was terrified that all my work would have been for nothing; I wouldn't be able to revive my research. Finding those who are resistant before they turn isn't easy, you know. And I still don't know how to heal a Rotter enough to restore their minds."

I sat up at his words. "Wait, you think that you could possibly reverse the necrosis of the brain?" I asked him. He looked past my face at the skyscrapers beyond.

"Not reverse, no… but I do think that human consciousness is more complex than modern medicine fully appreciates." He sighed, rolling over, trailing his hand lazily up my back. "Our numbers had dwindled down to almost nothing that winter. We had barely any doctors on staff. The people working with me were more fighters than scientists. We needed to press on, and we found a way. We're survivors, Clara. We'll make it through this virus, too. We can't lose hope."

"That must have been so hard," I said. His fingertips made circles on my hip. I leaned towards him, as his other arm wrapped around the small of my waist. His lips pressed against mine, and I became lost in the sensation of him: his hard body, his musky scent, the warmth of his body, heating up in the summer sunshine.

***

I was shaken from my reverie by a voice that came over the loudspeaker, instructing us to go to our rooms for counting. The huge crowd shuffled out the doors and up the stairs. The elevators were not in use, and I groaned at the thought of climbing fifteen stories before reminding myself that Kaye and Braeden were still fighting for their lives.

Sometimes, perspective is important.

As soon I got to my room, I stripped off all my gear. I

45

would return it after everything settled down. I threw myself on the bed and allowed the tears to come. I cried for ages until I was spent. By the end, I felt drained and tired but still couldn't sleep. I was too stressed. It was a knock at the door that forced me to stop the last of my weak snivels.

I opened it to Dr. Cottier standing in the doorway. My heart sank. "What?" I spat the word out, terrified about what he had come to tell me.

He looked a bit disconcerted as he shuffled from foot to foot. "Uh… Dr. O'Donnell and Dr. Runar sent me here to look at your hand."

Suddenly I felt light and hopeful. "Dr. Runar sent you? He's okay? Is Kaye okay?" I asked.

He blinked. For a moment, I felt bad for Dr. Cottier, whose coat and trousers were smeared with blood. He looked a little shell-shocked. Honestly, I think it was his first attack. "They're stable in the sixteenth-floor recovery wards." I felt an immense amount of relief as I let the doctor examine my hand. The rot spread beyond the cuts and was beginning to trace up my veins, indicating blood poisoning.

He announced that I would need a graft. "I'll put in an order for the specimen with Harvest. Dr. Runar had a note in here that he was considered your primary surgeon." Dr. Cottier frowned at the note, written in Braeden's elegant spiked handwriting, then shrugged. "I'll ask him about performing your surgery."

"Is he going to be able to?" I asked, picturing the decay that spread from his wound while he laid unconscious on the floor.

Dr. Cottier gave me a look that suggested I was stupid for even asking. "Dr. Runar is extremely capable, and if he finds himself unable to perform the procedure adequately, I'm sure he will find a suitable replacement." He sniffed loudly.

I bit back my tongue to stop the sharp retort from reaching

my lips. "What time should I see him?"

He sniffed again, "You'll be notified once things have settled."

Deciding that Dr. Cottier was probably on his last nerve, I held my tongue until he left. He quickly cleaned the pus out of my cuts and applied gauze around them. After he was gone, per my usual M.O., I waited patiently for a few minutes, making sure that I wouldn't run into him, before exiting the room.

I went directly to the sixteenth floor, pushing my way past a crowd of doctors and medical staff as they bustled throughout the corridors. When I entered the ward, I could see that Missy's face was wan and pinched. "Hey, Clara." She let out a fatigued sigh, combing her thin fingers through her hair. She didn't bother asking why I was there. "He's in room Sixteen Twelve."

For a moment, we were bonded over our shared grief.

"Is he okay?" I asked quietly. She lifted her bloodshot eyes to mine. Her lips formed a tight line, and she looked at me for a long while.

"He's awake." She finally answered. I swallowed down all the other unpleasant questions I wanted to ask and instead decided to stop stalling and go to see Braeden. "Password's 'vitiligo,'" she said. I repeated the word to myself as I exited the room and was swept into a rush of people.

I weaved through the crowd, trying to keep my patience and not shove them out of my way. I approached the door with Braeden behind it to see two armed guards were posted out front.

The guards eyed me. One opened his mouth; I was sure he was prepared to argue.

"Vitiligo," I said flatly. The guard snapped his mouth shut and stepped aside, gesturing me through the door.

The room was dim with the curtains drawn. A lonely

lamp provided lighting in the corner. Its dull yellow glow illuminated a desk that was pulled up next to his bed. Machines surrounding Braeden were beeping steadily.

In the bed, Braeden sat propped up by pillows, eating gelatin. He didn't spare a glance for me; instead, he stared fixedly at the blank wall as he shovelled the wobbling red cubes into his mouth. I approached him a little apprehensively.

"Hey, there." I moved into his line of vision and examined his face. His eyes seemed unfocused, almost glazed over. I felt a small spurt of worry as the hundreds of warnings I'd received about blank-outs played in my mind. *Once the rot reached the brain, the infected would start to forget who they are. Then they'd start to act strangely...*

My eyes travelled up to the bandage across his forehead where he was hit. *He could be concussed.*

"Braeden?" I asked him uncertainly. He continued to stare at the wall as though he hadn't heard me. I walked a little closer to him. "Braeden? How are you feeling?"

He blinked, turning towards me; his eyes searched my face. "Hello," he said pleasantly. "Were you speaking to me?"

I felt an immediate sense of relief. "Yeah, I was. How are you feeling?"

He glanced down at his body, currently clothed in a hospital gown and blankets. I couldn't see the wound, but there was a slight bulge from where the bandages wrapped around his torso. He blinked a few times, then looked back at me.

"Can I help you?"

"I asked how you were doing, Braeden," I said, unable to keep the concern from my voice.

His eyes opened in understanding, and his mouth formed an 'O.' "Oh! I'm sorry, I didn't hear you. I'm feeling fine." Small relief washed over me.

I scanned the room, trying to distract myself from the

anxiety pooling in the pit of my stomach. Amongst the books and scribbled notes in Braeden's familiar handwriting was a series of drawings. They were a bunch of large, uneven circles. A few of them vaguely resembled a clock. Some of them were misnumbered with multiple hands doodled onto them. Next to one, written in Missy's bubbly handwriting, were the words 'stimulus-bound error.'

The papers were disturbed when Braeden firmly set his empty bowl onto the desk. He held his hands out to me. I placed my own in them. His thumbs moved in familiar little circles over the backs of my hands. My relief was quickly replaced with a warm feeling, spreading from where he touched me. He pulled me in for a kiss, and I reminded myself that he was still in the recovery ward and needed rest.

Taking in his scent and feeling the warmth of his body, I crushed myself closer to him, sighing happily but unable to shake the jittery feeling of worry.

"So, you're really okay?" I whispered into his chest. His eyes followed his fingers as they traced along my lips and jawline. He leaned forward and hugged me tightly, resting his lips on my forehead.

Braeden breathed in deeply. "I feel fine, Clara. Thank you for finding me." I closed my eyes, smiling to myself. The rhythmic rise and fall of his chest relaxed me.

"Can I see it?" I gestured to his stomach. He looked down, with his brow furrowed. I quickly added, "If it's going to get infected or make it worse, then don't."

His long fingers slid the blankets down to his waist and he lifted the gown to reveal bandages covering his abdomen. He prodded them gently with his fingers. A yellowish stain showed on the white bandages.

"Hmmm." He muttered to himself, running his fingers along the seams. "How did that happen?"

"Does it not usually stain like that?" I asked, trying to

stay calm.

He tugged at the bandaging. From the corner of my eye, I could see movement. Missy had quietly entered the room and watched Braeden closely, but her face was unreadable.

Her voice was slow and clear, "How are you feeling?" Braeden tugged his shirt down quickly.

"Fine, Doctor." His voice sounded stronger than it had a moment ago. Missy took out a little flashlight. She stopped on the other side of the bed and asked him to follow the light as she moved it back and forth. She clicked it off, giving me a small disapproving look. I sat up a little straighter but didn't move off the bed. A grimace ghosted across her face.

Braeden yawned loudly and asked what was going on. Missy patted his hands before collecting the clock drawings on the desk beside him. She frowned when she saw them and said, "Okay, Braeden, can you repeat the three items I asked you to remember for me?"

Braeden's eyes unfocused as he searched his brain. "Apple?" he said with uncertainty. Missy's face did not betray anything. She simply jotted something down into her file and continued to look expectantly at him. "Desk." It may have been my imagination, but a flicker of unhappiness crossed her face before it fell back into an unreadable mask. She wrote something else down. Braeden screwed up his face as he searched in vain for the final word. My gaze bounced between Missy and Braeden as I tried to work out what was happening. Finally, his face smoothed over, and he shook his head. "It's there, on the tip of my tongue, but I can't get it. Give me a few moments, please," he said cordially. Missy gave him a small bow and retreated from the two of us. I stood up to follow her.

I tapped her shoulder and she turned, her eyebrows raised eagerly. "Yes, Miss Belford?" She asked in a clear, emotionless voice.

I leaned towards her and said in a hushed tone, "Are

his bandages supposed to be yellowed like that? Do they need to be changed?" I furtively glanced towards Braeden lounging on the bed. My voice dropped to a whisper. "Is he concussed, or is he blanking out?"

She waved me off impatiently and pointed at the door. "Clara, Dr. Inkerman would like to see you in her office; she's been worried about you since the attack finished. I'm afraid the information you've asked for is confidential." She sighed deeply and then added in a kinder voice, "You can come visit him again later tonight, but for now, he needs sleep, and we need to monitor him to ensure he makes a full recovery. Thank you for getting him help the way you did. I—everyone— is incredibly grateful."

I didn't say anything for fear that I was about to burst into tears. Instead, I gave her a watery smile before I quietly exited the room and headed towards Jade's office.

As I left the room, I heard him speak to Missy, "That young lady was very nice, wasn't she?"

"Yes, she was. Now, can you please spell 'world' for me, but backwards?"

"Backwards?" He asked. Missy's response was drowned out by the ruckus in the main hallway. The guards at the entry firmly clicked the door shut behind me as I left.

One sidled up close to me and asked, "So, what's going on? Is the Good Doctor okay?" I weighed up exactly how much to share. *Was he okay? He certainly looked fine, but then again, I wasn't entirely sure what to look for.*

"I think so?" I said in the most non-reassuring tone. When I saw his face fall in worry, I quickly added, "I mean, I'm no doctor, but he was up and talking and everything." The guard's face relaxed, but I could still see the signs of worry tugging at the corners of his mouth and eyes.

Not wanting to answer any more of his questions or make matters worse, I stepped away from the guard and into the throng of people, getting swept away from Braeden's room.

CHAPTER FIVE
The Ransacked Office

By the time I arrived on the second floor, a sheen of sweat covered me, and my heart thundered. Workers swept glass into glittering piles. I picked my way through the clean-up efforts towards a familiar door with a broken window. One of the engineers from the main floor gave me a sideways glance.

"She's in a royal mood right now. Just a warning." His voice was dour.

"When is she not?" I joked, pushing down my worry about Braeden.

Jade's door was ajar. The smashed window had paper taped over it. She sat in her office with her rifle in hand. An open bottle of oil sat on the table next to her. One of her fingers was jammed in the chamber; she wriggled the finger around and popped it back out. "Hey, Clara," she said cheerfully as she dismantled the gun into the upper and lower receiver. She put the lower receiver down and started fiddling with the upper. As she set it down, I noticed an array of old ID passkeys. Jade saw me staring at the cards, which she slid underneath a notebook and away from view, before turning her attention back to her gun.

"How many times did you fire that thing?" I asked her.

She didn't bother breaking focus from the bolt carrier. "Didn't even go through a whole clip, but the action was sticking a bit."

The firing pin was already on the table next to the other pieces of her gun by the time I sat down in the chair opposite of her. "So, I hear that you had quite the adventure. Missy looked like a wreck when I saw her earlier," Jade said as she poured oil onto a piece of surgical gauze. She ran the cloth along the metal. "I take it you were the one who found him?"

I simply nodded as I looked around the office. "No one got in here?" I asked.

Jade paused. The cloth had blackened. "A few tried," she said. "Did anyone check on Braeden's office? They ransacked the offices on this floor, but from what I can gather, it doesn't seem like anything was taken or accessed. I'm not sure what they were after."

A knot formed in the pit of my stomach. "We should check his office, just in case. I bet he'll want to know," I suggested. *At the least, it would be something to keep my mind off things right now.* Jade agreed.

On the sixteenth floor, the ornate wooden door to Braeden's office stood warm against the clinical hallway. Jade's face paled. Where the doorknob should have been, instead, was splintered wood and twisted metal. *Someone had shot out the lock.*

She reached her scarred hand out and pushed the door open.

Papers were strewn all over the floor, and several books were ripped from their bindings, leaving Braeden's office in ruins.

"We need to tell Missy about this," Jade said, wide-eyed. She prepared to leave but turned back when I didn't follow. My eyes were locked on the wreckage that flowed from Braeden's desk. Open, for the first time since I'd been at the Facility, was the upper-left desk drawer. The elaborate lock that usually kept it shut hung broken. Inside were mostly personal client files.

I moved to shut the drawer when something caught my eye. I paused, not sure what to make of it. One of the folders was labelled in Braeden's unique handwriting with the name 'Leonardo Samson.'

Confusion washed over me as I picked it up.

"What do you have there?' Jade asked.

I flicked open the file. Written atop the first page was 'Leonardo ~~Belford~~ Samson.' Except, this even bubbly handwriting was the work of Missy O'Donnell. Evidently, she recorded the wrong last name, then corrected it, meaning they knew Leo was related to a Belford. "Do you guys do blood tests to check for Redspot?" I asked.

Jade shook her head thoughtfully. "Not usually. Nose swabs are used for Wave Two. Wave Three is usually obvious from the transmission. Why?"

Numbly, I stared at Leo's smiling face. "Braeden tested both my mom and my half-brother?"

Jade shrugged. "I dunno." I handed her the file. "Looks like they were checking for a blood match." She frowned at the paper. "This has got to be one of the most complex blood matching processes I've ever seen. In fact, I don't think I've ever seen anything like it."

"A blood match?"

"Yeah. Both were crossmatch positive with Dr. Runar." she said as she handed back the file. At my blank look, she adds, "Neither your mother nor brother has the same blood type as Dr. Runar, so after your whole house became infected, there was nothing to be done for anyone except for you. Although… a simple blood test would have shown that."

"But he was definitely alive when they took the blood test?" I asked quietly.

Jade nodded. "Yeah, this was perimortem. He died here at the Facility. See?"

I held the folder in my hands; the emotions warring inside of me left me feeling strangely empty.

***

It was four months ago. I was in the recovery ward, groggy from spending the last few weeks battling fever dreams. My fever had just broken. Shaking off the last remaining traces of sleep, I sat up in the dark room. I tried to stand but noticed there was someone else in the room with me. The man was incredibly handsome, but so worn he looked almost like a ghost.

"Where's my family?" It was the first thing out of my mouth. "What happened?" Looking around the room frantically, everything was calm and quiet. My heart was racing. Something felt very wrong.

His eyes had searched mine as a look of pain crossed his features. I leaned towards him, silently urging him to speak. Finally, he said, "I'm so sorry to have to tell you this…" Seemingly without thinking, he reached for my hand and started making little circles with his thumb. I froze at the gesture, bracing myself for what I knew was going to come. He sighed, his eyes downcast. "You were the only one we found alive at the scene." The words hit me like a physical blow. Flinching, I shut my eyes as he continued, "The Aegis wasn't able to get there in time to save your brother or mother. The Resistance got there before we could stop them…We nearly lost you, too."

At the time, I flashed back to the attack. I could almost smell their blood and hear their screams as Rotters came in through the entrance. Everything faded into echoing silence after that.

***

Yet, there I stood in Braeden's office with evidence that my brother did not die at the scene. I stared at the file in my hands. Leo's unmistakable face in the hospital, a breathing tube in his mouth. *He said I was the only one they found alive.* I haven't been back to Oakville since they died. I had no reason to go and a lot of reasons to stay away. *Was my brother still alive?* I quickly crushed the thought. It was painful enough to mourn him the first time. *I didn't need to rehash old memories. Jade just said he died here at the Facility. But why would Braeden lie about where my brother died?*

Slipping the file back inside the desk drawer, I couldn't shake the uncomfortable feeling in the back of my head that something was off. I didn't recognize any other name in the drawer, just Leo's. Not exactly sure what to make of that, I shut the drawer and replaced the dangling lock.

The image of his face in the photograph stayed in my mind a moment longer. I sighed and forced back tears. My voice was wooden as I said to Jade, "Okay, let's go down the hall to find Missy and Braeden."

Once we arrived at the recovery ward, the strange numbness rapidly subsided and my appetite returned. My stomach rumbled loudly enough that even Jade gave it a glance. The gathering of people grew thick as we got closer to the surgical suites.

A smell moving through the halls suddenly became tantalizing, though it was laced with something that made my stomach churn. I couldn't quite put my finger on what, but focusing on the strange odour helped keep my hunger pangs at bay.

As we drew closer to the patient rooms, the enticing aroma grew even stronger. Soon my mouth was watering. I half-closed my eyes, inhaling deeply. It smelled better than anything I'd ever experienced.

The crowd here seemed thicker. People were barely

moving. Some just stood and inhaled. Annoyed, I pushed them out of my way as I continued to follow the delicious scent.

Distantly, Jade said something and grabbed my shoulder. She forced me around to face her, and I gave a dopey smile under half-lidded eyes. Briefly, I saw her eye roll towards the ceiling in exasperation before my cheek stung.

Confused, I stupidly blinked a few times, trying to shake off my trance. I barely registered what was happening as she drew her hand back a second time.

The next slap hurt.

"Holy geez. I'm fine! I'm fine!" I said quickly as she pulled her hand back for a third time. I rubbed my red cheek.

"Wait here. Breathe through your mouth." Jade commanded. "Those stupid bastards are trying to do emergency patches with uninfected flesh." She disappeared into the swarm.

Missy emerged from the recovery ward. She sprayed an aerosol mist into the air. "Get out of here, now!" She yelled, waving her arms to clear the way. Her mouth kept moving, but the scent distracted me.

Missy, too, went towards the smell.

See? She just wants it all for herself.

I vaguely registered the sound of glass shattering. Gagging, my eyes watered.

Jade crushed a vial of peppermint and splashed bleach along the hallway. Coughing, the crowd dispersed. She sidled up alongside me with an empty bottle of bleach, looking irritated as her eye watered.

"Dr. O'Donnell is handling discipline. These idiot surgeons were in the O.R., ignoring their patient, eating uninfected patches by the handful." She pushed her blond hair out of her face. "Obviously, someone rushed the patches before they were properly infected. Huge waste of good donor tissue."

"Do we infect the tissue before we use it?" I asked stupidly.

Jade's glare settled on me. Her brow briefly creased as she looked at my cheek, which I was sure was already bright red from her hand. "Yeah, otherwise everyone goes stupid, and the O.R. turns into a buffet."

"How come you and Missy don't seem as affected?" I asked. Jade shrugged as we pushed our way down the hallway towards the door where Braeden rested. The two new guards requested a password. I opened my mouth and shut it again, wordless.

I'd forgotten it.

"It started with a 'V'..." I muttered to Jade. "It was a medical term, I think."

"Missy likes those. Virion?" She tried. I shook my head, wracking my brain for the word. Jade began to guess. "Variola Major? Vaccine?"

"It was like 'viti-' something."

"Vitiligo?"

"Yes!" I turned to the guards. "Vitiligo."

Jade laughed and clapped her hands together. "Right-o, let's go in. Vitiligo… I bet Missy thought she was clever."

The room looked the same as it did on my first visit, though it had been tidied up since I was here last. The clock sketches and dirty dishes were missing from the desk. Braeden greeted us with a small wave.

Jade frowned at Braeden's pleasant smile as we entered the hospital room. "Hello," she said in a carefully neutral tone.

Braeden gave her a wide smile. "Hello." Jade's frown deepened briefly before she let her face fall into the same neutral mask that Missy had worn. Braeden turned his smile toward me.

"You're back," he said happily.

"I am. I just needed to go visit Jade. It turns out someone was trying to get into her office during the attack," I explained. Braeden's smile faltered.

"Excuse me?" All frailty had fled his voice.

Jade hopped up on the counter and crossed her legs. "Yeah, they tried to get my files, but I didn't let them."

Braeden stood from the hospital bed abruptly, and papers from the desk next to him went flying. The little clock drawings spilled out of his folder like leaves.

Braeden ignored the mess and strode out the door. Jade and I exchanged a look before we scurried after him. He was already far down the hallway, moving towards the elevators. We caught him as he waited for the doors to open.

The lights flickered, and the power briefly died. Realizing that he might end up trapped in the elevator, Braeden changed direction to the stairwell. I jogged after him.

He moved up the staircase towards the seventeenth floor. When he got to the door with the number '17' painted on it, he paused and looked around.

"Braeden?" I called out to him, panting and breathless. "Where are you going?" He kept bounding up the stairs. Stopping, I called again, "Dr. Runar?"

He paused and scanned the area around him. Shaking his head as if to clear it, he headed back down the steps. "Sorry, I got a little bit ahead of myself there, didn't I?"

He pushed past me and returned to the sixteenth floor. Seemingly disoriented, he turned in one direction, took a few steps, paused, then moved in the opposite direction.

I stepped towards him, but Jade placed her hand on my arm, stilling me. She watched him intently as he tried to orient himself.

He closed his eyes tight, his face screwing up in frustration. Finally settling into a pleasant composure, he headed down the hallway towards his office. Jade cocked an eyebrow.

"You keep an eye on him. I need to go check something. When you're finished here, meet me back in my office." she said cryptically. "Oh," Jade stopped and faced me earnestly, "I know you're confused right now, but you can't ask him about your brother's file yet. Look at the guy." With that, she sped towards Braeden's hospital room. I gave her one last look, watching as the guard stepped aside, before I rushed after Braeden.

I struggled through the crowd, which seemed to push against me. Braeden, on the other hand, moved through it easily. It parted for him like water, and some people joyfully called out to him. He raised his hands and greeted them half-heartedly. He disappeared around the corner towards his office.

I let out a frustrated groan and rudely shoved a few people aside, trying to catch up with him. Finally, I turned the corner and reached his office.

In the room, Braeden stood motionless behind his desk, mouth agape. His eyes met mine as he swayed on his feet. The colour drained from his face. He swooned, unconscious, to the floor. I tried to catch him, but it was too late.

"Help!" I screamed. As I made sure he was okay and lying down, I glanced at the desk drawer on the upper-left side. It was closed, but the lock was missing. I pondered this for only a moment until, like magic, Missy materialized at the door. Quickly, she placed Braeden's feet on a stack of thick medical textbooks. She gently disengaged me from him and placed his head on a cushion. Her brow was creased as she focused on her work.

Seemingly in moments, Braeden was in a wheelchair and being escorted back to the recovery ward. Missy was irritable but didn't say anything to me as I walked beside them into the hospital room.

When Braeden's eyes fluttered open, he glanced around in vague confusion. Missy arranged her face into a pleasantly neutral expression. Following her lead, I found myself smiling blandly.

When Braeden's eyes met mine, he gave me his usual heart-melting smile. Something about this made Missy smile slightly, instead of her usual glare.

Braeden's voice was breathy but sounded stronger than it had a moment ago. "Missy, when you have a free moment, I have a list of names on my computer that match the files in my desk's top-left drawer. Would you please ensure the files are accounted for? Then I'd like you to go prep the subbasement O.R."

Missy nodded, and without glancing at me, she vanished. Presumably to Braeden's office. Once she was gone, he closed his eyes and said, "You need to go downstairs. Into subbasement two for your operation." His last words were nearly a whisper as he drifted off to sleep.

Braeden gently snored on the bed before me. My heart thumped wildly in my chest at those words.

CHAPTER SIX
Undead Ends

Subbasement two… I was certain that the Facility had only one subbasement. I had asked about subbasement two when I arrived here, because once upon a time, when it used to be the Princess Margaret Cancer Centre, it did have one.

White noise filled my ears as memories crashed over me.

***

I went down into subbasement two to receive my radiation. Small and terrified, I held my mom's hand as we walked down the hallway, which felt far too large and echoing. At the end was Treatment Unit 4. A door was ajar, revealing a giant machine; its armrests had restraints, waiting for my thin arms.

The nurse's voice was distant as she chatted with mom. I eyed a stairwell at the end of another hallway, glancing back at the machine. The device's green lasers were off, but I knew the nurse would flip them on shortly after making sure I was perfectly aligned for direct radiation. Lights would shine images of a measuring tape down my torso. I tried to not let the apprehension fill me. I had done this plenty of times before. The thoughts in my head made it seem worse than it was.

I yanked my hand free from my mom's and sprinted towards the staircase. It was a short and only went up one floor, but it meant freedom. Then, I felt arms as strong as iron bands clasp around me.

***

Braeden's gentle snore brought me back to the present. I stared at his sleeping form, puzzled. I thought I trusted him completely, yet, as I watched the rise and fall of his chest, there was an apprehensive feeling in my gut. *Why would he say subbasement two? Why was Leo's patient file in the locked drawer?*

Weighing up how many files were in the drawer for Missy to count, I waited roughly five minutes in the recovery ward before heading back to Braeden's office.

The hallways were still chaos.

I peered through the wreckage where the doorknob used to be. Though I couldn't see the drawer, I saw that the blue folders from inside were stacked neatly on the desk. They were too far away for me to read the names. I knocked on the door. There was no answer, but the broken door creaked open.

Eagerly, I slipped into the office, my eyes on the prize. Immediately my feet hit a stack of papers on the floor, sending them flying. I cursed and jumped, realizing I was not the only one in the room.

"What are you doing?" Missy stood in the corner of the office with a stack of books in her hands. She proceeded to dump the books in a pile near one of the shelves.

I floundered. Missy knew Braeden hated other people in his office, even me. *Of course, she would assume she should tidy up his office while Braeden is injured.* Scanning the room, the chaos was nearly back in order. My stomach sank when I saw that sitting on the desk was another heavy-duty lock to replace the broken one.

"Oh, I was looking for you." I lied.

Missy cut across the room and gathered the files from the desk. "Clara, I'm very busy right now. What is it?" She shoved them into the drawer and slammed it shut.

A litany of lies sprang to my mind, each more preposterous than the last. I strolled around to the other side of the desk as I stalled, picking at the gauze on my fingers. I barely saw a flash of the list before Missy clicked off the computer screen and faced me expectantly. I tugged the bandage off. Unable to think up anything good, I settled on a half-truth. "Uh, I was just wondering what the deal was with my operation." I held up my injured hand with slices along the thumb and pointer finger and wriggled them. Well, sort of. I wiggled my three healthy fingers at her. My now black thumb and pointer finger just twitched weakly. *That can't be good.*

Missy rolled her eyes. "Do I look like your personal secretary?" She snapped.

Swallowing down my irritation, I changed tact. "Dr. Cottier told me that Braeden—Dr. Runar was going to do it... and, well, he didn't seem like he was in any condition to..." I trailed off. Even if I was a lousy liar, that one hit a little too close to home.

She sighed and said in a gentler tone, "Go check the listings on the first floor to see where your surgery has been slotted. The postings are next to the sign-ups for supply drops. I've already notified Dr. Cottier that I will be performing it." She raked her fingers through her wild red curls. "Clara, please go to the first-aid clinic after you check for your operation. You need those fingers rebandaged." She dismissed me by turning to face the computer but didn't flip the screen back on.

I dawdled in the doorway before exiting. She hadn't moved

a muscle.

"So, what were those files he asked you to check?" I tried to say casually. Internally, a wince. *That was lame.*

"Clara, those files have absolutely nothing to do with you."

"Can I see them?" I asked.

"No. Now can I help you with something, Miss Belford, or are you just bored? I have a lot of work to do, and your fingers need attention." Her tone was brusque. I raised my hand and thanked her. She didn't touch the computer until I exited the office.

I walked away quickly before an inevitable flush turned my face bright red. I knew I was a bad liar, but that was abysmal.

Unable to look at the file, I turned my thoughts back to subbasement two. *Maybe it was only used in emergencies?* I was trying to think if anyone ever mentioned another floor being opened after an attack by the Resistance, but nothing came to mind. I stared at the pus glistening on my wet hand. I went to check the O.R. surgery schedule so I could get my fingers patched up.

When I entered the elevator, just in case, I scanned for subbasement two. There was nothing to indicate that it even existed, let alone had an operating theatre.

I reported to the first floor. The doors opened to a wide atrium filled with natural light. The airy stone that filled the room had been shot to dust during the attack. The metal bannisters, which were usually brightly polished, were coated in white dust. Glass panels lined the balconies and stairs, which were either cracked or blown away into glitter.

Squad 4 was still heavily armed and guarded the outside of the drop coordinator's office. Inside the office were supply drop archives and the Drop Armoury: a smaller weapons cache designated for supply runs. I waved to Squad 4 and proceeded towards the first-aid clinic.

The line went out of the clinic and wrapped around the corner. I groaned, but the complete inability to grip anything made me wait. Missy's voice replayed in my head, 'With Wave Three, the longer a wound has been exposed to open air, the faster the necrosis occurs.'

Posters were on either side of the clinic. One said 'How to Spot a Bleeder' with arrows pointing to a character, red oozing out of its orifices. The cartoon had several distinct rashes on its skin where the disease manifested. I shuddered, thankful that hybridization was the exception and not the norm.

The other poster said, 'What to Do in Case of a Blank-Out.' I stared at the photograph of a seemingly normal Facility member with average skin patches, but the look in their eyes was lost, vacant. Their head sagged slightly. I remembered the first time I watched someone blank out.

***

It was during one of our shifts at the Butcher's Corner, where Evan and I periodically worked as meat sorters for the supply drops. Whenever the smell of meat became too overpowering, I loaded up on peppermint oil. It was incredibly effective.

That day, we needed to prepare approximately two thousand packages for the drop sites.

Next to me, there was a sullen-looking girl who made it painfully clear within the first few minutes that she was not there to make friends. At first, I thought she was anti-social, but the more I paid attention, the more it seemed like she was struggling worse than others when it came to the meat.

As I wondered if I should flag Evan down, the girl grabbed a thick portion of a ribcage and began gnawing on the gristle-covered bone. Unable to react, I stared at her.

Her eyes locked onto mine and she bit down into the bone with alarming ferocity. There was a loud crack as the bone broke. She started working into it with the enthusiasm of a starving dog, no longer paying attention to the task at hand. Her eyes rolled into the back of her head as saliva drooled down her face. The others were staring at her in mute fascination. Several were eyeballing the nearby meat, tempted to follow the actions of the girl. Work had completely stopped around my table.

Evan, sensing that something was amiss, came straight over to me since I was the newest meat sorter. "Hey, Clara, are you doing okay?" Without saying anything, I pointed at the girl who was crunching down on the bone like a breadstick, his face went pale.

A mix of blood and saliva dribbled down her chin. Initially, I thought it was blood from the meat until I noticed that she cracked one of her teeth. Evan called over security. Two burly men approached the girl cautiously. She cradled the bone close to her chest as she snapped and gnashed her teeth at the guards.

The others moved away from her and I followed in suit, while the two men worked out how to best approach her. I watched the reactions on the others' faces with curiosity. Most, like me, were looking around trying to get a read on the situation. A few were focused on inhaling their vials of peppermint, paying no attention to the altercation. Evan took note of these people; they wouldn't be allowed at the next sorting without tests.

One guard slammed the girl to the ground while the other grabbed her by the hair to keep her teeth away from their arms. She thrashed and growled; Evan ran forward to wrestle the bone away from her. He doused a rag with peppermint oil and threw it over her head. She eventually went still.

"What's happening?" Her voice was high-pitched and scared from beneath the rag. Evan cautiously rolled down the rag so that he could see her eyes. They were wide with panic. Apologetically, he placed restraints on the girl's wrists and ankles, citing it was just a precaution until we got back to the Facility.

The ride back was dead silent. Everyone gave the girl a wide berth, eyeing her with fear. She sobbed silently in the corner, blood still running down her chin from the broken tooth.

We arrived back at the Facility, and darkness cloaked the truck as we entered the underground transport bay. Medical staff awaited our arrival. The girl collapsed to her knees, begging them to not take her away. The staff held her down, while Evan, looking a little shaken, ordered each of us to get a precautionary medical checkup. He took the weeping girl and disappeared with the rest of the medical staff down the tunnels. I never saw her again.

***

I stood in line glumly for what felt like ages but was probably only half an hour. Finally, I neared the front and approached the reception desk where a woman sat, smiling widely at me. She stood and offered me her hand, introducing herself as Selena. Her ring finger was deeply bruised and sported a small wedding ring. I grasped her hand, making sure not to squeeze too tightly. *I had an irrational fear that doing so might pop her finger right off.*

Her smile widened. "Well, hello. My goodness! Your fingers look painful! You poor dear!" Her chirpy tone had me baring my teeth in what I'm sure was a piss-poor excuse for a smile.

"Hi." My mouth remained open, but I couldn't think of anything to say back to this woman, with her weird rotting ring finger. She paused for a moment before deciding I wasn't going to add anything. She hitched up a sugary smile and bobbed out from behind the reception desk. Her high voice trailed behind her as she gestured for me to follow. "Welcome, I'm going to take you into the back and get that fixed up for you! Come, come." She beckoned me with a flick of her wrist towards the back room.

She examined my fingers and dipped them into a numbing

solution. "I'm afraid I can't do too much, but hopefully this will slow it down," she said and snipped away at the meat on my palm. One snip burned and drew blood. I hissed through my teeth. "Oh good, pain means nerve endings," she said happily, as I held back a catalogue of expletives to scream at her. She smoothed a patch of skin over my fingers and bandaged them.

Her parting words to me were, "Go check the O.R. list for your time, sweetie. That will spread if it's not dealt with soon!" She waved me off and went to collect the next Facility member needing care.

Posted on the whiteboard was next week's surgery list. Out of curiosity, I scanned the list for subbasement two. Nothing. The operating theatres only went down to the BSL-2 Labs in subbasement one. I searched for my name to determine when the surgery was scheduled. Surprisingly, I was listed for tomorrow. I frowned and immediately felt guilty. Just because Braeden Runar and I had something romantic didn't mean I always deserved special treatment. Still, it was odd.

I skimmed the list for Missy's name and noticed something else. Dr. O'Donnell wasn't scheduled to perform any surgeries today. I took my finger and ran it along the list of doctors' names. Nothing.

I knew Missy was Braeden's personal physician, but surely the Facility wouldn't assign one of their top surgeons anywhere besides an operating theatre the day after an attack? There was also the question of the operation Braeden thought was happening downstairs. More and more intrigued by the lost subbasement, I made my way to the emergency stairs and went down them two at a time.

Stopping at the base of the stairs in subbasement one, where one direction led to the underground tunnel network, and the other led to BSL-2, I examined where the stairwell dead-ended. The bricks in place were painted the same colour as the rest of the walls but weren't made of the same material. I ran my hands along the rough bricks but couldn't find a single loose one. I wondered how to get back there.

I eyed the aluminum doors that led to the BSL-2 labs and operating theatres. They were kept under tight security at the Facility, and I had no access. *Yet.*

I took the stairs to level two.

I went in the opposite direction of the BSL-4 labs, towards Jade's office. Written on the door was 'Dr. Jade Inkerman MD MS FRCPSC.'

When I entered the office, Jade was seated at a little table. Books were everywhere. Unlike Braeden's office, where there was a semblance of order, Jade's office was a chaotic array of papers, books, and weaponry. I grinned to myself. Even though no one had managed to get in, it was in worse shape than Braeden's ransacked office.

"Oh, good, you made it in time!" she said brightly as she looked at the watch on her wrist. "I've got like five minutes before my first surgery." Her eye was bloodshot, and she cradled a mug of coffee in her hands. After most of the international trade lines were cut, coffee became a rare and prized resource. *Jade must have been having a rough one.* "Did Braeden calm down?" She asked me cheerfully, despite her exhaustion. Mounted on the wall behind her were blades, swords, and daggers. A crossbow leaned against the desk with an arrangement of bolts beside it. Metal gleamed at me from all sides. In contrast to the chaos of the rest of the office, the weapons were kept surgically clean and sharpened, looking almost new. The smell of fresh oil hung in the air.

"Yeah, he was napping when I left him," I said, not bothering to take a seat, convinced that exhaustion might overtake me if I stopped moving. I continued, "Have you ever heard of a second subbasement within the Facility?"

Jade shook her head and gave me a quizzical stare,

"The second subbasement took up too many resources, so it got walled off." she said. "No one can get into it."

Shelving my train of thought, I asked, "What did you look up?"

"Whether Leonardo Samson was ever recorded in the computer system as a patient here."

"And?"

"Nope." Jade looked deep in my eyes. "Look, it might have been because admin was lazy and knew he was a goner. I mean, his file said he was infected with Wave Three, but... it could be something else too. Like I said, I've never seen a blood test done like that before."

An anxious feeling grew inside me. "Jade," I said carefully, "could you please do me a favour?"

"What is it?"

I reached down to grab one of the numerous IDs Jade collected from Facility members who went to rot over the years. I chose the one with the highest security clearance and held the laminate card up between two fingers. "Can I borrow this?"

Her face broke into a mischievous grin. "Sure."

CHAPTER SEVEN
The Missing Stairwell

With one of Jade's ID cards in my pocket, I casually strolled back down the stairs towards the subbasement.

Mimicking the path I would have taken a decade ago if I were a floor lower, I retraced my way through the secured area near the BSL-2 labs. Not needing to enter them directly, I took the long hallway just outside of the suit room.

I remembered this hallway from years ago.

***

"Hey, hey, it's okay." The nurse said gently after she found me tucked behind the waiting chairs, crying. "You're feeling a little stressed, huh?" She got down on her knees, eye level with me. I nodded and wiped a silver trail of snot along my sleeve. "What room are you supposed to be in?"

"Four." My hysterical eight-year-old voice piped back.

"But you don't want to go right now?" Her voice was calm, and her eyes kind. I didn't, and she understood. She asked if I wanted a few minutes of time by myself, or if I wanted a hug.

"I want to be alone." I replied through hiccups, wiping

my puffy eyes. She smiled and held out her hand. She didn't care that my fingers were covered in tears and mucus as she walked me up the stairwell and into a small, empty supply closet, hidden between two hallways.

Both doors were shut tight, and the nurse produced a small footstool for me to sit on. "I'll come back in a few minutes to check on you, but take the time you need, okay? Your mom is just outside when you're ready." She said, shutting the door on my first of what was to be many crying sessions in that closet before my radiation.

***

At the end of the long and twisted hallway, I reached exactly where my spot was. Only, instead of a door, a large abstract painting hung on the wall before me. Wondering if this way had been bricked off, too, I grinned as I lifted the canvas off the wall to reveal the door behind it.

Through the small closet was an entrance to another disused hallway. The end of the hallway revealed a staircase leading to subbasement two. Littered in front, like an annoying obstacle course, were a few dozen gurneys and beds. I clambered over the gurneys to reach the stairwell.

I opened the door at the bottom of the stairs, leading to the disused floor, and my heart stopped. The subbasement looked identical to how it did all those years ago. I forced that thought down and focused on the important thing. *The lights were on.* I clung to the shadows on the wall as I darted my way down the hallway, ears straining to pick up any sounds. Hushed voices and quick footsteps came from the direction of the old radiation treatment units. Ignoring fears from years ago, I followed the noises.

Treatment Unit 4 was exactly where I remembered it being. Someone, whom I recognized as a nurse, moved in and out of it.

Dim lights flickered in the subbasement. The nurse looked harried; her hair was gnarled, and her eyes were bloodshot. Deep bruises ran down her face. If she hadn't been moving so quickly, I would have thought she was a Rotter. I froze for a moment before pulling myself behind a fake plant. The leafy green plastic obscured me nicely from view. She opened the door to the treatment unit, and Missy's voice floated out. "Are you ready to operate?" Missy asked.

Braeden's voice responded. "Yes, yes, I've done this before. I am going to be a little bit distractible, so please, nothing to break my concentration—" The door swung shut.

Checking that the coast was clear, I scampered over to the adjoining observation room, cloaked in darkness. The room was packed with machines and stacked chairs. It had been turned into another storage area. I shuffled some of the furniture around to keep myself hidden from view. I picked up a chair, but it slipped from my injured hand. I used my foot to cushion its impact before it could clatter on the floor. The heavy chair struck the bones in my feet, hard. Hopping around for a few moments, I wanted to shout, but I mouthed out curse words until the pain subsided.

I glanced at the ripped skin that peeked out from beneath the hastily applied bandages on my injured hand. Already, the torn edges were blackened and oozing. I tried to make a fist, but the pointer and thumb couldn't close all the way. Ignoring the injury, I glanced through the small observation window into the newly retrofitted operating room.

The room held the same array of monitors they had up in the BSL-4. A huge machine dangled from the ceiling, wrapped in plastic. From it, beamed a light that was eye-wateringly bright.

I made out Braeden and Missy in the centre, lit by the monitors dotted throughout the room. The glowing screens displayed brain scans and numbers from machines surrounding an empty silver table.

Missy wheeled a stretcher into the centre of the room. I

blinked a few times. *Kaye?* My brain sluggishly tried to piece this together. *Was he getting an operation here first?*

He laid on a stretcher, bound and barely conscious. Missy rolled him beside the empty operating table and locked the wheels in place to prevent it from moving.

Braeden and Missy shifted Kaye onto the table. Missy's hair burned like blood beneath the flickering bulbs. The regular lights dimmed slightly, while the fluorescent bulbs strobed chaotically throughout the room.

"Will you shut those lights off? I've already got enough of a migraine because of all the shit in my head." Braeden growled at Missy. She ducked her head and hurriedly turned off the overhead lights. A dull yellow filled the room and my eyes took a moment to adjust. I pulled back further into the shadows of the observation room.

"Make sure that door is locked." His voice sounded hard, and my heart broke for him. *I couldn't imagine trying to operate on my own brother.*

"*You ruin my concentration.*" The memory of his lips against my skin as he whispered that sent goosebumps to rise upon my flesh. I smiled down at the lighter skin patch that always got them first. Dotting up my arm was bruising that made my smile drop. My own memories were beginning to flicker in and out, just like those lights.

Kaye woke up and jerked against the bonds. His words were garbled and unintelligible. His mouth opened wide in a scream, and for a moment, it looked like he had no tongue, just a stump. *Had the rot spread to his tongue? Or even... his brain?* My heart thumped in my chest, making me feel more alert than before.

Braeden forcefully held Kaye's arm still as Missy lined up a needle with his vein. Kaye shrieked and thrashed harder as Missy swore softly under her breath. *He was acting like he'd gone to rot.* The restraints that tied him down were old, but they held.

Missy's eyes narrowed in concentration as she tried again. Finally satisfied, she quickly taped down the IV before grabbing a syringe of clear liquid to inject into him. Once Kaye stilled, the two of them leaned over him, like vultures picking over a kill.

My heart pounded as I tried to get a better view from my hiding spot. Finding another place to peer through, I could clearly see their hunched forms over Kaye's body. Illuminated on the monitors were brain imaging maps. Missy pulled vial after vial of his blood.

"You prep him while I get the heart-lung machine ready." Braeden turned to Missy and clasped both of her gloved hands in his. He looked into her eyes intently. "Remember, I'm trusting you. The Facility is trusting you. You can do this."

"You remember our deal?" Her voice was cold. Braeden gave her a pleasant smile.

"Of course, Dr. O'Donnell. And I will be happy to assist with your procedure when the time comes, but right now, let's focus on this operation."

"Have you ever done it this close to the spinal cord, Doctor?" For the first time, I heard a slight tremble in her voice.

Braeden swallowed visibly, "No, but we're sure to see a disruption in the ANS. We've got mild necrosis near the medulla."

Missy closed her eyes. She took a shaky breath. "I'll enter through the anterior median fissure," she said, nodding once, as though confirming her own decision.

Almost lovingly, she stroked back the black hair that clung to Kaye's sweating forehead. I stifled a gasp as she pulled out a huge pair of clippers and began shaving his head meticulously.

My heart was in my throat.

She pulled out wads of gauze and began to wipe him

down with a thick, bubbling, orange solution, which resembled drying blood underneath the gloomy lights. It was the same solution they wiped me down with when they did my patch.

Surely, they're not attempting to do a brain transplant on Kaye? I had asked about brain transplants when I was given my orientation tour of the Facility. Dr. Martinez, the man in charge of BSL-2, was showing a group of us around the labs.

***

He was a swarthy man with laugh lines etched into his face from spending too much time in the sun. He stopped in front of a doorway to the labs and said, "This is the room we've dubbed: The Rotter Pit." Behind the door were low murmurs of a restless crowd. Vaguely, through the slit of a window, I saw people milling about in a dimly lit room. "It's where we keep our active Wave Three subjects."

A sign on the door was half-covered with masking tape. Stamped in neat letters, visible beneath the beige tape, were the words 'Large Animal Holding Room' with a little biohazard symbol.

Dr. Martinez scanned his passkey and cracked open the door. Surrounding us were two dozen Rotters. They barely seemed to notice us. My heart hammered in my chest as I forced myself to remember that the infected weren't interested in me. *For all these things know, I was one of them.*

Even with the air conditioning toiling away, the stench of rot was rank in the air, almost overpowering. Despite the heat from the summer's evening, the room had been quite cold, especially compared to the rest of the subbasement. Dr. Martinez explained that this was to slow down the rot and to keep them in a near hibernation state.

I stared at the blank faces surrounding me. Dr. Martinez placed his gloved hand on a nearby Rotter's shoulder. The spot where his hand rested became dampened as the festering wound oozed through the cloth.

Dr. Martinez gestured towards it. "With Wave Three, open-air exposure speeds up the necrosis. The death knell of the virus is when the infection reaches the brain. We're seeing if proximity or tissue type affects the spread rate." A Rotter with a missing eye socket patted its hip, then its other hip. It looked down, thumb hooked to its pocket. It stopped and shuffled off. Dr. Martinez watched his test subject fondly as it went. "Once the rot reaches the brain, it's all over. That's when we have blank-outs, and then the condition worsens exponentially.

"Why can't we do anything once it reaches the brain?' I asked.

A dark look fell over his face, "The brain is much more complex than the other organs that we replace with grafts and transplants. When the rot reaches the brain, there is nothing that can be done. Medical science just isn't there yet."

***

I swallowed thickly as I looked at Kaye's prone body. His usual smiling face was smooth, devoid of any emotion. His chest rose and fell gently. Even beneath the dark sweep of his eyelashes, I could see the bruising that ran around his eyes. The purple veins that crawled up his neck were a testimony to how far the rot had spread.

Braeden's eyes bore similar bruises as he looked at his brother. His face was frightened as he reached out and ran his hand over the shiny skin on Kaye's head. He paused a moment and sighed heavily. Removing his gloves, he lifted his shirt, revealing a lean, chiselled body. I felt a warm flush as he arched over a large machine equipped with small tubes. He grabbed a blue surgical gown, and his bare chest was magnificent against the dim lighting. He pulled the gown over his body, tying it from the back.

Missy, meanwhile, positioned the light onto Kaye's shaved

head, projecting an array of lines and measurements. She readjusted the light a few times, according to the dimensions shown on the computer screens in front of her. I realized with unease that I could see Kaye's blood filling the machine attached to his left arm. *Wasn't blood supposed to go the other direction?*

A loud banging on the door startled me, as well as Missy. The light she had been adjusting swivelled off-centre, illuminating Kaye's shoulder. Missy and Braeden went perfectly still.

The banging on the door became more insistent. "Dr. Runar, if you're in there, you need to come out now. We have a situation." It was the grumpy nurse from earlier.

"I'm busy, Lacey. Surely this can wait." Braeden's voice was clipped and cold.

"No, sir. You're needed upstairs, now," Lacey replied with a slight note of panic in her voice.

Braeden sat upright; his face covered in shadow. He rolled his shoulders. "I'll be there in one moment."

Missy reached for his arm, "Doctor, we really need to do this as soon as possible." He shook her hand away.

"Yes, I'm aware of that, Missy." He snarled at her. "You know Lacey wouldn't interrupt without cause." He undid the gown, pulled his shirt over his torso, and exited the room.

Missy stood in the empty room and paced around. Occasionally, she would stop at the operating table and adjust the blankets covering Kaye. Other times, she would read from the monitors like she was trying to memorize what was on them. After a few minutes, Missy opened the door to the room and peered out; she glanced back at Kaye, clicked off the lights, and darted down the hallway. I pulled tighter into the shadows, holding my breath until her footsteps disappeared. Emboldened, I slipped out of the observation room and tried to enter Treatment Unit 4. The door was locked. I rattled the knob, hoping to undo the locking mechanism. I mused the thought of picking the lock for some time, but I was jerked away from my reverie by the sound of approaching footsteps. I slipped back inside the observation room, tucked away in the corner to be unnoticed.

Missy entered the room, wheeling a bed with a relatively healthy-looking woman asleep on it. Humming to herself, she leaned over and tightened the straps, holding the unconscious woman down. Gently, she brushed the hair off the nape of the woman's neck and dabbed at it with a piece of cotton doused in alcohol.

She slid over to the fridge and removed a vial rack with fifteen quivering glass tubes. She carefully selected one and pulled a syringe worth of fluid from the vial.

Still humming to herself, Missy picked up what looked like a little plastic gun with a thick needle attached on the front. She lined up her shot at the base of the woman's skull and injected the liquid. The woman shuddered and went still. Missy pushed her bed in line with Kaye's and locked it into place. She gently rolled Kaye over onto his belly, readjusting a mask covering his face that fell slightly. His shaved scalp poked out through a mess of sterile blue paper and plastic that wrapped around the machines and cabinetry. I noticed that she used some sort of pen to draw her incision lines, crisscrossing on the base of his skull.

Missy rubbed the orange solution over his lower back before picking up a sharp scalpel. The incision was made just beneath a dimple on his lower back. She pulled out an enormous t-shaped needle. Lining up the needle with her incision, she took a small silver hammer and knocked it into his hip, like a chisel. She pulled out a portion of the needle and seemed satisfied.

She picked up a recorder, clicked it on, and said, "Cortical layer of subject eight has been breached at 8:31 am." She clicked it off, placed it down, and screwed a barrel onto the needle. When she lifted the plunger, a swirl of frothy liquid began to slowly fill the container. After a few minutes, she switched the barrel out with a new one. Once several of these were filled with the reddish-brown liquid, she removed the needle and placed it on a little tray.

Looking over her utensils, Missy selected a plastic pen-looking instrument. She fiddled with it until the tip of the pen was glowing white hot. With the utensil in one hand, she grabbed a cloth with the other and wiped a small dribble of blood that oozed from the incision she made on Kaye's back. After inspecting the heated tip, she pressed it sparingly over the wound. Instantly, it fused shut. The smell of burning flesh reached my nostrils. I gagged a little bit and covered my mouth and nose with my hand.

Missy collected her vials and placed them into the nearby fridge.

Once this was done, she turned her attention to the unconscious woman and lifted her hair. I could see a dark spot forming where the shot had been administered. Missy rolled the woman onto her back and picked up her arm. Her eyes rolled up into her head, and she gurgled a little bit. I gasped when I saw the tell-tale bruising flowing up from the woman's fingertips and toes. She was a Rotter.

With the same deft movements from before, Missy wiped down the crook of the Rotter's elbow, lined the needle with a vein and placed an IV line. She injected another series of liquids into the woman, retightened her straps, and proceeded to take the woman out of the room.

I sat in the darkness, watching Kaye's still form beneath the harsh beam of the dangling overhead light. I was contemplating leaving when I heard Missy and Lacey return. The two women resumed prepping the O.R.

"Such lovely dark hair," Lacey said as she picked up a bowl filled with foam and wet, black locks of Kaye's hair.

Missy glanced over her shoulder at the bowl. "Yeah, all of his family has that hair. Just beautiful," she said. "What was so urgent that Dr. Runar needed to be called back upstairs?" Missy asked.

Lacey gave her a long look before answering, "His drawer with the files? That wasn't the only thing they got."

Missy went still. "What do you mean?"

Lacey was enjoying herself. Theatrically, she placed the bowl down and leaned towards Missy, "I mean, they breached the you-know-what in the tunnels."

Missy's face went sheet white. She excused herself and exited the O.R. immediately. *The you-know-what in the tunnels?* I turned this piece of information around in my head. *The tunnel network was massive. They could have been after anything. The armoury was in the tunnels. So was a lot of our medical equipment. Were they after our weapons? Maybe our research?*

I crouched behind the machinery and watched as Missy jogged down the hallway to investigate. When she disappeared, I emerged from my hiding spot and sprinted as quickly as I could towards the entrance to the tunnels.

There was a mass of people moving through the concrete tunnels. I bobbed and weaved throughout the crowd, wondering if I had missed her. When I turned around for the fifth time, I found myself nose-to-nose with Missy.

She said loudly, "This corridor is for soldiers and doctors, Miss Belford, of which you are neither." She stopped in front of me and crossed her arms, chin tilted up aggressively as she stared into my eyes. "I am aware Dr. Runar pulled you out of the field last night. What are you doing here?"

My mouth froze open as I scoured my brain for a suitable lie. "The lockers." I blurted out, pointing to the familiar room just behind her, "I was just clearing out my locker." I tried to keep my face as neutral as possible.

"Good." Missy's blue eyes leveled at me coolly. "Who gave you that clearance?"

"Dr. Inkerman," I grinned sheepishly. "I was medically sound, though."

Missy sighed and gave me a thoughtful look. "If we want to get through this pandemic, we all have to make sacrifices, Clara. Braeden's barely hanging on. He needs your support and needs you to stay safe," she said. "Sometimes you can do more for the cause by staying on the sidelines. Bullets can only stop a few people, but what Braeden is doing here, that could change everything."

She looked at me earnestly before taking a step back. It took me a moment before realizing she was waiting for me to make good on what I said and go into the locker rooms. Begrudgingly, I entered the busy room. It only took a few moments before Chase flagged me down. I closed my eyes, bracing for the inevitable demand to sign over all my gear, along with a tongue lashing for sneaking around Missy and potentially getting Jade in trouble.

Instead, Chase said, "Hey, I still haven't gotten your gear checked off. Have you returned it?" He eyed my civilian clothing.

"It's in my room," I replied.

Chase shook his head, tutting, "You know the protocol, Belford. As soon as the all-clear is given to your squad, you need to return all your gear to the armoury, ASAP." He hugged his clipboard to his massive chest and rocked on his heels, "Though Jade mentioned you were the one who found the Doctor. I can understand you being a bit rattled after that." I nodded as my gut did another flip at the thought of Braeden, wherever he was.

"I'll go grab it," I said, wondering if I might still be able to catch Missy and not quite able to believe my luck.

The main room in the tunnels was packed, but she was nowhere to be seen.

I made my way up to Braeden's office and, kneeling in the corridor, before the rich oak door, was one of the maintenance technicians. He was installing a handleset. The handle was a large brass flourish attached to a lock.

The new unit had a fingerprint scanner and keypad. My gaze moved to the other side, where I eyed relatively simple hinges. They were held in place by two screws apiece. I shrugged. *Maybe the new lock was mostly for show.*

I stepped over the technician's toolbox and poked my head into the office. Neither Missy nor Braeden was inside. Instead, another technician was crouched before the desk, presumably installing another lock. In his hands, he scrubbed the new hole in the drawer with fine-grit sandpaper. The guy didn't spare a glance from his work as he asked, "Something you need help with?"

I peered over the edge of the desk. The drawer had been emptied. After a quick scan of the office, it was apparent the files were moved elsewhere. "Um, I just came to check on how things were coming along for Dr. Runar." I craned my neck, trying to spot a flash of blue anywhere amongst the warm honey tones. For a second, when I blinked, the symbol of the flourished 'R' with a phoenix flying from it flashed before my eyes. I did a double take and stared for a few moments before realizing the technician was giving me a weird look. "Looks like everything is going great!" I said brightly, then awkwardly left the office.

Grumbling to myself, I made my way down to the fourteenth floor to retrieve the gear from my apartment. The lack of sleep and food had me exhausted to the point of hallucinating. *I'll ask Jade about the operating theatre tomorrow.* I collapsed into sleep and my gear remained neatly piled in the corner by the front door.

CHAPTER EIGHT
New Parts

The next day I sat propped up in a bed on the sixteenth floor. My wound had turned an ugly black and red. Yellow pus pearled along the slices on my hand. My thumb and pointer finger had gone black.

Missy was in front of me, her hair tied back in a tight bun. "Can you move these?" She asked, pointing to my blackened fingers. I curled three of them successfully. Neither my thumb nor pointer so much as twitched. "All right, your hand might be out of commission for a week or so."

Missy's face was still drawn and tired from the attack, but she looked much happier than she did yesterday. Though she assured me that she had a good night's sleep, it looked like she'd been working tirelessly since the Facility had been resecured. Most of the donor tissue had been lost in the attack, and several of the labs had been breached. BSL-4 laboratories were under partial lock down until repairs could be made.

Missy snapped on her gloves. I noticed several people were milling around the room as I was wheeled into the O.R.

Amongst the tools on the table were several that looked like long drills. I squeezed my eyes shut before opening them to stare at the ceiling with its blinding fluorescents.

My arm was wiped down with the orange solution, like the one used on Kaye. I felt a stab of worry. Missy refused to tell me what was going on with Kaye, saying annoyingly vague things like, "We're doing all we can" and "He can't have visitors right now."

"Brachial plexus nerve block, Doctor?" the block nurse confirmed as he sorted through the various bottles in front of him.

"Yes, as well as general anesthesia." I looked between the two of them with concern. The block nurse didn't look surprised by this, so I found myself relaxing as he lined a needle with my vein. They placed an IV in my arm and a mask over my face. My eyelids fluttered closed and their voices faded into nothingness.

I woke up in an empty recovery room.

My hand was heavily bandaged. Two of my fingers were immobile in a plaster. I stood up, realizing my lower abdomen felt tender. I pressed my hands against it, curious. My right hand was numb.

Missy entered the room, beaming. "Everything went perfectly. How do you feel?"

I held up my bandaged hand. "It's still numb."

She smiled. "Yes, it will be for a few days while the nerves regenerate. We'll remove the bandaging so that your skin can air dry while it heals."

She took large clippers and snipped the bandages off. The flesh on half of my hand was yellowish and light. The thumb and pointer were slimmer than my other fingers and the nails were long and ovalene compared to my short-clipped ones. I examined my hand. At first glance, the fingers looked like they might belong to me.

I attempted to remain detached and scientific about it,

but I always felt a little creeped out whenever I got a new patch. Missy helped me to my feet so that I could head back to my room.

"You'll need to see me again tonight so that I can re-bandage it before you sleep," Missy said. I dimly thanked her as I left, repulsed by my new fingers.

Back in my room, the pile of gear that I had yet to return sat in the corner, mocking me. As badly as I wanted to share with Jade what I saw the other day, I needed to get my stuff downstairs before the higher-ups discovered Chase was covering for my ass. Especially because I didn't know if I was kicked off Extraction Platoon or not.

Groggy from the drugs still in my system, I shrugged on my jacket before I clipped my weapons into place. Everything else was slung over my left arm while I carried the gasmask in my right. The rubber mask kept slipping through my numbed fingers down to the floor. Irritated, I threw the strap around my neck along with the lanyard for my Facility ID. Once I had gathered all my gear, I wandered down to the armoury.

The look of relief on Chase's face was immediate when he saw me. "Oh, don't ever do that to me again. Hakim would have killed me."

"Sorry, it's been hectic. I just got out of surgery." I held up my new fingers.

Chase jerked his head towards his bulging bicep, where a shiny new strip of white flesh wrapped around his arm. "You weren't the only one who lost flesh the other night. Sergeant Longboat got a pretty nasty scrape herself. She's been looking for you." His voice was neutral.

My stomach plummeted. "Did she say what she wanted?" I asked.

He shook his head. "Nah, man, Longboat only shares with people she wants to share with. But she told me she'd be up on the ninth floor, quote, 'If Belford has some reason to stop by today,' unquote." He said.

Something told me Piper had noticed the missing gear.

Once in the elevator, I used my ID card to scan onto the ninth floor. I breathed a sigh of relief as the elevator dinged shut and began to climb upwards. *They hadn't taken away my security clearance yet.*

Being one of the most secure floors in the building, the ninth floor looked like any other recovery floor, except posted at every intersection was one of the Facility's specialist deadeye marksmen. The guard stationed near the elevators was a self-described feisty country boy named Aidan, who gained his skill by picking off rats at the farm with a .22. He also lived on the fourteenth floor, and had two great qualities: his aim, and his ability to make a cup of tea.

"Hey, have you seen Sergeant Longboat?" I asked him.

He pointed down the hallway. "She's grilling the floor pretty hard for information right now." He sounded a bit dazed, which was understandable. Piper was great in the field, but she had an aptitude for pulling information from people that was almost breathtaking. I considered myself lucky to have never been on the receiving end of it.

"Everyone's on edge and wants answers," I replied vaguely to Aidan as I waved a greeting to the deadeye at the far end of the corridor. After the marksman greeted me back, I proceeded down the hallway towards him—no point in getting shot due to lack of manners. A door ahead of me creaked open, and a man with triangular skin patches on his cheeks, like a clown, gestured wildly for me to come close to him. "Hey, girlie," he said. His hair was split evenly down his scalp, one side curling and dark, the other wavy and white. He looked like a cartoon villain.

I kept my distance. "What?" My voice echoed down the empty hall. The Leuko flinched. It was noticeable that the white side of his hair was thinning. His scalp showed through in large patches.

He furtively glanced around and beckoned again. I planted my feet more firmly and raised my eyebrows to him in a challenge. Still not giving up, he wheedled back and forth, scanning the hallway, seemingly oblivious to Aidan standing only fifty feet away. "I'm heading north toward Newmarket after this. Just in case you're interested." He winked. Though the Facility banned Leukos from making any deals within its walls, they always announced their travel plans loudly in hopes of more jobs. Like everyone else with Strategy clearance, I ignored them. I snorted and shook my head with derision before continuing to find Piper. My palms were sweating. I was dreading this conversation.

At the end of the hallway, a door stood ajar. Inside, Piper was talking animatedly to a merc. Mona was in the corner, scribbling furious notes on the interviews. Piper glanced at me mid-question and held up a finger for a moment. After the Leuko repeated his whereabouts for the week prior to the attack, Piper turned her attention to me.

"Belford, come with me," she said as soon as I reached the doorway. She stomped towards the middle of the empty hallway. Once we were out of earshot, Piper stopped. She scanned me and said, "First of all, how are you? Had everyone not been talking about you and the Good Doctor, I would have worried when your gear wasn't checked in this morning." *I knew she noticed.* "Holding up okay?"

I inhaled deeply, thinking about the last two days. "Things were a little shaky. I'm doing better, though."

Piper smiled. "I'm glad to hear it." She glanced around, then leaned towards me. Her voice was low when she said, "So, in the craziness of Dr. Runar getting injured and everything, no one's brought up pulling you from the squad. Braeden hasn't said anything; neither has Commander Dekkar. No official action has been taken." I swallowed down the bitterness at the thought of being off the team, sitting idly by, while the Resistance tried to destroy the Facility. I opened my mouth, but Piper cut me off, "We might be in the clear if we're smart about it. So, you're going to take a few weeks off for bereavement and to heal up your hand. When the higher-ups have completely forgotten about it, I'll bring you back into the mix."

I nodded thoughtfully. "So, what's the news with these guys?" I asked as we walked along the hallway back to Mona and the Leuko.

Piper gave me a long stare before saying, "You know, Belford, that sounds an awful lot like a question that shouldn't be asked by someone staying out of the mix." I bit my cheek and nodded again, trying to wrestle down my frustration. This was the biggest attack on the Facility since my arrival, and I was being benched. There was a part of me that wanted to grab a gun and just hunt them all down, one by one. *Bullets can only stop a few people, but what Braeden is doing here, that could change everything.*

I turned the words Missy said to me earlier over in my brain before saying, "Fine, but have they at least been honest?"

"Do mercs ever behave with honour?" Piper quipped back as we slowed in front of Mona.

"They do when you pay them," Mona interjected as she met eyes with the merc. "As long as you pay them enough."

The two of them went back to their interview. As I left, I added quietly, "Hey Piper?" She turned around, her eyebrows raised. "I'll skip the scouting missions happily, but only if you promise to cut me in on the next big mission."

Piper grinned. "You can count on it."

Feeling lighter than air, I practically floated down to Jade's office.

Jade was sitting at her small breakfast table, looking exhausted. She had been in surgery all night. She cradled a mug of tea. Every few moments she took a sip, smacked her lips, and set the mug back down with a clunk.

"I'm sorry, Clara, can you please repeat that?" she asked for the second time. I clutched both hands to the sides of my head and took a deep breath, preparing my nerves. I slowly repeated what I had seen from the other day.

"Was Kaye listed for any surgeries?" I asked after I finished explaining. If Jade found any of this mysterious, she didn't show it. Though if I hadn't known she was drained, I would have been worried she was blanking out.

Jade slowly pulled herself to her feet and stretched. "We can take a look," she said as she pulled the computer closer to her, "but it's possible they haven't updated the electronic files yet."

Her fingers flew over the keyboard as she pulled up the lengthy surgery listings. Hundreds of names were loaded on the screen, each assigned to different operating theatres throughout the hospital. She blinked slowly as she scrolled.

Yet again, there was no mention of subbasement two or Treatment Unit 4. My heart started to thump wildly. Jade must've caught the excited expression on my face because she said, "I don't think it's as mysterious as you're making it out to be. The Facility didn't have enough resources to keep that floor operating, and then, after a big attack, they used the theatre for an operation. I mean look at the schedule," she ran her fingers down the list, "Every operating theatre has been running nonstop since the attack. There haven't been any breaks aside from sterilization protocol."

She sighed and looked at me, "As much as I love a good conspiracy theory, I think they may have opened the theatre because it was an emergency."

"You think that two of the Facility's top surgeons thought their skills were best used in a dingy, forgotten basement the day after an attack?" I asked her incredulously.

Jade shrugged, "Braeden's been known to do some pretty stupid and despondent things when his family gets hurt." She got quieter. "Just before you arrived, his sister died. He had a mental breakdown for a few weeks, roaming the hallways and calling for his nephew, even though he died five months prior."

She sat down at the small table and stirred her tea. "Missy intervened at that stage, and she kept him isolated from the rest of the hospital until he got control over himself, but it was scary for a while. I'm just saying, Missy taking Braeden away when he's stressed out, or acting unusual, isn't exactly unheard of."

I sat down heavily, feeling deflated and a bit silly. Maybe I've been feeling a little stressed out and despondent myself. "Could you pull up Kaye's file and see?"

Jade swivelled back to her computer and tapped the information into the search key. Jade frowned as she perused the list of names. "That's odd; I don't see him here."

I sat upright. "Excuse me?"

She spun the wheel of the mouse, jumping throughout the list. Shortly after names in black, came a long list of ones labelled in red. She stopped when she came across the name *Kaye Runar* and muttered, "Well, that can't be right."

Next to every name in red was one word.

'Deceased.'

My vision narrowed as I stared at the word. "What can't be right?" I asked faintly.

"You're sure you saw them take him into subbasement two?" She asked.

My brow furrowed. "I'm absolutely positive." *Though, now that I thought about it, he had been far away from me. I knew for sure the patient was male and had dark hair, but… that could be anyone.* "Why?"

"It says here that the only place they moved him was to Missy's recovery ward upstairs… and that he's still there. Let's go."

Once we got to the recovery ward, a feeling of grief and fear gripped me. Kaye's beautiful, blank face made it appear as if he could be sleeping. The machine that breathed for him grew distant as white noise filled my ears. The room, with its blue curtains and little mint plants, faded away.

His chest rose and fell. *He was breathing.* I reached out to touch Kaye's chest, placing my hand over his heart. It beat with a steady rhythm.

The little ring of pale flesh on my wrist stood out more than usual as I ran my fingers along his face.

No reaction to my touch.

My heart rate picked up a little as I tried to quell the feeling of panic taking over me.

"Clara?" Jade stood behind me in the doorway. Her brow creased, nose turning pink as tears began to make her eyes sparkle. "I'm so sorry, Clara."

An odd ringing sound filled my ears and drowned out the rest of her words.

"But, he's breathing," I said stupidly. *He was still breathing. He had to be okay. Dead people don't breathe.*

Jade shook her head sadly.

My mind was spinning as I tried to process what was going on around me.

Kaye... dead...

He looked so peaceful. So still. I looked frantically between the bruising on his face and the arms of the Rotter next to him. *He can't be dead. He didn't even turn full Rotter.* Kaye had some bruising on the bags of his eyes, but he didn't look far gone enough to have succumbed, not fully. He didn't look like the other people I knew who were doomed to die. "Kaye's dead," I said in a hollow voice. Yet, as I looked at his still form, it was the faces of my family that flitted through my mind.

My stomach tied itself into a knot when I recalled where I was and what that meant. For me, for Kaye, for everyone who goes through this place. Kaye won't have a grave, and I won't be able to rest flowers on it.

Jade wrapped her arms around me and pulled me in for a tight hug. "Oh, honey, I'm so sorry." I let myself be held by her, feeling tears form in my eyes. She held me for a long while as tears silently poured onto her shoulder. I cried for what felt like ages, not even entirely sure what I was crying for. Kaye and I hadn't been that close.

Eventually I pulled away, and my sobs turned into little hiccupping gasps. I left a large wet patch on her shirt.

I apologized to Jade, but she impatiently waved off the apology and pulled me back into a hug.

I felt stupid. I didn't usually let death affect me like this.

Once she let go, Jade took my thigh holster and knife and helped me clip them into place. I'm not sure why, but this small gesture made me cry again. I rested my hand on the grip of my knife until I quieted myself.

Back in my little apartment, I sat still on the bed, staring at the glass flowers in the courtyard outside my window. Rays caught the bulbs and bathed the room in purples and pinks. As the shadows grew longer and the light turned to soft, dusk hues, my marks seemed to fade. Shutting my eyes, I remembered Kaye's chest rising and falling.

CHAPTER NINE
An Experiment Gone Wrong

The next few days were a confusing blur. Braeden seemed just as out of it as I was. If anything, the loss of his brother made him seem a little unhinged. I only saw him briefly, skulking around the shadows.

While I tried to sort out my emotions, I started working out more and threw myself into training sessions. I didn't run into Braeden much; he spent most of his time locked away in the library, poring over anything from old diaries to medical journals. It seemed like he was determined to relearn everything he'd ever known.

One day, while I was in the gym, Braeden finally approached me. He looked tired. His normally pale skin now looked translucent, revealing bruises under his bloodshot eyes from sleepless nights.

I put down my weights and embraced him. He enfolded me in his strong arms, holding me tightly. I let myself feel his reassuring warmth and the firmness of his body. Despite looking fragile from exhaustion, he was still solid.

He wore a black hoodie and a beanie pulled down over

his ears. It was the first time I had ever seen him wear a hoodie. "Everything okay?" I asked uncertainly.

He cleared his throat and looked out the window onto a burnt-out Toronto skyline. Braeden choked up as he spoke. "Kaye is being unplugged tomorrow. He's going on ice, but…"

I felt a rock in my throat.

I finished his sentence in a hollow voice, "We can't have a funeral."

"We'll hold a memorial for his friends here at the Facility." He observed the backs of his hands, flipping them over to see his palms. He frowned slightly before putting his head in his hands. He looked at me from between his fingers and gave a watery smile. "Did you know that grief can manifest itself in physical aches and pains? I've had a splitting headache all week." I gave him a sad smile back. His light tone dropped. "When he gets moved tomorrow, we'll hold a service."

The next morning was bright and sunny, but I kept my room dark. I groaned, throwing the blankets over my head before forcing myself to get ready for the memorial. It felt like an insult to everything that had happened, how cheerful the day was. The sky was cloudless with seagulls swooping through the air. I wished it was raining.

I got up and sluggishly moved around the room. My brain stubbornly refused to believe that the last of Braeden's family was dead. *I saw him breathing.* I slid on my black pants and top.

I closed my eyes tightly, willing my memory to stop recalling the image of him lying so unnaturally still. I was not allowed to see his body before they took him to wherever the donors were held on ice.

I swept a thick brush through my spiky auburn hair until it laid reasonably flat against my head.

There was a general mood of mourning throughout the

Facility on the day of the memorial. Hung throughout the hallways were traditional black banners. The atrium looked bleak. The usually white airy stones were darkened with the colours of mourning.

Kaye's memorial was going to take place that afternoon on the fourteenth-floor sitting room, just outside the Healing Garden. That evening, we would attend a Facility-wide service for all the victims and fallen.

After lunch with Jade, we went upstairs for the memorial. The elevator doors opened, and a large sitting room spread before us, filled with black and white couches. The courtyard full of glowing flowers filled in as a backdrop to the stark waiting room. We stepped out of the elevator and walked towards the Healing Garden through a small glass door. The hot air felt like a pillow over my face as we stepped outside.

The garden itself was vibrantly multi-hued, laid out to form a rainbow. The flowers were bulbs of spun glass sitting atop large metal poles. Green plastic hedges lined the walkways and embraced the flowers in swirling geometric patterns. The glass sparkled in the muted light. In the centre was a large skylight, illuminating the atrium below.

Aidan milled around the bulbs in the garden, looking disconsolate. He and Kaye were extremely close. Both were relaxed and had the same easy laugh.

"Hey, Aidan," I said softly.

He gave me a sad smile and resumed staring blankly at the plastic hedging in front of him. "Hey, Clara." His voice sounded heavy. I stood beside him and silently stared off into space. After a few moments, he broke the silence by saying, "It never really occurred to me that Kaye wouldn't make it. I had thought about it, but I had always felt deep down that he would pull through."

I nodded silently. I had been to so many of these over the years. For some reason, I was always surprised after losing someone. *You'd think we'd be used to loss by now.* I reached out and placed an arm around his shoulders. He hugged me back tightly.

Aidan began to cry, and I just stood there, like Jade had the other day, offering comfort.

The people behind us milled and traded soft words of support to each other. A few stopped and offered their condolences to Aidan. I gave him one last hug after he finished crying, and he gave me a watery smile. "Thanks."

I shrugged, "I needed a good hug-cry myself a few days ago. Feeling any better?"

He nodded, still staring blankly at the hedges. "A bit."

I patted him on the back. "I can stop by your room tonight for a cup of tea if you'd like?" I offered. Aidan's apartment was two doors down from mine. We often had late night chats over cups of tea when sleep was being elusive.

"Yeah, that sounds perfect," Aidan said. I had to agree. The first Facility memorial I attended felt powerful and overwhelming, but with each passing one, it began to feel more and more pointless. After leaving Aidan, I continued to wander around the garden, mindlessly. I spotted many familiar faces, but none I was especially close with.

I examined the memorial wall inside the sitting room. A gold plaque displayed the name 'Kaye Runar.' It was solemnly added beneath the names Anita Valyiff and Deniz Valyiff, Braeden's sister and nephew. Like Jade said, Anita had passed in March, just before I arrived. Deniz had fallen much sooner, back in September of last year. The names of other Runars were listed above them. Braeden had lost so much and so many.

I felt a punch to the gut when I realized I never looked for the plaques of my family. I didn't even know if there were any.

I scanned the memorial hallway and courtyard where people were walking amongst the glass flowers. I couldn't spot Braeden anywhere. Keeping an eye out for Missy too, I felt strange when I realized neither were present.

Determined to double check, I casually went back outside and strolled around the perimeter. *Why would Braeden miss his own brother's memorial?*

It was likely he just needed some time to himself, or he had thrown himself into his work, as he was known to do when tragedy struck. I still couldn't shake the uncomfortable feeling in my gut.

When I told Jade, she quietly excused herself. "So where do you think he is?" she asked me.

"I think he's back in the subbasement. Do you have that card by any chance?"

When I arrived at subbasement one, instead of retracing my previous path, I diverted at the centre fork towards the BSL-2 laboratories and scanned the borrowed ID card. The hallway within BSL-2 ended with heavy aluminum doors, which opened to a bright white space. I followed the usual twisting mess of hallways until I arrived at the ugly abstract painting that hung over the closet door.

I slipped through the closet, making my way past the maze of gurneys until I emerged at the staircase leading to subbasement two. Excitement made the blood pound in my ears when I noticed a light emanating from the vacant floor.

I bit my lip and crept along the wall towards Treatment Unit 4. Apprehension and fear slithered up my spine as I slowed to a crawl.

I unsheathed two inches of my wicked blade, and then sheathed it again, hearing the satisfying *schwing* of the metal. I took a deep breath. The air smelled like antiseptic and rot.

My breathing and footsteps echoed in the empty hallway. The dim lights created shadows that looked like lurking monsters.

A blood-curdling scream disrupted my thoughts.

Nora Ashe

I quickly pulled out my blade as I heard another scream behind Unit 4. "Please! Help me!" I rushed to the door and pushed the handle down, but it was locked. I threw my weight against it until it gave way and I tumbled into the room.

A Rotter lay on a machine that once administered direct radiation. New equipment had since been added from a few days ago. Monitors decorated the room, as did trays of medical tools. It looked haphazard and overcrowded, like the equipment wasn't designed to be in here.

The dangling light was pointed at the Rotter's skull, taking close-up images, and displaying them on the surrounding monitors. A few screens presented brain scans and 3D models.

I wondered if this Rotter was one of the BSL-2 pets; it looked healthy and appeared to have been a woman. *Or was it still a woman? Was she the one who'd screamed for help?* Her skin had so many different patches that it was impossible to tell what ethnicity she was. Her eyes were relatively clear—one was grey, and the other was a deep hazel. The myriad of replaced parts led me to wonder if she used to be a doctor at the Facility.

"Hello?" I tried cautiously.

She didn't seem to notice me. She lay on her back, staring up at the ceiling. Dainty porcelain hands with swarthy fingers rested in the old stirrups beside her head. The same ones used to restrain Kaye. In her arm sat an IV. The bruise, which ran along her vein, was stained many colours, changing beneath each patch of skin. Her head was shaved on the side where the light reflected. There were also thick stitches and an ugly wound that ran from above her eyebrow, curving over her ear, and down to the base of her skull. Pus seeped from beneath the stitches.

My body was still, but my eyes flew around the room, trying to determine who screamed. *We were the only ones*

100

there. The Rotter sniffed the air. Catching my scent, its eyes rolled into the back of its head as it let out an animalistic snarl. It leapt from the machine, only to fall back by the restraints on its arms.

It thrashed viciously and freed one wrist. The thing reached to the other binding and clawed at the stitching beneath the plastic cuff, tearing itself free. The IV ripped from its arm and blood spewed as it turned to face me.

My knife hung uselessly at my side as the Rotter ran at me full tilt.

It launched itself towards me, and I screamed, kicking it hard until it stumbled backwards, farther than I expected. My strength had grown from the intense surge of adrenaline that flooded my system.

The thing recovered quickly. I scrambled away as it lunged again.

I kicked it in the jaw and lifted my knife. The blade, magnificent in the fluorescent lights, didn't deter it. Its pupils were drowning pools of black as it threw its head back in a shriek. I slashed wildly, feeling resistance as my knife sliced its side, and the Rotter howled. It stumbled throughout the treatment room in a rage. I flipped the knife around in my hand, preparing to strike a blow to the heart, when it doubled over.

The Rotter started clutching at the sides of its head, screaming. The screams lapsed into silence for a moment, then a guttural voice rose from its throat.

It repeated itself a few more times until I could understand what it was saying: "You're infected." The Rotter's voice grew clearer and clearer, sounding more like the voice of a young woman.

In horror, I backed away.

I kept the grip on my knife tight, but I couldn't seem to will myself to strike her.

Somewhere in there was a brain that could still think.

I looked at the stitches on the Rotter's head with a new curiosity. It lunged for me again, but this time I grabbed it around the waist and threw it back onto the table. The Rotter was so wraithlike, it almost seemed to be a skeleton wrapped in skin.

It leaned forward, teeth gnashing as its crazed eyes rolled back into its skull. Its speech shifted back into a roar.

I captured its wrists in my hands and began pinning it back to the bonds. It struggled, but I was more coordinated and focused. The Rotter hissed and spat at me as it convulsed. It seemed to realize I was putting the restraints back on and started to calm down, guiding its hands into the stirrups at its own will. I tied the broken wrist restraint back into place clumsily, hoping the knot was strong enough to hold the little plastic cuff in place. I quickly fastened the other bonds, adding an extra belt across the thing's chest, along with the leg and ankle restraints.

It regarded me curiously with its heterochromatic eyes.

My heart frantic, I stepped back and exhaled slowly.

"Help me. Please. Before she comes back." Again, the Rotter's voice sounded like a young woman's. She began to sob, tears rolling down her sickly face. The cries reminded me of the girl from the Butcher's Corner who blanked out.

I eyed my clumsy knot. The cloth was badly frayed on the underside. *That's probably not going to hold… but she's restrained for now.*

I pulled a chair towards me and the scraping of the legs across the linoleum sent the Rotter into a frenzy. A litany of curses fell from its lips. I could only catch a few words like "monster" and "diseased," but the rest became a garbled mess around the rotted vocal cords in its throat.

Its eyes focused on me with an alarming intensity. Its skeletal chest rose and fell frantically. Almost reluctantly, I pulled my gaze from the Rotter and scanned its body. Plenty of old bruises were speckled across its skin, especially at the contact points for the bonds. I was sure that it had been restrained before, multiple times. *What was it doing in here?*

A quick search of the room revealed a manilla folder with the name 'Meredith Robertson' on it. I flipped it open. Inside were dozens of images. One picture was titled 'PET Scan' with a sticky note on it, on which was scrawled 'Resembles Alzheimer's.' I recognized the bubbly handwriting; it was the same lettering from Leo's file.

In another scan, the brain looked to be more whole. There were fewer dark areas. I double checked the dates. The healthier brain scan occurred after the image with the sticky note on it. I continued to flick through the notes and pictures.

There were some colour photographs as well, and a little disk marked 'Surgery 1.' The photographs showed various stages of brain surgery.

My stomach clenched unpleasantly when I saw the "donor." The woman in the photograph looked whole, aside from missing half of her skull. The nails of my left hand were digging into the new skin on my shoulder. I forced myself to relax and let go.

The file showed several shots of damaged brain tissue that was removed in surgery. Scrawled on the back of the photograph in Missy's handwriting were the words 'intracranial cytokine storm.' I paced the room, trying to make sense of the photographs.

Like a flipbook, CT scans showed her new brain integrating with her old brain. The images took a rapid turn as something clearly went wrong. Black spots lined with white, almost like burn spots, grew on the brain. I replaced the folder.

Her head suture had knitted itself closed with a thin strip of new flesh acting as glue. The Rotter struggled and spat at me again. A thick wad of bloody saliva didn't clear its chin. The Rotter's raspy throat gurgled unintelligibly.

"Get away from that!" Missy's voice made me jump

nearly a foot in the air. I automatically held my hands up before realizing she wasn't pointing a gun at me. *Old habits.*

Missy's face flushed red, and she was shaking as she tried to speak calmly. "Is that blood?"

I glanced down at the Rotter's blood spattered on my arm. "Your science project attacked me." The colour drained from her face quickly; I worried she would pass out. Missy sat herself down, clutching her chest. Forcibly, she took a very measured breath.

"Please come with me. We'll need to get you looked at." Her voice was faint.

"It's not my blood. You might need to get her looked at." I jerked my head in the direction of the woman.

Missy's face clouded over. "She's not important."

A weight settled into my stomach at her words. "Yes, she is. She's not mindless like you think. She cried out for help… and recognized that I was bitten. She knew it. And she knew who you were." Missy looked panic-stricken at my accusations.

She swallowed thickly, steadying her nerves. "It's complicated…" Missy said, taking a deep breath as she looked into my eyes closely. Her eyes looked even worse than they did when I first saw her. The redness had bled into both eyes, and I now realized that it wasn't just from her tears. I blinked a few times.

"I've been trying to do these experiments for a while now," she said, running her fingers through her gnarled red hair. Deep bruises stood out from underneath her eyes. "The virus damages the brain last. That's how it manages to spread itself so effectively while it'll destroy organs and tissue; for some reason, it manages to semi-control the brain of those infected. I've theorized that introducing human brain tissue could have the same results as our other transplants, to significantly delay someone turning 'full Rotter.'" Her words made me feel tainted.

"And?"

Her bloodshot eyes glistened as she shook her head slightly. "No success. The immune rejection always occurs anywhere from minutes to hours. At first, they'll be aware of what's happening and who they are. Then, the breakdown occurs, and the subject becomes even more dangerous. Blood samples afterwards have shown incredibly spiked catecholamine levels." She took in the blank look on my face. "Adrenaline. The levels are high enough that they actually look similar to post-mortems I've seen from an epinephrine overdose. The virus affects the body's ability to cope with excess adrenaline. Once the subjects reach this point, they no longer discriminate between infected or not. Everyone is a target. Within hours, the subject dies."

Missy sighed and touched the arm of the woman on the table. "With her brain swelling, she won't last the night." My stomach churned as the Rotter blinked languidly at the ceiling, unaware of its own impending death. Missy turned on the tap of a small sink in the room and gestured towards it. "Wash your hands, please, so I can confirm you don't have any injuries."

Obediently, I trotted to the sink. The water flowed red as I rinsed the blood from my arms. As I washed, I heard Missy tapping away at the keyboard. What she said next surprised me, "I'm also going to need Mario Hernandez's key pass back." She held out her hand expectantly.

I dried off my hands slowly, my mind raced and came up blank. I pulled the ID card out of my pocket. *I'll just have to apologize to Jade later for being a terrible liar.*

"Where did you find this?" Missy asked as she gazed down at the I.D.

"I found it ages ago," I replied. Missy didn't believe me, but she probably knew I wasn't going to tell her the truth, so she let it go.

"I'm confiscating this for obvious reasons," Missy said.

"I also want to reiterate that you are not allowed in any of the Authorized Personnel areas without special clearance. I'm going to need you to tell me how you skirted the Facility's security." My heart sank as I slowly navigated her towards the empty supply closet.

Missy gazed around the hallway filled with the gurneys and asked, "What made you crawl past all of this, into an area you were clearly not permitted anyway, to poke around? I thought you had more common sense than that."

Suddenly, staring around the closet where I spent so long crying, I finally managed to come up with a lie that might be somewhat convincing. "This supply closet is where I used to come to cry before my cancer treatments," I said slowly. "With everything that happened, I just wanted a place to be alone for a while."

"Surely, when you needed to steal an ID card, you knew you were out of bounds?"

"I thought it was out of bounds because it was disused. Jade told me that this basement was empty and sealed off, so I figured no one would notice."

Missy held up her hand. "Jade is not privy to all of the inner workings of this hospital, nor are you, Miss Belford. You should know that some of the Facility's research is top secret. You were part of the squads, were you not?" Missy asked me.

I swallowed, recalling my oath when I took up the Aegis Shield.

Finally, I decided on a half-truth. "I've been trying to work out what happened to my family after... the attack," I said finally.

Missy blinked at me. "Your family was killed by the Resistance."

"Were they ever brought to the Facility?" I asked her directly. "Were my mother and brother kept on the ninth floor with the Leukos?"

"No." She paused, searching my eyes, then added softly, "Both had passed before we arrived on the scene."

I remembered the mask over Kaye's face. *Maybe Jade misread the file. Maybe he already died, and the mask was just there to preserve him as a donor.*

I tried one more time, "So did... did you use them as...?" I couldn't bring myself to say the word 'donors.' Missy crossed her arms and watched me with detached curiosity. "Did you... were they... where are they?" I finally manage to choke it out.

She swallowed thickly and placed her hand over mine. "Oakville was quarantined. Those who didn't make it were..." she trailed off. I needed to hear the truth. *Maybe I just needed closure with my brother.* I wanted to hear that they were used as donors to keep others alive.

"Those who didn't make it were what?" I asked.

"They were placed into the incinerator." She looked tragic. I fought to keep the confusion from my face as her eyes began to tear up. She continued, "We couldn't risk an outbreak. All the dead were cremated. I'm sorry you weren't told sooner."

After a moment, I realized my mouth was hanging open, dumbstruck. I closed it quickly and nodded my head as though I accepted her story.

Liar.

CHAPTER TEN
An Unexpected Party

Warm weather faded, and with it, the deep feeling of loss. What didn't fade were my suspicions, and a burning desire to uncover what happened to my brother after he was brought to the Facility.

It was still technically late Autumn, but outside felt like winter. After Kaye's death, I had become restless, trying to figure out the "you-know-what" that got breached. It was difficult for me to explore because Braeden became even more protective since Kaye's passing. In the time after his memorial, Braeden stabilized and stopped acting so bizarre, which meant that he had fallen back into his routine. Jade and I knew his schedule well enough to slip away regularly.

We explored another branch of the tunnel system, hoping to find some clues, but wound up burning off steam in the empty streets. After a quick jaunt outside, Jade and I clambered back through the tunnels, breathless and laughing. She slung her crossbow across her back. The tunnels were warm, and I could feel a fine layer of sweat forming on my face. Although my fingers were stiff from the cold, my cheeks were warm and flushed.

I asked Jade the same question for the millionth time. "Are you absolutely positive there were no breaches where the Facility keeps its donors?"

"Clara, I scoured the inventory records myself, not even a blood bag went missing from Harvest during the attack. I have no idea what Lacey would have meant when she told Missy that."

"Well then, we must be missing something in the tunnel network." I sighed. "Let's try again in a few days when Braeden's scrubbed up in BSL-4." I handed Jade back the crossbow that she had lent me.

"What are your plans for this evening?" Jade asked me casually, wiping her upper lip.

"Strategy," I said simply.

The biweekly meetings had become a haven for me once Commander Dekkar overrode Braeden's decision to bench me, keeping me on Strategy and Scouting just like Piper said. After his brother's death, Braeden was deemed too unstable to make that decision. "How about you?"

"Work, work, and more work," Jade replied, heading towards the Facility while I turned to Strategy. "All right, Clar', I'm off to the lab. The virus waits for no man! No matter how devastatingly beautiful." She gave a superfluous flip of her hair and sauntered off down the tunnels.

The Strategy room was empty, except for Piper. She sat where Commander Hakim Dekkar usually sat, with her boots crossed on the table in front of her, playing with her knife.

The map that usually sat atop the table was gone, revealing polished mahogany instead. I tapped the blade on my thigh, hidden beneath my black sweater dress.

"We're not in here today." Piper's voice echoed in the room. She pulled her feet off the desk and stood up abruptly. "We had an unexpected visit from a group of Leuko mercs."

"Plural?" I asked with my eyebrows shooting up.

"Yeah, it stinks to me, too. They're in the ground-floor library." Piper said as she walked past me, gesturing to the door. I exited, with Piper at my back. She shut the heavy door with a clang.

"Do we trust any of them?" I asked her. She gave me a sidelong glance.

Piper spoke to me in a low voice as we walked through the tunnels. "Look, I don't trust these guys for anything, except Jasper. And Jasper's not with this group."

"Jasper?" I probed.

"An old friend who's had my back in a few sticky situations. He doesn't usually flock when the other mercs do. Out of all of them, he's the only one I trust to do the honourable thing," she said resolutely.

As we made our way closer to the elevators, Piper ran through what Cynthia had already told her. "We don't know what these Leukos are here for. They showed up injured and Medical had to patch up quite a few deep wounds."

"So they're just here to get fixed up? Swapping info for medicine?"

"No, Commander Dekkar doesn't think so. Nor does Dr. Runar. He says the blood loss doesn't match the wounds or the distance travelled."

"He can tell that?" I found myself impressed.

"I dunno if he can tell normally, but these guys should've bled out if their story was true." Piper shrugged. "We collected all their stories separately, and they matched up. So, either these Leukos rehearsed it perfectly, they're all prone to over-exaggeration, or they're just the luckiest bastards ever."

"Or the doctor was wrong," I added quietly.

Piper cocked an eyebrow at me. "Then it would be the first time since I've been here."

Piper was unusually tense as we got into the elevators;

her movements were stiff and jerky. She handed me a small pistol that was holstered under her coat. "Here. That knife you've got under your skirt isn't going to be enough." I felt a little shocked that she knew I had my knife, but then I remembered our first conversation.

***

We were in the shooting range when Jade introduced us. Piper's cotton clothes were pristine, contrasting with my slightly stained outfit. I wasn't coping with the loss of my family very well.

Piper stared fixedly at the knife on my thigh. "That's not one of the Facility weapons," she said bluntly. I touched it, a little defensively.

"No, it's mine."

A ghost of a smile passed over her face.

"How long have you been wearing it?"

"Since I was fourteen."

"Always have it?" she asked inquisitively. She already knew the answer.

"I sleep with it," I responded.

Piper nodded in approval.

***

Now, in the tunnels, I eyed Piper's clothing, vaguely wondering where she kept her own blade. It had disappeared somewhere between Strategy and the tunnels.

I clipped the pistol and holster onto my belt. Once I shrugged my jacket back on, she looked over me with approval. The little gun disappeared behind the folds of black leather.

"All right, good." Piper smiled as the elevator doors dinged open.

We stepped across the atrium to the old library. Security gathered, giving our visitors a customary welcome of guns and unsmiling faces. The guards clutched their rifles as we walked by, giving Piper a salute.

I immediately felt the hairs on the back of my neck rise as we entered the room. A multitude of chairs were pulled around a make-shift desk to mirror the one up in Strategy. However, the chairs remained empty as both the Facility's command and the Leukos stood, sizing each other up. The tension in the room was palpable. I eyed the lines of their ripped clothing, wondering what we missed. The muddy leather was bulky, easy for a knife or a small gun to go unnoticed. Hakim and the others stood in a semi-circle, partially surrounding them. Even though their weapons weren't visible, every other soldier from Strategy was armed.

The scrappy crew of Leukos—three men and two women—eyed us, seemingly unhappy with their less-than-warm reception. Their scowls, combined with artistic body modifications, gave them a feral menace. An array of skin tones marked their bodies.

One woman had a pattern of light and dark circles on the side of her skull. The effect looked somewhat like a soccer ball, which gave me an insane urge to giggle. I kept my composure, unwillingly admiring the pattern of her multicoloured mohawk. It fell like a waterfall, obscuring half of her face in a splash of blacks, reds, and golds.

I wonder if she picked out the Rotters she slayed specifically for their hair colour? Piper's mouth tightened when she saw the woman's mohawk and her nostrils flared. Other than that, there was no sign she noticed.

Automatically, I found myself pulling at the zipper on my jacket, trying to hide my own marks. I couldn't shake the unsettling realization that, if not for the Facility, I could have easily been standing with this group. My dress and shining leather jacket looked dainty compared to their muddied, torn clothing.

A leuko leered at me, licking his lips. I balled my hands into a fist to prevent myself from reaching for my knife. Or my gun.

Exhaling slowly, I forced myself to remain composed.

Bandages were wrapped around their torsos and thighs, potentially where major arteries or organs could be hit.

Those wounds would have made the necrosis spread quickly.

The Leukos gave a convincing performance of being beaten and tired, but I was having trouble taking them as harmless. Their colorful skin looked barbaric underneath the bright lights. The Leukos looked around shiftily, like cornered animals in the pristine Facility.

Commander Cynthia Ho, a scowling woman with straight black hair, stepped forward. Her hands were on her hips, flaring her jacket wide open. The effect made her seem tough yet unarmed. Her voice ran loudly in the quiet library. "We've been told you have information." Without offering anything else, she let her sentence hang.

The woman with the mohawk spoke, "We know where the humans are hiding."

"There are lots of humans," Hakim replied, pushing his glasses up his nose.

"The Resistance. We know where the Resistance is." The woman growled.

Hakim moved to reply, but Cynthia cut across him. "Please tell us what you have to share." Her tone was neutral, but there was a certain deadly quality to the way her gaze flickered between the Leukos, like a wolf eyeing up which rabbit to kill first.

The woman spilled everything, starting with an abandoned-hotel-turned-merc-hideaway. We discussed this hotel in Strategy before, but the Facility by and large left it alone—it wasn't close enough to be considered a threat.

This group decided to risk the Rotters; they were caught out in bad weather and needed somewhere to stay for the night. "When we got there, we noticed someone had already been running the backup generator. It was nearly depleted," the woman said. Something in that line made Piper's face close off.

I wondered if she was going to speak up, but she followed Cynthia's lead—don't give them any information to adjust their story.

The merc continued, "When we got onto the main floor, everything seemed normal. We were prepped for Rotters, so we did a patrol and purge. During the PNP, we came across humans camping in the ballroom… and…" Her voice cracked and she turned to her male companion, burying her face in his chest, sobbing. Her friend took her in his arms and finished the story. "We lost two groups in the ambush. They chased us into the streets." I felt a pang, recalling my own losses over the past few years.

"How did you know they were Resistance?" Hakim asked. Cynthia nodded her head vigorously, waiting for the Leukos to elaborate.

They exchanged looks, and Cynthia narrowed her eyes at them. A bearded Leuko spoke up, "Who else would attack a group of mercenaries? We don't have problems with any other humans."

"So, you're saying you're not sure."

"We just assumed it was the Resistance," admitted the woman. "Either way, hostile uninfected this close to the Facility was something worth knowing, right?" She looked hopefully at the members' faces.

"Where were you attacked?" Hakim asked.

"In the Crystal Room, on the seventeenth floor." The others nodded. Everyone else in the room seemed to understand what that meant, and I made a mental note to ask Piper about it later. "Look, it's been whispered about for ages amongst the mercenaries that the Resistance was thinking of moving into the downtown. We just didn't think it would be in our territory." She shrugged, but sounded unapologetic. "Frankly, with how much they were bombing you, we figured they'd move into one of your buildings."

I bristled at her words but didn't say anything.

She glanced between everyone. "Look, if the Resistance is held up on the seventeenth floor, you guys have a clear shot to exterminate them. I don't know how much more of a silver platter we can give you!" She whined, her eyes searching for someone in Strategy to believe her.

None of us spoke, waiting for Cynthia. She was quiet for a long time before saying, "Charlie, Oscar, please escort our guests back to the ninth-floor ward so they can rest up properly. We may have some more questions for them later."

Two men guided the Leukos out of the room. The guards posted at the doorway circled the group, and they all trudged towards the elevators. After a moment, the Strategy members relaxed. "All right, everyone," Cynthia said, "Let's regroup in five." With that, she paraded out of the room, and others followed her lead.

Piper stopped as everyone filed out and placed a hand on my shoulder. "You holding up okay?" She asked the same question every time we finished a Strategy meeting.

"Yeah, I am." I smiled at her gratefully. She kept me out of Strategy and on scouting missions for the last few weeks. Luckily, I hadn't missed anything major; otherwise, I would have probably gone stir crazy. The colonies had been oddly quiet for some time now.

Piper gave me a reassuring smile and patted my arm. "Good." She glanced around the atrium, but to my surprise, she did not head towards the tunnels. "Follow me. I want some intel before we talk with the others."

My curiosity mounted when Piper disengaged the group. I followed her.

As Piper and I left the library, I asked, "Is this about the issue with the generators?"

Piper grinned. "You caught that, did you?" She nodded her head and answered, "We did a sweep near that portion of the Path last week with Falcon Bravo. There was still power being supplied to the hotel by the main line." Her brow was furrowed as she strolled towards a room on the other side of the atrium.

"The engineers?" I asked as we approached the corridor. She nodded. Her voice was a harsh whisper. "I need to know if there's been any disruptions in the power supply." She glanced around surreptitiously to make sure we weren't being overheard. "I don't think there have been any, but maybe they left one undocumented in one of the unpopulated areas. That might explain the missing petrol."

"And if there aren't any outages?"

"Then either our Leukos are lying, or we've got something using power that they don't want on the grid." Her voice was grim as we approached the dark hallway where the engineers spent their time. "And if it's the Resistance, like the Leukos said, then they're probably preparing for another attack. Hell, the humans might not even be there anymore. They might have packed the place full of Rotters and bailed."

"Why would they waste fuel to control the climate of a building full of Rotters?" I asked, puzzled.

"You know how we've been finding traces of Wave Two particles in those cold nests?" Piper asked. I nodded. "I think they're lacing those nests with Wave Two in an attempt to hybridize the virus themselves. They must be using abandoned hideaways to run their experiments."

"Why would they want to hybridize it?' I asked with horror.

"The Resistance doesn't exactly abide by the Geneva Convention." She looked at me meaningfully, "We're a group of people who, so far, can't catch Wave Two, and are resistant to Wave Three. Why do you think they'd want to hybridize it?"

"You think they're going to try to turn the entire Facility into Bleeders?"

Piper shrugged. "Wouldn't you if you were them?"

I thought about what I've heard about hybrids. The virus rips through the system so quickly that the insides of the infected are liquified before they succumb to rot. Jade always said hybrids weren't a threat to us because they die too quickly, before they can pass it on. *But if they managed to infect a hybrid who didn't die immediately...* I shuddered and stopped outside the entrance to the Engineering Quarters.

Piper disappeared behind the doors, and I waited outside while she finished asking questions. She returned, looking grimmer than before. I lifted my eyebrows at her, and she shook her head. "No power outages marked in that area. If they were using the generator, they were using it for something off the grid."

"Could it have been leaking?"

"Possibly. The equipment's old and it's not like we have a lot of them lying around. It might have been a defect, but..." She trailed off.

"But?"

"There's too many unknowns right now. We need to get back to Strategy and discuss this with everyone else."

We moved towards the elevators, and thoughts swirled through my mind. We were the last to arrive at Strategy. Most of the members already shed their jackets, revealing the host of weaponry they had hidden on their bodies. Between the holster straps and blades that glinted on the table, it seemed the Leukos posed a far more serious threat than I realized. One man even fidgeted with a little coil of piano wire.

I tapped my blade as Piper and I took our seats at the table.

"Does anybody buy their story?" Piper said once everyone unarmed themselves.

Cynthia's eyes flicked between us. "Not on your life. I think they've got something in store for us at that hotel, I just don't know what."

Everyone began to speak at once.

"What, you mean the Leukos or the humans?"

"How do we know they weren't working together when the Facility was attacked?"

A man, who I'd never heard speak before, cleared his throat. "I say we keep everyone here." Silence fell as he brought himself to his feet. Standing a head taller than everyone else, with a white beard, he projected an aura of authority.

Cynthia looked grimly at the man, "Gerard, I don't think we can just ignore this."

"Why not? This isn't the first time these lunatics have sent us on a wild goose chase. Last time, their decoy cost the facility dearly."

Hakim stood up. "I don't think we can ignore the warning, even if we've had a few false flags from the Leukos before. Yes, there was an attack on the Facility, but the Resistance went after the power plant, too. We didn't have bad intel, necessarily, we just didn't have all the intel."

Piper gestured to a large map on the table in front of her and began explaining her theory of how the nests were placed strategically. She placed markers around the map where squads have discovered nests.

Cynthia's frown deepened as Piper continued placing markers.

Silence seemed to stretch in front of me. The pinpointed areas with identified Rotter nests were all located downtown, effectively forming a blockade between the Facility and the loading docks.

Hakim gestured to the map. "Have we sent scouts into

any other areas, or just through Old Toronto? It looks like we've either got an infestation, or someone is deliberately trying to block us from Sugar Beach."

"We've done a few missions in the north, but I don't think drills have taken place anywhere other than downtown," Cynthia replied. "So far, we've found nests, but that isn't unusual."

"But never this many, in a concentrated area, within such a short time period." Piper insisted, jabbing her finger at the harbour. "Hakim is right, they are deliberately trying to block us from Sugar Beach, and if they succeed—"

"Then they've disrupted the supply drops."

"Exactly. At the very least, we need to change loading to somewhere west of Bathhurst Quay. We can't let them disrupt the supply lines."

Cynthia sighed and glanced at Hakim. He gave her an almost imperceptible nod. "All right, I'll speak with the drop supervisors about moving our boats over to the marina near West Island."

Hakim turned to the rest of the group and asked, "So, with all that in mind, does that mean that we trust the information provided by the Leukos?" Again, the group began arguing.

"According to their story, the group was outnumbered by the Resistance, but they were able to escape and find asylum at the Facility."

"Right, and they lost two men."

"Maybe three squads, prepared and fully armed, would be enough to take out the Resistance stronghold."

"If their intel is good. We have no idea how many Resistance might actually be there."

"So the first step is a scouting mission," Piper said finally, directing the attention her way. "Then we can confirm their intel. They didn't suggest the Resistance was preparing for an attack. They just happened to fall into their territory. If they are preparing an attack, chances are they will strike soon."

"It only took them a month and a half to regroup after the attack in September."

"Yeah, and the casualties they suffered at Darlington were much more severe," Piper shot back.

"All right." Cynthia's voice rang out with finality; we stopped bickering amongst ourselves. "Piper, you oversee the scouting mission. Will you need any additional support?"

Piper cocked her head thoughtfully, "If it's only a scouting mission, I'll need my fireteam and possibly someone who knows the area and layout of the building. Do we have any mercs that we can use as a guide?"

Gerard spoke up again. "You're not suggesting we use one of those Leukos? If nothing else, they're injured."

Piper looked coolly at him. "I was asking if we knew of anyone *else* who might be of some help. I don't want to use any of those five; something about their story doesn't sit right with me."

Cynthia looked thoughtfully. "I believe Dr. Runar has contacts that we could look into. I'll check with him. Otherwise, is your fireteam good to go in solo?" Piper nodded. "All right. We're sending in Falcon Bravo One Three. I believe Bravo did the most recent scout of that area?" I felt my stomach drop in disappointment. That stupid phoenix flashed through my mind. I clenched my fist and my nails bit into my palm, distracting me from saying something regrettable.

Cynthia glanced over as Piper cleared her throat.

Piper looked at me, then at Cynthia, and said, "Actually, I would prefer to use Falcon Alpha."

Goosebumps erupted over my skin, and my heart did a flip, but I kept my face impassive.

I could already feel the heady spike of adrenaline. *It was only a scouting a mission. I wouldn't need to pull the trigger this time.* My eyes met Piper's, and we exchanged excited smiles.

I balled my hand into a fist, preventing myself from unsheathing my blade and tossing it between hands. Piper looked to me, "Go get dressed, and meet me back in the locker room in forty-five minutes for the debriefing." I gratefully took my leave.

As soon as I was out of sight of Cynthia and the others, I unsheathed my blade and twirled it between my fingers as I went off to get changed.

CHAPTER ELEVEN
The Scouting Mission

My fireteam sat quietly in the back of the truck as we jostled our way through Toronto. The squad was at MOPP 0, so my mask rested in my hands. I looked at the two new men in the van with us. The one sitting across from me looked like someone I knew. I kept staring at him, trying to make sense of why he seemed so familiar.

On his arm was a tattoo: a rod with a snake entwined around it. He noticed me staring, "Bet your doctor boyfriend would love this tattoo, eh?" he said. I jerked my head up and looked at him.

What did he just say?

Evan leaned close to Brad and me and said, "That's one of the Leuko mercs we work with sometimes when we need some extra firepower. He's good."

"You've worked with him before?" Brad whispered back, apprehension creeping into his words. "*The last time we needed Leukos, we were outnumbered fifteen to one.*" Evan's voice played in my mind as I looked at the strange man in front of me with renewed interest. His fingers were tipped with ebony and his knuckles were a lighter shade of pink, whereas the fingers themselves were a deep olive tone. The effect was beautiful.

"Yeah, the mercs do good work when we need some help. They like to keep up a good trade arrangement with us. Everybody wins."

The Leuko's stunning green eyes caused my breath to catch a little. They looked like Leo's. Panic flared inside of me as the similarities became more apparent. I ran my fingers along the patch on my forearm and forced down the concern.

Whatever happened to Leo happened four months ago. Besides, what are the odds that the eyes of the man across from me belonged to my brother? Still, I couldn't quite shake the feeling that something was off.

A squat knife was sheathed in his boot. My stomach did an unpleasant squirm as I recognized the short skinner—a blade used for skinning a carcass after hunting. *Something told me he didn't use that for deer hide.* I eyed the patches that decorated his arms with distaste, imagining what he had to do to get them.

We continued the short ride in silence. In a blink, we arrived at our destination. The truck pulled up to an intersection about a block away from the stronghold. The driver, a man Piper called James, cut the engine. My team and the two mercs got out of the van.

Deserted buildings were lit up in the night sky. Riding heavy on the crisp air was the promise of snow. Wispy clouds full of ice crystals sat above, forming a halo around the moon. Darker, ominous clouds lurked further away on the horizon.

The green-eyed man headed towards the other Leuko.

"Wait," I commanded.

With a lazy smile, the merc stopped. "Yes?"

I grabbed him by the chin and looked deep into his

eyes. They slightly widened in surprise, but he recovered his shock with a lusty smile. I inspected each iris carefully. There was no red freckle on either eye. I breathed a sigh of relief and released his face. *Those weren't Leo's eyes.*

Taking a few steps back, I awkwardly thanked him. He gave me a puzzled look before joining the other Leuko. The two of them whispered between themselves before looking at me with alarming intensity. Feeling uncomfortable, I rejoined my fireteam.

Mona ran us through our movements for inside the hotel. The map was covered in Kowalski's notes from the previous sweep. Piper and Brad already broke off to investigate the generators. As Mona finished instructing our floor-by-floor sweeps, they returned.

"The generator is low. It was running recently," Piper announced.

"Wait, they weren't lying?" Suddenly, I was a lot more apprehensive. *If that was true, what else from their story was?* My hands tightened around the barrel of my rifle in excitement.

"I'm still not convinced," Piper said. "It's not that hard to drain petrol from a tank, and as a fuel source, it's valuable as all hell right now." She raked her gaze over the rough sketch of the floorplan.

"To be safe, we should operate as though there will be a nest in there. My guess is if there is one, it'll be in the lower levels, over here." She pointed at the large room marked 'Kitchen.' After she checked with Mona, Piper told us to move out.

The fireteam moved quietly along the dark, abandoned street. We turned the corner, and the hotel towered over us. I scanned the building. No traces of light emanated from within. *Did the Resistance abandon it as soon as the Leukos fled?*

The old hotel had vestiges of grandeur, though now a

decrepit, abandoned feeling permeated the worn stones. A black dome awning was ripped and faded. Remnants of gold lettering were visible, but the words were illegible.

We entered cautiously. Massive statues of chess pieces stood tall in the lobby. They were cracked and faded in the moonlight. The moth-eaten furniture was blood-stained. Dead leaves swirled across the dusty floor, while webs hung from crumbling columns. The air smelled musty, and water damage stained the carpets. An industrious fern spread itself beyond its pot. Little seedlings sprouted throughout the cracked tiles.

A sweeping staircase with an intricate wrought iron banister swirled up to the second floor. My eyes curved along the balcony that ringed the room. It held nothing but more dust and cobwebs.

Our footsteps echoed in the old hotel lobby. I ran my fingers along a small side table, leaving black rivets in the dust. It didn't look like anyone had been in this building since the outbreak, let alone earlier today. The room grew dark as the bright moon became shrouded in clouds.

As we moved through the deserted room towards the emergency stairs, our scope lights landed upon empty corners and dusty furniture. My apprehension rose. The Leukos said there was a large fight, but this place looked like no one had been here in months.

Piper noticed too. "Something's not right." Her low voice came over my comm. Those words sent me on high alert, and my heart started thumping. I stroked my gun to calm myself as my ears strained for any noise beyond that of our little group.

"New plan?" Mona's voice crackled into my ear.

I pulled Piper over and whispered to her, "Look, they said the fight was on the seventeenth-floor ballroom, right? There are kitchens on that level as well. We should try to investigate a potential nest."

Piper gave me a thoughtful look before she comm'd to the rest of the scouting team, "The end goal is the seventeenth-floor ballroom. Let's sweep the floors in pairs, each group with a Leuko as a guide."

I was paired with Mona and the green-eyed Leuko, assigned to clear several of the lower levels before we rendezvoused with the others.

We pushed through the partially rusted doors to the stairwell. It was dank from water that seeped through the concrete walls in the summertime. The desolate atmosphere that cloaked this place made the entire squad jumpy.

Our group split off from the squad a few floors up. I naturally took the lead, and Mona brought up the rear. We didn't say it, but we both knew if the Leuko stepped out of line, Mona would shoot first and ask questions later—I might've hesitated.

We exited the stairwell to a decrepit hallway; most of its walls had been removed. Some of the rooms were completely gutted. Whether from fights, squatters, or fire, it was hard to tell. Two toilets, once from separate suites, sat back to back off to my right. Mildew and frost lined the bowls.

We entered a large room that must have been the gym. My scope swept along the floor. Wooden planks peeled up, swollen from moisture. Rusted exercise equipment sat against the wall. A cold breeze blew in through the shattered windows, letting in flurries of light snow.

I saw movement in the corner of my eye and swivelled, aiming my rifle, only to see my own reflection pointing my gun right back at me. I raised the barrel and shook my head. *I was too jumpy.* Something about the mirror seemed off. Unlike the rest of the gym that was covered in dust, the ones along the columns of the room were polished to a high shine. I approached my reflection and examined it curiously.

I quietly comm'd the rest of the team. "Mirrors had been cleaned recently in the gym." Mona looked closely at one of the columns, the beam from her scope reflected off and lit up the floor some five feet behind her.

"Anyone see anything more useful than shiny mirrors?" Piper snapped. I shared an annoyed glance with Mona but kept my mouth shut.

"Clear. Next floor." Mona led us out of the desolate gym.

"Guys, you're going to want to see this," Evan's voice crackled on the earpiece. Mona and I jogged back to the stairwell, holding our equipment in place.

My lungs were burning from the cold by the time we reached the seventeenth floor. The stairs we took led us directly into the ballroom. The air felt pleasant compared to the icy temperatures of the lower floors. The rest of the squad gathered.

The ballroom was large and lined with windows. Columns decorated the walls, tipped with peeling gold leaf. In the centre of the room hung a magnificent chandelier.

Remnants of camps were visible in the otherwise empty and spacious ballroom. Several of the hotel's mattresses were stacked high in the corners, forming a makeshift shelter within the open room. We spread in a wedge formation as we swept the area. My skin crawled as we passed by the mattress pile.

Mona's nose wrinkled when she smelled it. "What the hell is that?" She sniffed again and gagged a little. I inhaled the air and suppressed the urge to vomit. It was rank with the smell of mould and human flesh.

Evan evaluated the smell cautiously, not inhaling as deeply as either Mona or I did. His mouth curled downward in distaste. "All units, this is Reihman, masks on. You said there were kitchens around here?"

"Are you saying what I think you're saying?" Brad's voice was uneasy.

I refrained from losing my lunch, but dry heaved a bit. "Anyone think to bring extra peppermint?" I asked over the mic as I pulled on my mask.

Piper stalked ahead of us towards the kitchens and we fell in line behind her. The windows seemed oppressive. I suddenly wanted to throw them open to tempt in the cold air, both for the freshness and chill.

The faded carpet disintegrated from the ballroom along the hallway, revealing the concrete underneath. Water pooled on the floor. I looked at it uneasily. It appeared brown and scummy. The doors to the kitchen were wide open. We entered, leaving behind the Leukos.

Several corpses were chained to the stainless-steel appliances. I bent and heaved, barely avoiding emptying my stomach. Bloated and greyish, their bones jutted out from their gaunt faces. Evan held his hand over his mask and took in the scene in front of him.

"What is it?" I asked, attempting to appear unaffected by the state of decay. He glanced over to the bodies pointedly. "They don't have any rot marks. It's possible that they were infected and then killed quickly, but look at how starved they are. I think they were left here to die," he said darkly.

A large industrial freezer sat in one corner of the room. Its door was ajar, and water leaked from inside.

Piper stepped around bodies on the floor, trying her best not to disturb anything. She cautiously pressed her hand against the freezer's silver door, letting it swing open fully. Both she and Brad aimed inside, taking a moment to make sense of the horror scene within. Piper scrunched her face, but kept her aim, sweeping the freezer.

Brad, however, doubled over and began to retch. Mona clapped him on the back while he calmed himself. Piper gestured us to move out of the kitchen and back into the hallway. "Clear, guys. Let's move the hell out." She pointed her finger skyward and moved it in a circle. "That nest was down… the freezer off for ages. And it's defrosted, meaning someone was running the heat up there recently."

We headed for the stairs, taking in fresh air as we left the ballroom

Evan's voice was low in my ear as the mic crackled to life again. "That doorway wasn't open on our way up. Belford?" I looked down the staircase and saw the door. Clutching my rifle tight, I focused on Mona in front of me.

"Not us either," I replied, my heart racing.

"We need to move out. Now," Piper whispered urgently. We moved quietly and quickly down the stairs, but the sounds of our boots echoed through the stairwell.

We reached the ground floor and entered the main lobby. There was movement in the darkness. It was only when the clouds parted, and the moon's brightness spilled into the room, that I could see the mass of lurching bodies filling the lobby.

The moonlight illuminated the Rotters as they poured in through the side doors. Piper pulled out her radio and screamed into it, "James, what's going on out there?" Whatever the response was from the other end caused Piper's face to turn ashen. "Defensive positions!"

I ducked behind one of the iconic columns; the sweeping staircase was to my left, and doors to another room were behind me if I needed to retreat.

I took careful aim around the stone pillar and picked off the Rotters one by one. Quickly, they swarmed me, pulling me away like a tide through the doors to my rear, snapping vainly. The merc with the green eyes was forced in the same direction I was.

After a moment, I realized the Rotters weren't attacking me. In fact, they seemed to be trying to get away from something. Hoots and hollers came from the direction of the lobby. I was pushed further away from my squad and deeper into the room with upended tables and chairs. Broken booths lined the walls.

The merc sidled close to me. "There are doors that way!" He cried over the gunfire. I dimly made out the direction he was pointing to, as we both ran from the wave of Rotters. His hand grasped my arm roughly, and we stumbled our way through the doors. I realized belatedly that we ran into the kitchens.

"Wait!" I said, planting my feet as he tugged at my arm. "The nest!"

"Screw the nest!" He snarled, opening his satchel to produce a hunk of meat covered in plastic. My eyes widened. Saliva flooded my mouth. "Easy there, girl, this is for them." I reluctantly pulled away from it and stared into his eyes. For a split second, it almost felt like I was looking into Leo's eyes again. The spell was broken when the sound of snarling Rotter pulled me from my reverie.

"Focus," the Leuko commanded me.

The other merc entered the room after us. He hurled a hunk of bloodied meat back into the old restaurant. The Rotters in the doorway behind him scurried after it like a pack of dogs.

The merc limped in and his eyes fixed on me. The grin in his face reminded me of a jack-o'-lantern. Two Rotters broke through the doors, distracting us from each other. They snapped, punching and scratching as they staggered into the room, dangerously close to me.

The limping merc pulled out his gun and took aim at the duo. He fired before I could shout at him to wait. His shot went wide of the Rotters, and the bullet hit my calf directly. I swore as I sunk to my knee. The wound was a clean in and out, missing my artery. I hissed between clenched teeth. It hurt like hell. A second shot, then another, and both Rotters fell to the floor. His gun clicked empty. I watched as he holstered the gun before turning my attention back to my calf.

"Sorry about that. Just winged ya." He grunted, "Put

some pressure on it; I've got bandages." Silhouetted by the moonlight spilling in from the doorway, he stepped towards me. "We'll get you to your medic, no problem, girlie." His shadow directly over me, I saw him quietly reach for the machete at his back.

A moment too slow, I lunged out of the blade's way. His machete sank deep into my thigh, exactly where my neck had been a moment before. I grunted at the impact and my hand automatically reached for my knife.

I unsheathed my blade and stabbed the Leuko in the gut. Reactively, he punched me hard in the side of the head. My ear was ringing, yet the grip on my blade remained iron tight.

The Leuko wrenched the machete from my leg and blood began to pour from the deep gash. He raised it, ready to deal a fatal blow, when the other Leuko ripped the weapon away from him.

"What are you doing?" he snarled. "We need this one."

"To Hell with Blaise and to Hell with his plan. We *need* to kill her!" the one with the bleeding stomach shouted at the other. Then he called to me, "You see, girlie, I liked Oakville. I had a family there. And when your arrogant little boyfriend razed it to the ground to get you—well, now I have a score to settle." He leered at me. "Eye for an eye."

I crawled away from them, clutching my blade. Crouching, I put most of my weight on my good leg. My injured leg wobbled dangerously underneath me.

The merc I stabbed made to rush me again. I launched forward and arced the blade upwards. It sank through the soft flesh under his jaw and through the roof of his mouth. I twisted it for good measure before pulling it out.

He gurgled as he fell to the ground. The other Leuko didn't even blink.

Guess they weren't friends, after all.

"Big mistake." His voice was soft and deadly as he

pulled out a narrow gun. Recognizing it to be a tranq gun, I threw myself behind a metal table and heard a *ping* bounce off the cabinet next to me.

I clutched my rifle and peered around the table. The Leuko was no longer paying attention to me. The smell of blood from the dead merc and my leg attracted the Rotters. They were sluggish and poisoned, but obviously starving. His eyes widened. It was a unique thing; to see so many different shades of skin pale simultaneously.

He paused for a split second, unsure if he should waste precious time by switching from the tranq to his real gun, and a Rotter fell on him, swiping at his face. He shot a dart directly in its hollow chest.

One Rotter broke free of the horde and fell upon the other merc's corpse. I scrambled away from it, leaving a trail of blood in my wake. It threw its head back with an animalistic moan, dark blood shining on its mouth.

It locked eyes on me before turning its attention back to the dead body. Another Rotter came around the corner, and it too fell upon the corpse with relish. Not bothering to wait for the entire horde to show up, I realized I needed to call for backup immediately.

My finger went to my ear to hit the comm button, but it was empty. The Leuko knocked it out when he punched me in the head.

Frantically, I looked around the room. There were two exits, one was blocked by Rotters, and the other was on the far side of the kitchen. Blood still freely coursed from my leg. There was no way I would be able to make either exit in time. More Rotters entered.

Amongst the shiny metal tables, I noticed another door; it was thick and led to a walk-in freezer.

I crawled over to it, hoping this one wasn't made into a nest as well. Behind me, grotesque slurping and ripping sounds came from the Rotter's feast. I reached up for the door and twisted the handle as something grabbed my hair.

I was jerked backward, and the door flew open. I looked into the eyes of a crazed Rotter. Its teeth were bared as it threw me to the ground. I cried out in pain as I struggled to regain my footing. Blood spurted out of my leg with renewed force. The Rotter dropped to its knees and began lowering its head toward the wound on my thigh. Disgusted, I slashed at the thing's head and scrambled away. I got inside the walk-in freezer with the Rotter clawing at my heels.

CHAPTER TWELVE
The Freezer

I slammed the freezer door shut, gasping. My hands fumbled with the latch; the bolt was stuck. There was a jerk, and the door came out of my hands. I grabbed the handle and pulled it shut with all my might. My left leg planted firmly on the floor, against the wall. The door opened half an inch as the Rotter tried to get through it. Its fingers slipped through the cracks. I tried to plant my right leg on the ground to get a better wedge, but it spasmed underneath me and gave out.

"Damn!" The word came out as a strangled shriek as the door slipped half a foot. The Rotter's arm slipped between the door and the frame. I pulled it even harder. The door was not going to close unless I got this thing's arm out of the way. Gritting my teeth, I kept all the weight on my left leg and used my right hand to draw my blade. I somehow managed to avoid the blackened fingers that groped blindly, hoping for my flesh. I slashed at its arm, repeatedly stabbing near the crook of its elbow. I didn't think I'd be able to get it to withdraw its arm with pain, but hopefully, I could sever it.

The arm was rotted enough, it should fall apart relatively easily.

The blade sank in the Rotter's arm, up to the hilt. I withdrew my blade, leaving a ragged hole behind. There was a sluggish spurt of coagulated blood that let me know I struck an artery. I thrusted the knife in again, flesh hung loosely from its elbow. Several of its fingers had stopped moving. My blade had severed its tendons.

I flipped the knife around in my hand and started sawing at the bone with the serrated edge. The thing on the other side of the door howled with rage. They made me work even more feverishly to sever the arm. My hands grew slick with the thing's blackened blood. It pulled away before heaving itself at the door again.

The door lurched, and I almost lost my grip. With my knife still in my hand I pulled the door hard. The blade sliced through the pinkie finger my left hand. I hissed through gritted teeth but didn't let go of my hold. Blood poured downwards, coating my hands and wrists.

The door inched shut. I grinded my teeth as the knife sliced a little bit deeper, but I didn't dare adjust my hold. I would have sliced my entire fingertip off if I had to.

The blood slicked my hands, and my grip became precarious. I gave one last mighty pull. There was a nasty crunch as the fragile bone splintered, and the steel door slammed shut. I pushed the latch into place and the severed arm hung limply from the doorframe.

Panting, I collapsed backwards. My arm hit the shelving of the freezer with a clang. I didn't care. Sweat poured down my face. I ran my hand through my damp hair and hissed as the sweat touched the deep wound on my finger.

Several of my hairs were entangled in the wound. I swallowed hard and dropped my hand onto my lap. I jumped at the sound of Rotters on the other side trying to break down the door.

The arm in the doorway swayed uselessly in front of

me. I willed it to drop to the floor, but the arm just hung there. It flopped a little with each thud. I took a deep, shaky breath. Tears welled up hot in my eyes, matching the sensation of hot blood gushing from my wound. I blinked the tears away and went to assess how badly damaged my leg was.

My leg gaped open, showing pink flesh amongst a flood of red. *At least it missed the artery. I'd be dead by now otherwise.*

I couldn't see any bone through the torrent that poured out of me. *That's a good sign.* Darkish blood smeared up my leg in rust coloured strokes. My skin looked horribly pale and clammy underneath. I pressed my hands onto the wound as I looked around the room for something, anything, to use as a bandage on my leg. My hands couldn't stop the flow as blood poured from between my fingers. I started muttering to myself, "Oh, damn. Damn. Damn. *Damn.*" I whispered the word like a chant.

This is bad.

I pressed at the wound harder, hoping that the virus would glue the flesh shut. After a few moments, I tentatively removed my hands. The flesh held for a second before it popped open again like a bursting fig. I tried a few more times with no luck. My heart beat faster, and another spurt of blood came from the wound. I started crying.

At this rate, I didn't need to worry about the necrosis; I was going to bleed out.

Nothing in the freezer served as a suitable bandage. Instead, I pointed the tip of my knife at my shirt and sliced at the fabric. The tough outer exterior wouldn't cut, but I realized with relief that I didn't bother taking off my tank top while getting geared up. I sliced a long strip of fabric from the bottom. It tore unevenly, but I didn't care as I began to sway.

I tightly wrapped my leg shut until nausea overpowered me. I leaned over to my right side and retched. My meagre supper laid in a puddle beside me. I coughed a few more times until only a thin stream of bile dribbled from my mouth.

Wiping my chin with the back of my hand, I sat upright against the wall, panting. I finished tying the knot around my leg, but blood was already starting to soak through the dirty fabric.

I wistfully fantasized about my mic, sitting somewhere in the kitchen beyond. *If only one of my team would come and find me. The Rotters nearby should've made it easy.* I stopped panting and held my breath, ears pricked for any sounds. There was simply silence.

I cocked my head, trying to hear anything. *A faint shuffle. Breathing perhaps. They couldn't have left already—* Thump. *Ah, there they are.* The Rotters were right outside the door. *They'll know exactly where I am.*

Blood began to flow onto the floor. My bandage wasn't doing a damn thing, and short of a tourniquet, I was not sure what to do. My gaze roamed around the room. I felt an uncomfortable pulse of blood running down my leg with every beat of my heart. It started to beat quicker, struggling with my blood loss.

The world violently tilted. I raised my blood-slicked hands up to my face. *This might also be the last time it tilted if I don't do something.*

My vision went fuzzy, and I slapped myself, trying to stay alert.

I thought about Jade's scars. *She cauterized them herself, right?* I scanned the freezer with my gun mounted light. By a sheer stroke of luck, a few bottles of clear grain alcohol were on a low shelf nearby. Boxes filled with cutlery supplies and other odds and ends sat on the metal racks.

I pulled myself along the floor. My arms shook badly, and I had almost no colour left in my skin. I opened one box. Inside were faded yellow receipts and some other bits of paper. Angrily, I threw the box. Papers flew out and drifted, like snow, into the river of blood behind me. I felt nausea rise but didn't bother trying to vomit, nothing was left in my stomach anyway.

My muscles quivered with fatigue as I kept myself propped up. I found nothing useful in the next box, either. Finally, I got lucky with the last one. A long-reach lighter was inside the box. Thrilled, I clutched it to my chest as I crawled over to the bottles liquor. I untwisted the cap, and the overpowering smell of alcohol made my eyes water. I didn't even bother checking what the proof was; it was plenty strong enough.

I doused my leg with the alcohol. Tears started streaming from my eyes.

Damn, that stung.

My arms shook even more violently. I heard a weird groaning noise and realized it was coming from me. I promptly snapped my mouth shut. My teeth were chattering but the noise didn't completely stop.

On the other side of the door, I heard the Rotters scratching. They shrieked in frustration, trying to penetrate the steel.

Thank goodness for walk-in freezers.

I pulled myself over to my blade. I doused it with alcohol and lit it to clean it. Once the flames died off, I held the blade in the steady flame of the lighter. It began to get hotter and hotter. I put it down and clumsily undid the knot in the cloth.

"You stupid idiot," I muttered angrily to myself under my breath. "Should've just cut it off before you heated the knife." As I scolded myself, I fumbled with the fabric. Sweating a bit, I finally got the knot undone. The fabric was bound so tightly in my leg; I could see the compressions from where it was tied. My leg was half-sunken from the pressure.

That can't be good.

I picked up the knife and held it in the flame a little longer before pressing the flat side of the metal on my wound.

Screams rang throughout the small room, echoing back to me in a cacophony of sound. I punched the wall with my left fist but kept my leg still as the knife pressed against it. I howled until my throat felt raw. My leg twitched involuntarily, and I pulled the knife away. My flesh was smouldering and continued to bleed. Tears freely poured down my face as I heated up the knife again.

The stench of cooked flesh lingering in the air made me feel nauseous. Bile threatened to rise in my throat. I swallowed hard, focusing on the flame licking the edge of my blade.

Pressing the knife back onto my leg, I bit my lip hard enough to draw blood as I tried to hold it steady. My vision narrowed dangerously, and everything turned grey. I didn't want to pass out. *I was going to bleed out for sure.*

I jerked the knife off my thigh.

I blinked a few times and waited for the colour to return. Gradually, the floor regained its bright red-smeared appearance, and I exhaled slowly.

The sickening, charred smell was even stronger. My flesh sealed itself, forcing me to retch.

The wound on my leg was mangled. It was a rough job, but I didn't care. I needed to stop the bleeding, but the pain nearly knocked me out. *I can't afford to pass out right now.*

Limping over to the window in the freezer door, I pressed my ear against it. There was silence. I wondered if they were still licking up my blood or if they'd moved on. A groan from the other side answered my question. Resigned, I lowered myself to the floor. The air suddenly felt icy. I sat in a drying pool of my own blood, knowing the stench of my fresh meat was going to act as a lure for any nearby Rotters.

I began to rock, wondering if my team was going to come. I thought they would.

I noticed after a while that the silence was beginning to

press in on me. There were no longer any groans or thumps from behind the door. I remembered the perfectly clean room in the Facility after they had been fed. Shakily, I pulled myself up the door.

Peering through the smudged window, I saw that the blood puddle was cleared up. Behind me, blood pooled on the floor. Red streaks ran down from the wreckage of my leg. The smell alone was going to bring them right to me.

I popped the cap off the alcohol and flushed the floor with it. The powerful scent of the liquor masked the smell of blood. The fumes made me slightly dizzy. I made sure that the lighter was far away from the puddle of pinkish alcohol, more out of paranoia than any real danger of a fire starting.

The Rotter arm hung by the door's latch. I gingerly pinched it by the wrist and tugged. After a few moments of wiggling, it reluctantly came unstuck. I tossed it onto the floor behind me with distaste. A few strings of flesh still hung from the door.

I wiped the sweat out of my eyes as I twisted the latch. I was shaking, cold, and desperately hoping I could find my mic.

I pushed my full body weight against the door, and it groaned open. I crawled out from the freezer on my hands and knees and shut the door behind me. Hopefully, the smell wouldn't carry too far, and the alcohol would mask it.

The kitchen was licked clean. Tongue marks occasionally smudged along the surfaces. All that was left of the two Leukos were some of their weapons and bits of cloth.

I looked around in vain for my tiny earpiece. I lay flat on the floor to peer beneath the cabinets. Finally, I saw it sticking out from beneath the counter.

"Oh, come here, you beautiful bastard," I whispered to it. Holding it up to eye level, I could faintly hear crackling noises. Breaking out in a grin, I popped in the earpiece. "Hey, guys," I sighed into the mic.

"Holy shit. Belford? Are you all right?" Mona's voice was clipped and excited.

"I've lost a lot of blood. I'm in the restaurant kitchens. I need medical attention, stat."

"Jesus. Okay. All right, we're on our way. And Belford?"

"Yes?"

"For fuck's sake, don't lose your earpiece again." With a burst of static, she cut the connection. I grinned. Sighing in relief, I leaned against the cabinets. Near my hand rested a folder that looked similar to one a Leuko was carrying earlier. My suspicion aroused, I pulled the folder out from underneath the table.

My hand shook violently, and a few of the pages slipped from within the folder. Sticking out from the most prominent page was a face that looked frighteningly familiar. I pulled the sheet out and blinked a few times until the image came into focus.

I stared into my own eyes.

Adrenaline surged into my veins briefly, sharpening the fuzzy aspects of the image. I could see my name, written blurrily at the bottom of the picture.

I squinted at the rest of the fuzzy lines, hoping they'd focus into words. The squiggles danced around a little but refused to turn into anything legible. I swore and flopped the folder on the ground.

I needed to know what this said.

Evan and my team would be arriving soon, and they'd also be able to read it for me. I felt relaxed momentarily, followed quickly by another surge of panic. The Leuko's words about Oakville echoed in my mind: "*Your arrogant little boyfriend razed it to the ground to get you.*" Suddenly paranoid, I decided that maybe I didn't want to share this folder with anyone until I knew what it said.

My breathing was shallow as everything swirled for a moment. I was going to pass out, and they would take me to the hospital, strip my belongings off of me, and find the file. I couldn't afford to keep it on me.

My eyes flicked around the kitchen, trying to find a good hiding spot. Shaking, I shifted myself away from the cabinet door that I was blocking. Inside, there was nothing but rusted out saucepans, coated with dirt and dust. Curling the file into a tube, I slipped it into the largest pot and put the lid on it. The metal scraped against the rust and settled, but it didn't entirely hide the folder from view. I closed the cabinet and pulled open a drawer. Feeling its underside, I realized I could slip the folder underneath, effectively hiding it from view. I slid the drawer open and shut a few times before I was satisfied that the folder was invisible. I committed its location to memory.

At this small exertion, my nausea came back with a vengeance. My arms and legs began to numb. My heartbeat was erratic, feeling indecently frantic for how sluggish my brain felt.

I looked down at the hole in my leg. I swallowed my nausea and imagined how big the scar would be. My vision faded in and out. Realizing I was about to become unconscious in open Rotter territory, I got a small burst of adrenaline, which allowed me to look around the kitchen. I could barely put weight on my leg, and I was going to be unconscious any second, but I crawled over to the metal shelving.

Painstakingly, I hauled myself up as high as I could. I was slightly above head height when I decided I couldn't climb anymore. I rolled onto an empty shelf, panting, feeling cold strips of metal pressed against my bare flesh. Spots danced in front of my vision, and my breathing sounded oddly tinny.

I passed out.

Everything was blurry when I came to. *Was I moving?* Instantly, I sprung awake. My hand flew to my right thigh where my fingers grasped at an empty neoprene holster.

"Easy there. Jesus, Belford." The profile of Piper's angular face swam into view. I was lying across her shoulders in a fireman's carry. My eyes darted around, but I was unwilling to turn my head. Evan stood off to my right and held my dagger.

"Piper thought it might be best if we disarmed you." He handed me back my knife. Once the initial adrenaline rush wore off, my limbs suddenly felt fragile and shaky. I tried to slip the blade into its sheath, but it took me a few stabs before managing to slide it home.

I took a deep breath and settled onto Piper's strong shoulders. I felt like I should be embarrassed about being carried around like this, but I was so cold, and my body felt so far away. Plus, this was going to be the second time in a few months that I had most of my blood drained.

Something slightly pinched my left arm. I groggily looked over and saw that Evan already hooked me up to a blood bag, which he carried above his head as we walked. My vision tunnelled as he changed the blood bag over to his other hand. I felt a rush of gratitude. I began to say something, but my voice sounded echoey and distant. Piper said something that dimly faded before I lost consciousness again.

CHAPTER THIRTEEN
The Blank-Out

I came to in a hospital room. There was a familiar beep and whir of machines surrounding me. The curtains were pulled, separating me from the other beds.

I blinked a few times, trying to gather my thoughts. A sharp pain stabbed from the base of my skull. I moved to sit up but found my body unwilling to cooperate. Remembering the machete wound, I pulled aside the starched white sheets and saw the mess of bandages that covered my leg.

My thigh was still pink and shiny. I traced my fingers over the rough, melted tissue, realizing that there was no new patch. Jade entered and gave me a wide smile. "Hope you don't mind; we thought we'd save ourselves a spare part. There's no shame in being a little bit scarred up." She gave me a broad smile that lit up her whole face, even though the scar tissue itself didn't move. I felt a small surge of pride as I looked at Jade's cauterized wounds. Today, her scars seemed larger and more numerous, as though the agony I felt amplified them a hundredfold.

I moved to stand up again, and this time, felt a little tug

at my ankles. I flipped off the blanket completely, revealing thick plastic cuffs chaining me to the bed. I looked at Jade questioningly. She gave me an unapologetic shrug.

"You lost a ton of blood. It was a good thing that you cauterized the wound. Otherwise, you would probably be one of the shambling horde by now."

I felt a bit of nervousness tickle down my spine. "Are you guys going to let me go?"

Jade leaned against the counter with her arms crossed as she looked over me. "Of course. This is just a precaution on the off chance you might be feeling worse than you look. Besides," she pulled herself away from the counter and sauntered over to me, "Braeden specifically requested that we hold you in the hospital until he can look at you." I felt my stomach drop.

She gave me a saucy wink before she saw that my face had fallen.

"You okay?" she asked with a real note of concern.

I shrugged; my hands nervously picked at the threads of the hospital linens. "I figured Braeden was going to discover that I was a part of the raids sooner or later. I had hoped that he would have found out while I was still in fine fighting form, preferably after I had helped secure the Facility a major victory." The image of the hidden file swam into my mind, as I swallowed down my guilt from lying.

She laughed a little. "Ah, you mean instead of banged up and half-dead in the hospital?" She gave my good leg a reassuring squeeze. "Don't stress too much. Between Piper and I, you've got plenty of people to sing your praises."

I looked over myself, scarred and hooked up to machines and IVs, having just barely made it out of the hotel alive. There was no way he'd let me go on any more raids. "What exactly does he want to look at me for?" I asked. My attempt to sound casual failed, as my voice came out unnaturally high.

Jade gave me a knowing look before she replied, "We can pretend that it's just the Good Doctor's ego at work, but I think he is actually worried about your well-being, Clara."

"His worry should be *his* problem. Why does he keep making it into mine?" I groaned.

Missy entered with her new assistant before Jade could reply. He smiled and said, "Hey, Clara, heard you got a little roughed up." I smiled half-heartedly at him, trying to conceal that I had completely forgotten his name again.

Missy flipped open my file and frowned. "That's weird."

My heart rate sped up. "What's weird?"

"Huh? Oh, nothing. It's probably just his ego." She turned to her assistant. "Can you grab Dr. Runar for me? Apparently, he needs to be here."

He waved over his shoulder at us as he left.

Missy leaned over me and prodded at the patch of skin on my calf. My breathing came out as a hiss through clenched teeth. Something that was not quite pain radiated from where her fingertips touched, like a bubble that was straining to pop. The skin itself was loose and wobbly. "Don't worry," she murmured, not paying too much attention to my distress. "As soon as we see what Dr. Runar wants, we'll put you under and get you a nice new one. Can you move your foot at all?" I managed to lightly wriggle my toes and do a small circle with my foot. She prodded my calf once more, and the uncomfortable feeling came back. I gasped. Missy stopped touching me. "Easy there. Don't hurt yourself. Well... don't keep hurting yourself. You're lucky it was a clean in-and-out." She buzzed two assistants to fetch her an appropriate specimen. She rattled off a series of measurements while simultaneously jotting them down on a piece of paper.

"YOU LET HER GO ON A RAID?" Braeden's voice echoed down the hallway. I felt myself tense up. Missy and Jade shared a look.

The door flung open and Braeden exploded into the room. His short hair was mussed, eyes wild, as he scanned the room and saw me lying on the bed. I hastily covered up the scar on my leg with the blanket. He moved across the room in three strides before he was at my side, cradling my face in his hands. I had to physically stop myself from recoiling. The Leukos words about Oakville wouldn't stop repeating in my brain. *Razed it to the ground?*

"Clara, are you okay? What happened?" Braeden said gently, his eyes searching mine. I pulled aside the hospital blanket, uncovering my calf. The patch attached messily to my clammy skin with blackness lining the seams.

His pale fingers traced over it. Unlike Missy's, his touch was gentle and probing. His brow creased with worry. As he examined the patch, he tsked and frowned. I felt a little bit defensive of Evan. All things considered, he'd done a great job.

Braeden ordered the donor list from Evan's Medi-kit to be brought to him, along with the remaining patches. His two assistants bowed awkwardly and quietly crept towards the door, as though not to disturb him. He looked up from his examination and snarled, "Run! Go! Now!" The two of them took off like cats on a hot tin roof.

Missy and Jade both stared at him, not moving. In a low growl, he said, "Go make yourselves useful elsewhere." Jade looked disgruntled but didn't say anything. Missy wore a look of consternation. Neither doctor argued with him, and after a moment's hesitation, they exited the room.

Once they left, he turned his full attention to my injury. He ran his fingers over the smooth, slightly sunken piece of skin, muttering to himself. Finally, his two assistants returned. One carried a list, the other, Evan's Medi-kit. Braeden snatched the list and quickly read down it. He snapped his fingers at the assistant holding the case, "Patch from specimen seven, is it accounted for?"

The shaking assistant clicked open the cold portion of the kit and began to inspect each patch. She reached the bottom and went back through it again. Finally, in a quivering voice, she said, "N-no, no, sir. The specimen is unaccounted for."

Braeden closed his eyes and rolled his neck. "Bring me specimen two or five. I need to replace this patch." I bolted upright at his words.

He was planning on doing what to my patch?

Braeden swallowed and looked at me with apologetic eyes. The growing disgust I'd been feeling for him grew again. I simply said, "Do you have to?" He nodded. I took a deep breath and settled myself against my pillows. I looked up at the ceiling and said to the room, "All right, let's get it over with. Do it. Cut me open."

Braeden put down the list and went to wash his hands. While he prepared himself, the assistants gathered the necessary supplies for the operation, and I, attempting to not think about my upcoming debridement, picked up the list to look over the patch donors.

There were descriptions of physical attributes attached to each patch.

When Braeden reappeared, snapping on latex gloves, I held up the list to him, "What was wrong with specimen seven?" Not stopping, he collected the scalpel from his tray and began to wipe my calf down with cold antiseptic that coloured my leg a rusty orange.

"It's the wrong blood type," he said in a low, almost hypnotic voice while he focused on my calf. "If you want an organ transplant to be accepted, you should always use the proper match. If it's cross-match positive, it'll be rejected, and your condition will worsen." He tossed the little swab away and began applying a numbing agent to my leg. "You and I are both lucky because we've got AB positive blood, the universal recipient, so we can take donations from anyone. But it's always better to have a perfect match, it slows down the spread of necrosis." The scalpel reflected the fluorescent lighting like a mirror. I squeezed my eyes shut and clenched my jaw, preparing for the pain.

Instead, I only felt a gentle pulling sensation on my calf. Fighting against my better judgement, I peeked an eye open. Braeden was methodically sawing the scalpel underneath the flap of skin. Even in the short time it took to return to the hospital, the patch had almost completely integrated with my flesh. I felt the bitter tang of bile in my mouth as I forced myself to look away from the hunk of meat that was my leg. I swallowed it back down and started thinking of random things to distract myself from the soft tugging where my leg was being skinned.

Eventually, I felt something being smoothed onto my leg, and then, slowly, the feeling came back into most of my calf. I opened my eyes and looked down. Braeden lightly prodded at it. I had complete sensation everywhere except my new patch.

The skin was already starting to seal itself. I also didn't see any bruising. There was another flutter of hope in my chest that Braeden might actually find the cure for this thing.

He wiped the wound clean and bandaged it. I eyed his face while he worked, admiring the dark stubble on his strong chin. His touch sent electric shocks up my skin.

"Okay, you're all good to go." He snapped off his gloves and gave me a warm smile. His lips looked good enough to bite. I paused at the thought, and then shoved it down.

I wasn't entirely certain, nor did I want to know what had driven that particular impulse.

He sat down on the bed next to me, his hand resting on my thigh.

When he released me, it took me a moment to catch my breath. My eyelids fluttered open as I inhaled deeply, trying to regain my composure. Braeden straightened his clothing,

149

out of breath himself. He looked at me with heavily hooded eyes. "I'm glad that you're okay." His voice was husky.

"Me too. In fact, I feel great," I said, surprising even myself with how good I felt.

Braeden gave me a doubtful look. "I can't let you go out on those raids. You could have been killed, Clara."

The urge to protest rose, but I stopped myself. I stared into his eyes with feelings of doubt and dread.

Did he raze Oakville to the ground?

Realizing he was waiting for an answer, I nodded meekly, my head full of thoughts about retrieving the hidden file. Rather than belabour the point, I asked, "Can I at least keep my knife on me?"

He smiled. "After everything you've gone through? Of course you can keep some extra protection on you." Braeden seemed pleased by my obedience.

He jerked his head to the bedside table, and I pulled open a drawer. Inside were two bags—one that contained my soiled civilian clothing from the raid and another that contained my knife and thigh sheathe. The knife bag had a little smiley face drawn on it. I really appreciated Piper's attention to detail for her squad members.

I clipped it into place and felt my muscles fully relax.

He gently smoothed my hair back from my face with one hand, his other interlocked with my fingers.

Feeling emboldened by this, I asked, "Can I go to Oakville? Just to see it?" The smile dropped from his face as his hand released from mine.

"Look at where you are." His voice was cold. "Look at the ankle restraints. With your injury, we were worried you had gone to rot, and you want to go around the uninfected?" I opened my mouth to protest but decided it was wiser for me to remain silent for now.

Instead, I choked back the retort and said, "You're right. I'm sorry." The words felt like bile in my mouth.

Braeden frowned as his eyes rested on the blade.

His anger melted away in a lightning change of mood, and he smiled warmly at me, taking my hand again. "Missy is probably going to give you one last look over, and we'll get someone to wheel you to your room. I'll see you later, okay?" He gave my hand a gentle squeeze. I immediately felt a warm rush, despite my trepidations, as he disappeared out the door. I smiled and smoothed down my blankets, clinging to the warmth I felt deep in my chest and ignoring the rise of panic in my gut.

Suddenly, Missy stood in front of me. I blinked a few times in confusion, not entirely sure where Braeden had gone. *No wait… he had left, right?*

She approached and tried to put her hands on me. Nervously, I took a few steps back. *When did I leave my bed?* I rubbed my eyes hard until white spots appeared. I couldn't remember what I had just been doing. The woman looked at me with wide blue eyes. "Clara, listen to me." She wore a medical insignia. "Are you feeling confused?"

I looked at her, then around the room. "Where am I?" I asked her finally, feeling a tremble starting in my shoulders as my panic was peaking. I felt so adrift… I couldn't remember.

"You're just having a bad reaction to some medication. I have something for you that will clear it right up, okay? You can trust me." Her voice was low and soothing. I stared at her and nodded.

She gave me a relieved smile and pulled out a little briefcase. The inside of it was lined with little vials. She removed a syringe and took a measured dosage of clear liquid. "It's just a quick shot, and it'll all be over."

I held out my arm and gasped a little as the needle slid into my flesh and felt a weird cooling sensation as she pressed the plunger. Within minutes, I felt like I'd been pleasantly removed from my body.

Distantly I heard, "We should do the MRI while she's out."

I opened my eyes to my little apartment on the fourteenth floor. I patted my thigh, and my heart rate picked up. My knife wasn't there.

I tried to stand up and realized my left hand had been handcuffed to my bed. Panicked, I began to thrash. The steel handcuff screamed against the metal of the bedpost. The door flew open, and Aidan entered. His hands were on me, and he was shushing me. Braeden came in shortly after.

"Braeden," I was almost weeping. "It's happening."

His brow creased. Panic rose in my chest as I looked into his worried eyes.

I couldn't recall my mother's voice. I thought back to the last day in Oakville, but I could only remember her cooking. She seemed like a blurry shape, just out of focus. Tears began to form in my eyes. *Was this the start of it?*

He brushed my hair back and looked at me as though he was mesmerized by my features. He sat with me for the longest time. Unfamiliar faces came into the room. I didn't want them to see me. I jerked my arm a few more times, trying to get free.

Braeden calmly examined my face. "Do you know who you are?"

"I'm Clara Belford," I replied.

He smiled at me. "Good." He took a set of keys and unlocked the handcuffs that were cutting into my wrists. "I'm glad to see that you're lucid again."

I nearly wanted to cry. I finally asked the question I had been too afraid to ask before. "Was that a blank-out?"

He gave me a solemn nod, and I closed my eyes tightly.

"Can you please leave me alone right now?" I asked him softly. He gently ran the back of his hand along my cheek before placing a gentle kiss on my temple and leaving the room.

Realizing I didn't have anything left to lose, I was more determined than ever to find that file in the hotel.

CHAPTER FOURTEEN
Returning to the Hideaway

My heart pounded as I waited for the darkness to fall in my room. I listened to the radio as I waited. My hand kept lazily rubbing along my thigh. The shiny scar was still sore, but nothing compared to what it felt like twenty-four hours ago. The bruising along the scar mirrored the ones that were blossoming along my hands. The rot was spreading faster.

I lay in my bed and stared at the ceiling. Orange and yellow lights reflected from the glass flowers outside. I drew in a deep breath and tried to shut my mind off. I passed the last hours of the afternoon, lazing in my bed and daydreaming. Time seemed to crawl.

Occasionally, I tried to get up and do something, but I was lethargic. I needed to form a plan to get to the hotel.

I was lucky. The hotel was close enough that I could use Toronto's underground pedestrian walkways that zigzagged throughout the Old City to get there without worrying too much about the cold. If it was any farther away, I probably would need to work out finding a set of wheels for myself.

I sat down and tried to read one of the books that Aidan

lent me. I was unable to focus on the words. Irritable, I threw myself back in my bed and closed my eyes. Hopefully, I could sleep.

Sleep, however, never came. After ages, darkness finally fell, and I slipped out of bed.

I made my way over to Aidan's room in my pyjamas. A sense of relief washed over me when I saw the warm orange glow emitting from underneath his doorway. I raised my knuckles and gently rapped on his door. Aidan creaked it open. His bright blue eyes peered out at me through the crack, before I saw his scar crinkle up as he smiled. He opened the door wide. "Hey there, Clara. What can I do for you?"

I hitched what I thought was a genuine smile on my face and shrugged my shoulders nonchalantly. "I couldn't really sleep, and I was hoping I could bother you for a cup of tea. If you're not busy, of course."

Aidan gestured for me to come inside and began busying himself with a tea kettle. His room was much more decorated than mine: he'd filled it with little odds and ends, trinkets from his adventures outside. In the corner was a little shrine with a woman's photograph, surrounded by dried wildflowers. She smiled widely at the camera and had flowers woven into her long blond hair. The photo itself was faded and worn.

Aidan looked through his collection of dried flowers and herbs. He selected a few different jars before mixing a new tea. It was filled with dried purple flowers and green leaves. Soon the smell of mint and perfume filled the air. I gratefully accepted my cup from him.

He settled himself down in the chair opposite me. I held the steaming mug up to my lips, grateful for the warmth seeping into my fingers. The smell of mint immediately soothed some of my frazzled nerves.

Aidan and I made pleasantries, lightly gossiping about

the latest news in the Facility. The more he regaled me with the latest drama, the more relaxed I found myself. It was easy to forget my plans for the time being, sitting in the warmth of his room as the snow gently fell outside.

My eyes continued to scan his room until they landed on his large keyring.

It took four mugs of tea before Aidan got up and excused himself to go to the restroom. I watched him closely. Once the door clicked shut, I sprang up from my seat towards the keys.

Deftly, I pressed my hand over them, clasping them all, so they didn't jingle as I picked them up. I quickly found what I was looking for: two large brass keys with a little piece of tape labelling them as D-XW and D-XA—the same keys I had seen him use before to unlock the Level 1 Drop Armoury and the weapon's safe. I slipped these two off the ring and quietly placed the keys back into position.

I was lowering myself into my seat when the door opened again. I palmed both the keys before slipping them into a pocket-apiece of my flannel pyjama pants for safekeeping.

As Aidan settled back down into the armchair, I did a theatrical yawn and announced that I was exhausted. I thanked him for the tea and said my goodbyes.

Once his door closed, I scampered back to my room. Ripping off my pyjamas and pulling on a black pair of jeans and top, I clipped my thigh holster into place and slipped on my knee-length coat. My hair was tucked underneath a toque, its wool covering my ears.

I grabbed a few of the extra pillows and sheets from the closet and piled them roughly into a human shape on the bed. Once I pulled the covers up, anyone who felt like checking in on me would think I was lying there sleeping. For good measure, I left the radio softly playing.

I turned off the light and locked the door behind me. The hallway felt even darker and more oppressive than usual.

My heart was racing when I reached the elevators.

I made it into the bright and empty atrium without running into anyone. Pausing, my eyes searched each of the floors above and below me. There were quiet whispers being carried from the ground floor. Holding my breath, I peered over the glass railing and strained my eyes to see who it was. My breath came out in a rush when I saw two lab techs wandering across the lobby towards the blood lab. I heard a thump as a door opened and shut behind them. Frozen, I sat in silence a moment longer, until I was satisfied that there was no one else wandering around near the atrium. Retreating into the shadows, I slipped past the empty information desk by the first-aid clinic and made my way over to the storage room.

The large brass key fit into the door nicely. The lock gave with a small click. I pushed it open and scrunched my face as it let out a loud creak. The opening was barely big enough for me to squeeze through.

I heard footsteps and froze, wedged partway through the doorway. I held my breath again, praying that no one could see me in the cloak beneath the shadows. After a moment or two, I realized the sound of footsteps was once again coming from downstairs.

I gritted my teeth and pulled myself fully through the doorway, breathing easily once I was inside the storage room. Grey trunks lined the walls. I picked my way through carefully until I found the weapons cache.

Pulling out my second key, I opened a crate in the back corner. Barrels glinted from the dim light of the doorway. Feeling through the dark, I found a rifle scope to turn on. A tiny spotlight illuminated the inside of the chest. I ran my fingers over the spare bullets, the empty magazines, and the guns carefully placed in the lining.

Moving quickly, I examined the weapons until I found a rifle and two pistols that sat nicely in my hands. I began quietly whispering the number as I slid the bullets into their magazines. *Sixty-three bullets. Two kilometres there, two kilometres back.*

The guards stationed at the main entrance talked loudly. Their voices echoed throughout the empty atrium. Feeling confident that their noise would drown out most of it, I shut the door quickly. It produced a loud shriek and the voices went quiet. After a moment or two, they resumed. I pulled the door fully closed and locked it. I mentally vowed to return the keys to Aidan in the morning as I slipped them into my boot for safekeeping.

Hugging the walls, I pulled as far away from the atrium as possible while I made my way to the tunnels in the basement. Reluctantly, I scanned my passkey to get into the tunnels, secretly wishing I had thought to swipe one.

Once I entered the large underground room, I turned on the lights. I covered my eyes as the bright fluorescents flickered to life. Blinking a few times, my vision eventually adjusted. I strode confidently over to my locker and entered my combination.

I quickly traded my clothing for my raid gear. I hissed as the cold cloth slid against my skin. I hopped from foot to foot to increase my circulation. *The walk should do plenty to warm me up.* I gathered up my weapons and arranged myself. Once everything was clipped into place, I rolled my shoulders a few times and proceeded out the door.

Moving away from the Facility, I entered the tunnels and began my long walk. Without my teammates' banter, it seemed to take forever. Eventually, I found myself in front of the door where I had my first training session three months earlier.

I undid the deadbolt and stepped inside the abandoned building. Once I left the tunnels, the fresh air bit into me. My breath formed around me like a ghost. I was thankful that it was nearly a full moon. The silvery light permeated the empty building, giving me an idea of where to step to keep quiet.

I strained my ears for any groans or sounds of shuffling. The wind ruffled a few of the dead leaves in the next room, but otherwise, all was silent. Clutching my rifle closely to me, I proceeded up the steps into the room beyond.

I stopped in front of the map that Piper had used to mark our trails, examining it closely, trying to work out the best path back to the hotel. After closely examining the map, I decided the quickest route was through the Path. If I could take it through to the plaza, I'd only have to move a block or two above ground to get to the hotel. Once I memorized the route, I slipped outside into the night.

The moon glared in the night sky overhead. Its brightness caused deep shadows to cut across the ground. The light desaturated the world into garish black and white.

Frost lined the dead autumn leaves, glittering in the moonlight. I lightly pressed one boot into the frosty leaves and was relieved that the snow had dampened them. They were soft, and my footsteps, silent. Feeling optimistic, I began to sneak my way through the streets.

I kept my ears pricked for any sounds. Wings fluttered overhead, causing my heart to hammer in my chest.

I slipped through the streets, accompanied by the low groans of an occasional rotter, and some lonesome howls of a coyote in the distance. The snow-dusted streets were almost completely deserted.

I approached the opening to the Path. Roars and shrieks echoed from inside the depths of the tunnels. I realized my folly—most of the Rotters had gone underground from the cold. Only a few opportunistic ones still shuffled around out in the brisk air.

Despite the chill, I decided to keep to the streets, away from the warmer tunnels. Based on the growls coming from underground, I was sure that many of them were nested, waiting for some poor creature to venture in from the cold, into their awaiting jaws.

I moved easily through the middle of the cracked streets as the frost sparkled in the moonlight.

I breathed a sigh of relief as I saw the ripped black awning of the hotel. I quickly moved up the small steps and through the doors. A cold sweat broke out down my back as I entered the old lobby. The giant statues looked like ancient sentinels instead of chess pieces. Everything was now in shades of grey.

The furniture, so orderly before, had been overturned and scattered. It looked like it had been ransacked. My light added a small splash of colour to the dull world. I quickly scanned it around the room, wondering if I would see any new splotches of red.

My finger rested on the trigger, but I kept my barrel pointed skywards. Aside from the pounding of my heart, I heard nothing. Whatever had disturbed the furniture didn't appear to be nearby anymore. It may have even happened during the raid. This room was teeming with Rotters.

I retraced my steps to the kitchen. When I entered, I stifled a small gasp. In the beam of my light, the kitchen was in ruins. Rusted-out pots and pans laid in a heap across the room; their cabinet doors still stood ajar, as though flung from their places by some vengeful spirit.

I took a few small steps into the room as I surveyed the damage. Everything had been searched. The insides of cabinets and drawers had been thrown into a pile.

Someone had come through here again after I left.

Shaking, I got onto my knees near the partially opened drawers. My trembling fingers reached underneath the bottom drawer, and relief flooded my veins. I could feel the silky-smooth texture of the manila folder. I gently dislodged it from its hiding space. The papers had been crumpled a little bit—probably from when the drawer was wrenched open—but nothing was torn.

Though I desperately wanted to read through it, I simply opened it and saw that the documents were in there, as well as my photograph, and I closed it again. I forced down my curiosity and promised myself that I would read it the second I got inside the Facility tunnels, out of open Rotter territory.

Still holding my rifle in one hand, I clumsily shifted the file around, realizing too late that I had forgotten to bring something to carry it in. Unwilling to waste any more time, I smoothed it out and slid it down the front of my pants for safekeeping. With my jacket zipped shut, I was certain it wouldn't be going anywhere.

I slowly exhaled and willed my heart to slow. In its state of disrepair, this haunted place felt even more malevolent than it had been when it was teeming with the infected. I shuddered as I thought back to the Leukos. My thigh twitched unpleasantly as the hairs on the back of my neck tingled. I reached up and rubbed along the nape of my neck, thankful that the blow hadn't struck where it was meant to.

Having spent a lot of the last few years running away from death, it felt like I was tempting fate as I stood in the place that had almost became my tomb.

I couldn't let them kill me before I found out what happened to my family.

A hopeless thought tried to enter my mind but was quickly quashed. *I would find out without issue. I knew it.*

I couldn't bear to consider the alternative...

I walked through the abandoned lobby, carrying the gun tightly to my chest to securely hold the file. Within those pages was the information as to why I was nearly beheaded, I was certain of it. I took in deep breaths of cold air as I walked outside.

A shiver shook my being, and I felt the exhaustion I had been resolutely ignoring take hold of me. Suddenly, nothing in the world seemed more pleasant than laying my head down in the snowbank and resting. I blinked slowly and looked around for a moment before I slapped myself.

"Focus, Clara," I muttered to myself. The dark entrance to the Path yawned in front of me. I could hear the Rotters rustling through the warmth from the underground. Realizing I didn't have a choice if I wanted to make it back to the Facility without hibernating, I clicked the safety off.

I moved into the street and fired off two shots before scampering to an alcove near the entrance. It wasn't long before the Rotters that camped in the tunnels, moved out from their hiding spots.

They came forward, looking half-starved. As they lurched by, a few of them caught my scent and shuffled towards me. As they got closer, they could smell my infection and continued to move past me. *Good, they weren't hungry enough.*

I slipped by them and made my way into the tunnels, clicking on my scope light. Most of the nest cleared out. The few that remained in the tunnel behind did not show me any interest. They were either hibernating or dead; I didn't care to find out which. I picked my way past the piles of bodies. The feeling of warmth began to seep into my skin, and I was much more alert than before. As my focus came back, I noticed a flickering light down one of the tunnels.

CHAPTER FIFTEEN
The Leuko Camp

I peered my head around the corner to see that I had almost unwittingly run into a group of camping Leukos. My gut tightened with fear, as I pressed my hand protectively over the folder. Four of them sat in silence around a small smokeless fire. One held a pistol in his hand. I turned off my scope light and drew into the shadows.

Shaken that I hadn't heard them, I paused to gather my wits. My fingers were numb, and the barrel of my gun was icy.

I jumped when I heard one of the Leuko's deep voice, "It was probably just some dumb human." Goosebumps erupted down my body as I crouched near the ground and tried to move closer.

"You don't think it was Facility?" another asked.

My ears pricked up.

"Nah, mate. It won't be Facility. They're still licking their wounds from the other night." The three of them snickered. I felt my blood turn hot but willed myself to stay calm, fighting the usual surge of adrenaline.

The third Leuko spoke, "When are we going to have another shot?"

The first one who spoke laughed. "Are you kidding me? From what I saw, and the way they dragged her out of there, she's going to be harvested within a week. Good riddance, too." I squeezed my eyes shut and held my rifle tightly to me as the scar on my leg seared with pain. I contemplated the gun. Taking out my hit squad and getting to warm up by the fire sounded like a win-win, but I cut the idea short. Even if I were a deadeye, it'd be suicide to try to take on four armed Leukos at once.

"Can't believe Marcus got himself killed over that," the second one said.

The deep-voiced Leuko snorted, "He didn't just get himself killed. He did it while screwing up everything Blaise had set in motion. And the girl made it back to the Facility."

My blood turned cold. *Blaise.* I said the name repeatedly to burn it into my memory.

"Do we have any more food?" one asked. The conversation turned away from the Facility and the raid. I resisted the urge to fire off a few more bullets out in the street to try to get them back to discussing whatever they had been talking about. Unsure if it was the virus affecting my brain or if I was just feeling reckless, I reminded myself that I had gotten lucky that they hadn't inspected the noise the first time.

I guess I am going to have to take the long way.

I set aside my frustration and instead chose to be grateful for the warmth of the tunnels, which permeated all the way down into my bones.

I took the opposite route from the camp of Leukos. The light from their fire flickered along the walls of the Path. Their laughter followed me, echoing eerily back at me from different directions. Silently, I cursed them as I saw a few Rotters appear from the abandoned stores ahead of me.

Three Rotters stumbled into the main hallway. They

looked around eagerly, hunting for the source of the sound. Their milky, bloodshot eyes fell on me. This trio was particularly skeletal. They hadn't feasted properly in a long time, which made me doubt I could get by them unscathed.

I quickly weighed my options. If I fired a shot, the mercs would absolutely hear it. I then thought about my knife. There were three Rotters, all too close to each other. Taking out one would mean exposing myself to the others. I was also becoming sluggish and stupid from the cold. I needed to get back to the Facility before hypothermia got to me and I tried to burrow into the snow like the other Wave Three infected.

I didn't have any other options.

I let out a string of curse words under my breath as I lined up my crosshairs with the closest Rotter. I exhaled and fired off the three shots quickly. *One, two, three.* I was already sprinting past their corpses before the third one had finished dropping. Immediately, behind me, I heard the Leuko group roar with confusion. Within moments, they would be after me.

Sprinting flat out, my footsteps rang along the hallway. A blast of cool air let me know I was running by an entrance to the outside. Tears from the frigid air whipped my face. My breathing was ragged, and the cold made my lungs raw. I could feel my muscles burning, but I didn't dare slow down.

My cauterized leg still hadn't fully healed, and as I ran, it felt like the muscles were being torn back apart. I slowed down to a limping jog and pressed forward. I came to a fork in the Path, continuing deeper underground. Hopefully, I would lose the mercs, but if need be, I had a better chance if they could only come at me from one direction.

My thigh burned, and I could only keep it up for a short while before I settled on an awkward hobbling powerwalk, trying to baby my inflamed injury. A few more twists and turns allowed me to feel confident enough to click on the scope light. The place was still empty and decrepit.

In my panicked run, I hadn't paid much attention to where I was going. Luckily, I recognized this part of the Path. We had hidden here during one of our drills, while we cleared a nest at street level. Eagerly, I moved towards the stairs to get from the underground. My walk was uneven, as my injured leg jerked underneath me.

The cold air hit my face in an unwelcome blast. Tucked into the white stones was the dark metal that entombed the nest. Though, as I crossed the street, something in the metal looked off. I stopped in my tracks before pulling myself tight into the shadows. Where before solid metal sealed the nest, now stood a hole. The bolted-down pieces of sheet metal had been ripped wide open. I approached it carefully and reached out to touch the jagged edge of the metal opening. It looked like it had been pushed inwards.

Whatever got through that seal had definitely come from the outside. I felt the hairs on the back of my neck stand up again. *Possibly other Rotters? Hopefully not humans trying to get through...* I shook off those feelings.

Now was not the time to get distracted.

The longer I was outside in the cold, the more tired I felt. Fatigued from the cold and worn out from my desperate run, my energy was completely sapped. I stumbled a little bit as I moved away from the empty nest. My thigh burned angrily.

A strangled half-laugh, half-sob escaped my throat at the sight of the dark buildings that stood over the entrance to the Facility's tunnels. I limped as fast as I could across the street and hurled myself down the steps. It was only once the heavy metal door clanged shut behind me that I took a deep rasping breath and finally sat still. I assessed my leg. A little bit of blackness seeped from between the shining pink scar. The wound gaped open slightly, but no blood poured forth.

I gritted my teeth in annoyance.

I would probably have to get it cut out and patched when I got back into the Facility.

After I sat in the darkened tunnels for a long while, where the only sounds were from me greedily gulping down air and the rushing blood in my ears, I struggled to my feet.

I took a shaky step, dragging my injured leg behind me. It felt like the muscles may have severed again during my sprint. Unable to move it properly, I limped as I made my way through the deep tunnels. I touched my stomach, feeling relieved that I could still feel the smooth paper of the folder.

Pausing, I glanced surreptitiously around. No one was coming in my direction. Deciding I had waited long enough, I slid the folder from my stomach, and clicked on my scope light. Detaching it from the barrel, I awkwardly held it in my mouth as I flipped through the folder.

At first, I couldn't make much sense of the documents. There weren't any additional notes on them, just a few forms and a photograph of me taken back when I had cancer, along with a glossier, more recent photograph. The more recent photograph was after I joined the Aegis Shield; I recognized the blue jumpsuit.

However, I was not the only person in the dossier.

Written on a form, with my name labelled as 'recipient,' was Braeden Runar's name, listed as a 'donor.' The date listed was several weeks before I received my chemotherapy treatment.

I remembered those weeks too well. I had been waiting for a suitable bone marrow donor for ages. They had been having trouble finding anyone. Neither my mom nor Leo was a match for me, and my dad, at the time, was nowhere to be found.

In the end, the doctors chose for me to donate to myself.

Yet Braeden had been a match for me…

I felt a dull throbbing in the back of my skull as I tried to puzzle out the link between Braeden being a bone marrow match for me and the Leukos attacking my fireteam.

I managed to find the only handwritten note in the entire document. Stamped on the back of the new photo taken of me when I was at the Facility, in cramped handwriting, were the words:

Donor ~~Seven~~ Eight, DoD(Est) ~~September~~ February - Final.

I flipped the photo back over and examined it. I looked healthy and human. My hair was still short, and I was laughing. It was with a slight chill that I realized in the background, I could see the colourful blurs of flowers in the cobblestone courtyard.

This photo had been taken at St Michael's Cathedral Basilica, the same day as the attack on the Facility.

I closed the folder and slid it back underneath my shirt. I vainly tried to recall if the Leuko had said anything else to make sense of this. *What did Braeden being a bone marrow match for me have anything to do with Oakville? Is that why the Resistance attacked me in May?* I fiddled with my pistol, feeling like some answers might be found at my old home.

Razed to the ground… what happened to Oakville? I didn't know whom to trust anymore. I needed something more concrete than this.

Gazing at the weapon, my eyes slipped over to the guns I had borrowed from the supply drops, and suddenly the answer seemed too obvious. The Facility kept extensive records about all the colonies for the drops, including Oakville. I took off down the tunnels again, back towards the Facility.

My leg throbbed while I searched through the rows and rows of manila folders before me. I was in the drop coordinator's office on the first floor. For a moment, I couldn't recall what I had done with the Leuko's file on me. I spun around, confused for a moment. My mind couldn't recall anything between the tunnels and how I got here. I squeezed my eyes shut, fighting with my brain to recall the memory. *You left it under your shirt last time.*

I patted my sides and stomach. Relief flooded over me when my hands touch the hard paper of the folder. I closed my eyes and willed myself to relax.

She's going to be harvested within a week. The Leukos words dance in my head as I strode over to the catalogued list of colonists for the supply drops. These blank-outs were starting to scare me.

I flicked through hundreds of order forms and supply sheets. I muttered the settlements aloud to myself. "… Mississauga, Milton… Oshawa." I flicked back and forth, checking in case it had been misfiled. Frowning, I picked up the Butcher's Corner order history. "… Mississauga, Milton… Oshawa." I picked up another pile. "C'mon, Oakville, where are you?" With my rising panic, I tried to keep calm and orderly as I searched through the individual papers.

Eventually, I gave up. There was not even an empty folder with Oakville stamped on it. It simply did not exist.

My mind was reeling.

Someone out there thought I was important enough to mark. I rubbed my hand along my pants where the scar sat. *Scratch that, someone out there thought I was important enough to kill.*

And now there was no sign of Oakville in the Facility's files.

I took a deep breath as panic threatened to overwhelm me. I needed to know what was going on, and I didn't know whom to trust.

The room warped a little bit, and the walls felt like they were closing in on me. Hyperventilating as I staggered backwards, I turned away from the folders. My feet moved one in front of the other until I was hobbling through the first-floor hallways, faltering as I went. My leg was still not fully cooperating.

I didn't stop moving until I was safely back in my room. I ripped off my clothes and shoved them into the back of my wardrobe.

Quickly throwing on the same pyjamas I had worn to Aidan's room, I sat down on my bed and opened the folder, ignoring the spasms in my thigh.

I searched in vain over the file one more time.

My brain then clicked into place something I didn't want to consider before.

I looked at the piece of paper with my name and Braeden's, as his low soothing voice danced in my memory: *It's always better to have a perfect match. It slows down the spread of the necrosis if it's with a match.* A thrill of fear ran through me as I gained a new sense of determination.

I needed to find people outside of the Facility who I could trust.

I needed to go back to Oakville.

CHAPTER SIXTEEN
Back to Oakville

Jade covered for me while I got my leg patched up by Missy. The three of us agreed it was unwise to bother Braeden with this injury, although she sternly told me to be more careful weightlifting.

Even though my leg was weak, it healed quickly. The next morning, I could support my weight again. Feeling relieved, I eased more onto it. Though I couldn't feel the pain, I could tell that my muscle wasn't reacting properly. It would probably be wise to take a few more days to let it heal, ideally a few weeks, but something told me I didn't have the luxury of time right now. The blank-out was still fresh in my memory. Still, I had no idea how I was supposed to get to Oakville.

I wandered through the hallways in a bit of a daze. The people might as well have been ghosts as I moved past them. I could feel my heart beating unnaturally fast. With each pump, I was painfully aware that there was something wrong—or maybe very precious—about the blood that pumped through my veins.

The Facility had an urgent air about it that morning. It was with a jolt that I realized I hadn't been briefed on anything after the failed scouting mission. Since I was not sure how to go about getting out of the Facility, I figured Piper and the raids would be my best shot, even if Braeden forbade it. *After all, what he didn't know couldn't hurt him.*

The tunnels were empty, as was the shooting range and the Strategy room. I got lucky when I decided to visit the Engineering Quarters. Piper's strong voice bounced along the empty corridors.

My heart stilled as I could finally make out their words echoing down the hallway. "How long is that Leuko going to keep using up our spare parts?"

Piper's voice cut across the sullen engineer, "For as long as he keeps being a good ally to the Facility."

"After what those other bastards did at the hotel…"

"Jasper is and has always been honest. Just because he has mods doesn't mean he's with that lot." Piper spat on the ground for emphasis. I could almost feel the engineer's desire to argue back with her, but at the heat in her words, he held his tongue.

There's a mercenary in the Facility.

Their voices grew closer, and in the split second it took for me to decide if I wanted to speak with Piper, she and the two men turned around the corner. She stopped dead in her tracks when she saw me; her two companions coming to a halt behind her. "Belford, I've been looking for you." She turned to them. "Hey, guys, I'll meet up with you back in the lounge. Give me one second." As the two men left, my hopes surged. *Maybe word about Braeden's rule hadn't reached her yet.*

"Hey, Belford." Her voice was casual. "I hear you've been taken off the raids."

So much for that hope.

I shuffled a little awkwardly, trying to act how I normally

would. After flipping through the emotions, I settled on disappointed. "Oh, you were already told?" I asked.

"More like got my ass chewed out for twenty minutes by the Good Doctor himself," Piper said dryly. "I'm not usually one to question the man, but…" She glanced around the hallway to ensure that we were not going to be overheard, "I think he needs a serious reality check. We're all in danger, every day. Keeping you out of the fray isn't going to save you. I mean, look at Kaye."

At the mention of his name, I felt like I'd been punched in the gut. I swallowed thickly and gave her what I hoped was a sympathetic look. "Sorry about the ass-chewing."

"You know, you never mentioned you weren't cleared for raids to begin with."

I didn't bother apologizing. "I wasn't exactly *not* cleared. I just decided not to mention it."

Piper chuckled and shook her head. "Splitting hairs, Belford. I just wanted to let you know that I'll miss having you on my squad. And that you're more than welcome to join us at the shooting range." My eyes must have lit up because she added quickly, "Firing range *only*. No more outside drills." She sighed and ruffled her grey hair. "Anyway, is there anything more I can do for you? I've got to meet with the engineers before I get back to Strategy."

"There's a Strategy meeting?" I asked, hopefully. Piper gave me a long look.

"Not for you, there isn't. That was also discussed during the aforementioned ass-chewing." Piper said grimly. My heart sank, but I didn't have time to care about that right now. "I think you and Evan are still on food-sorting duty later this morning. So at least you've got that." I gave a weak chuckle and bid her goodbye; my mind very much focused on a million other things besides working in the stupid Butcher's Corner.

I needed to get to Oakville first and foremost, which

meant right now, I needed to find that Leuko.

I made my way carefully through the Facility. I couldn't remember how I usually acted around people.

Do I usually wave and smile at them? Where do I look?

My palms perspired as I casually made my way up the atrium staircase to the upper levels. The polished bannisters gleamed in the early morning light. I stopped by Jade's office on the second floor. The thrumming of the BSL-4's immense air-filtration system made the floor feel smaller than it was. Her door was cracked open, with a steaming mug of tea on the desk. The office itself was empty. Taking the ID she usually let me borrow, I hobbled my way back down the hall.

My weak leg prevented me from full-on sprinting to the elevators like I wanted to.

I went to the ninth-floor ward, where they were treating the outside mercs. The layout of the security detail had changed since the ambush at the hotel. Instead of being placed at the intersections, armed guards were individually assigned to the Leuko's rooms.

Still attempting to be casual, despite the sweat now pouring out of me, I weaved through the hallways, trying not to draw attention to myself. For the most part, people didn't take notice of me. A few of the medical staff asked about my well-being. Unsurprisingly, it turned out Braeden's outburst had not gone unnoticed.

An armed Facility member stood in front of a closed door.

I'd found my mercenary.

The same guard who I threatened to shoot when Braeden was injured stood before the door. He gave me a surprised look as I approached. "Hey, Belford. I hear you lost clearance for raids."

I shrugged. "Might be bumped from raids, but not from Strategy. I need to talk to the Leuko behind that door. Jasper's in there, right?" If he was surprised that I knew about Jasper, he didn't show it.

I produced the Strategy ID badge Cynthia had given me during my very first full meeting. The guard frowned and looked over it. He then shrugged and stood aside, allowing me access to the room. I kept a straight face, unable to believe that he didn't call my bluff. I guess accessing the ninth floor added credibility to my lie.

I slipped into the room to find the Leuko, Jasper, pacing in agitation. His face was lined with a hundred thin strips of uneven flesh, almost mimicking tree-bark. His eyes were mismatched, blue and black, in his gaunt skull.

Piper trusted this guy?

"What do you want?" His whole body tensed. He was hunched over, partially turned away from me. His expression clearly showed that I was not wanted there.

Ignoring the unpleasant greeting, I held out my hand. "I'm Clara Belford. My commander Piper spoke highly of you. I wanted to introduce myself."

Jasper looked me up and down, smirking. His gnarled face was distrustful. He grasped my hand and jerked me close to him. Leaning forward, he whispered harshly in my ear, "All right, Belford. What's really going on? I already know you're not cleared to be in here. People talk, and unlike that guard out there, I wasn't born yesterday." I bit my lip, deciding how much to tell him.

"I need to go to the Oakville Camp," I finally said to him. He cocked an eyebrow but didn't say anything. "Tonight."

My heart hammered in my chest. I was hoping he didn't alert anyone.

I could just say that I was homesick, right? That shouldn't be an issue.

He scratched his chin thoughtfully.

"And just how, Miss Belford, are you anticipating you'll be getting to Oakville? Because I usually only travel between here and Newmarket; going south is a big ask."

I swallowed. "What would it cost me? I can get you weapons. Whatever you want."

His face broke into a wicked grin. "Oh, I already have weapons. I want meat."

I immediately shifted a little bit away from him. His eyes dropped to my waist then back up at me again. "No, not that kind of meat, girl. I mean *meat* meat. I hear you work in the slaughterhouse." Understanding dawns over me. *I can get meat.* "I want five kilos."

Feeling relieved, I agreed.

He shook my hand, telling me where to meet him at 10 p.m. sharp. I silently slipped out of the ward, making my way upstairs. For the first time since I'd come here, I was ecstatic to be a part of the Butcher's Corner.

The day passed quickly. There were a few announcements for the squads, which I ignored. Only when dusk approached did my excitement and trepidation begin to really hit me. At a quarter to 10, I grabbed my things and moved into the darkness, slipping past the guards during their change in rounds.

I went to the rendezvous point.

I shuffled irritably and pulled myself even deeper into the shadows. The eerie blue of night contrasted against the warm glow of the Facility. I resisted the urge to check my watch. The backpack I stuffed with steaks, which I had slipped off with during my shift earlier, now sat at my feet. The frozen meat started to warm up from sitting in my room. I could feel the dampness seeping through to my shoes.

I tugged my fitted jacket closer to me. My shoulder holsters and borrowed pistols ruined the line of my coat. Earlier, I returned the rifle I had taken from the drop containers, but without it, I felt strangely naked. My fingers drummed on the handle of my knife.

Looking up at the moon, I uselessly tried to discern how much time had passed since I'd slipped by the guards.

Jasper said he would meet me here by ten. My breath fogged in front of me. The sky was brilliantly clear, with stars shining like glitter embedded into black velvet.

The cold was starting to seep into my bones, and the dreaded exhaustion was settling in. Despite it being chilly, though, I just felt tired. *Another perk of being so close to rot.* If it weren't for the near-constant bruising around my nails, I would've almost forgotten that this virus was my death sentence.

That and the blank-outs.

I glanced back up at the moon. It had risen higher while I waited, transforming from a heavy yellow orb into a silver disk high up in the sky.

If Jasper didn't show up within a few more minutes, I was going back to bed.

I thought longingly about my warm, soft bed up on the fourteenth floor. I pushed those thoughts down. I needed answers, and I would get them tonight.

I hopped from foot to foot, trying to keep myself warm. *After all, just because I was numb and couldn't feel myself freezing, didn't mean I wasn't.*

"Hey, princess, over here." Jasper's rough voice emerged from the darkness. I hoisted the damp pack onto my back and followed the sound of his voice, blindly. My knife was unsheathed as I ran my hand along the rough stones. As I exited the alleyway, I saw him holding a small flashlight towards a side street. "Your chariot awaits." He gestured to the minibike next to him. "You'll be riding pillion." I raised my eyebrows as I took in the tiny bike.

"This is how we're going through open Rotter territory?" My voice was incredulous. He gave me a nonchalant shrug.

"If you think you can do better elsewhere, then by all means." He grinned at me. Knowing I was stuck, I threw the backpack into the open saddlebag and waited for him to climb on. He straddled the bike, and I uncomfortably slid in behind him. "Hold on," he called over his shoulder as the bike roared to life.

My heart leapt into my throat as it kicked off. My arms wrapped tightly around Jasper's leather-clad body. He coaxed the bike to higher and higher speeds through the abandoned streets of Toronto.

He was trying to scare me.

We weaved through the streets and the sight of an occasional Rotter flashed in front of the headlight. Jasper navigated around them with ease.

Shortly, we got out to the old Queen's Highway, where the Rotters were few and far between. The crumbling asphalt was covered with potholes due to the harsh winters. As we pulled off the roadway towards the smaller streets, snow began to fall.

"Stop here," I commanded. My blood was ice. The fence that surrounded the Oakville Camp had been torn down. The lights, which would usually dot the houses, were all black.

I got off the back of the bike and walked up to the torn edges of metal. It had been cut cleanly, probably with some sort of tool. Jasper sauntered over next to me. He eyed the cut marks dispassionately. "Those weren't done by Rotters."

I bit my tongue to refrain from saying something sarcastic back to him. My eyes swept the gloomy neighbourhood before me. "Have you come past here recently?" I asked him, wondering when all this happened.

"Not in months. I stick to the northern colonies," he replied. I pulled my hand back from the jagged metal.

Had Braeden done this? I couldn't think of a reason why the Leuko would lie to me. Then another, warmer thought came to me as Leo's face flashed before my eyes. *What other things had Braeden been lying about?*

I needed to see my old home.

We silently got back onto his bike and continued through

the streets. The feeling of foreboding increased as we went past empty house after empty house, but I clung to the small hope that my brother was still alive.

As we rode through the familiar, yet dark streets of the old colony, I noticed something foreign on the horizon. A glowing red light was floating just above the treetops, stationary.

"What is that?" I shouted to Jasper, leaning over him as I pointed toward it.

"That's a bounty posting near a hot site! If someone has a bounty and they think someone nearby might have info, they'll put information up on those poles."

"How come I've never seen one before?"

"Mercs don't mess with Facility territory unless we're invited," he laughed. "Mind if we check it out on our way back?"

I didn't reply immediately. The scar on my thigh was burning. I glanced around at the ruins of my home and had a bad feeling about whose name might be on that posting. "I really want to get back to the Facility quickly. Check it out on someone else's dime," I said, trying to sound both jovial and tough. Instead, I think Jasper found it off-putting. We continued the rest of the ride in silence.

Finally, we arrived at the street of my old home.

The small house looked the same from a distance, but as we pulled closer, a feeling of dread settled over me.

In the wintery night, I could see that the usually tame garden beds were overflowing with dead leaves and weeds. The front window was still broken. My heart sank into my stomach. If Leo were still alive, I felt certain he would have come back here.

A panicked feeling rose in my throat, and I felt tears beginning to form in my eyes. For some reason, it felt like I was losing him all over again. Jasper followed me, so I swallowed down my emotions. It wouldn't do me any good to let this Leuko see me crying.

I opened the front door to the very still entryway. An abandoned, musty air permeated the house. The furniture was covered in a thick layer of dust and debris.

I moved through the empty house like it was a museum. My footsteps echoed loudly in the rooms.

I opened the fridge and no light came on, but my flashlight revealed that it was empty, neither food nor mould was inside. *Was it picked clean by scavengers, or had it been cleaned recently?* I felt a small bit of hope as I shut the door, even though I tried not to entertain it. *Hope for the best but expect the worst.*

The master bedroom was desolate. The hole in the ceiling looked cavernous; grey insulation from the attic covered the room like snow.

As I moved from room to room, all the signs indicated that the house had been empty for a long time. The only people that had passed through were rifling for valuables. Aside from the weapons being gone, my room sat the same as it had been the night of the attack. My Kevlar wristlets still hung on my bedpost from when they had finished drying.

I searched through my belongings carefully, hoping that maybe if he did survive, he might've left some signal or clue as to what happened to him or where he went. The only clue I had was that my room remained frozen in time, like a shrine to a memory. I found nothing out of place, unlike the rest of the house which had been disturbed.

Jasper surveyed the room with me. His mismatched eyes looked around with interest. "You have a lot of trashy romance novels," he observed, flicking through one of my books.

"Time's change," I replied. After a few moments, I exited the room in silence. He replaced the book and followed me back into the hallway.

"Are we almost done here?" Jasper asked. "I've got other

things to do tomorrow and wanted to enjoy a warm, safe sleep tonight."

"Yeah," I said. "I just have one more thing I need to see."

Eventually, I went to the one room I had been avoiding. The door to the basement was shut. I grasped the knob and took a deep breath. I'm not sure why I needed to see it, but I did. Opening the basement door, I crept down the steps. I clutched my gun tightly to me, leading with the spotlight. I barely breathed. There was evil to this place, like something toxic hung in the air. I got to the bottom of the stairs, breath held, to where I had witnessed the attack on mom.

My brow furrowed as the beam from my scope light revealed a smooth, painted wall where the Resistance's insignia should have been. I scanned the room more thoroughly. Someone had even scrubbed it clean.

I shone the beam around the tidied room. My heart sat still. In one corner, there were chrysanthemums, mom's favourite flower. *Did someone leave her a memorial?* My mind spun faster. *And if they left a memorial, why only for her?*

I heard the door creak as Jasper joined me. It seemed like his patience had run out.

"Okay, okay," I said, turning around.

He leaned against the doorway, several pieces of paper in his hands. I felt a moment's excitement. *Did he find something?*

"What's that?" I asked him.

Jasper held a piece of paper in his hand, frowning. "Oh, there's a problem now," he said. My heart sank. I suddenly had a sneaking suspicion I knew where he disappeared to.

"What do you mean?" The hairs on the back of my neck stood up. I quietly clicked off the safety.

"See, you never mentioned there was a bounty on your head." He held the page up. There was the photograph of me taken at St Michael's Cathedral Basilica, and with it, a

181

hefty reward for bringing me in alive.

I took a step backwards, hoping to whichever god listening that Piper's instincts were right about this guy. I held my hands up. "I didn't realize I needed to let you know," I said carefully.

Jasper chortled and shook his head at me. "If we ever do work together in the future, Miss Belford, I'd appreciate a head's up if assassins might be following us." My ears perked up. *Work together in the future? Did that mean he wasn't going to turn me in for the bounty?*

"You know, I was wondering, why would someone who is so comfortable being holed up in the Old City, want to brave open Rotter territory in the dead of night to make a trek to Oakville?" Jasper continued, enjoying himself. He paced around the room, my scope light followed, creating eerie shadows on the wall behind him. He said, "Then I learn that the Oakville Colony has been dead for months, but it's all hush-hush. So now, I'm checking the merc bounty postings and the mark on your head wasn't all I found, Miss Belford. Do you know what else I found?"

My mind was swimming as I tried to make sense of what he was saying.

He showed me another piece of paper. My trembling hands reached out for it. I took it gently in my fingertips, as though it might disintegrate into powder.

It was a flyer, with a photo of Leo on it. The request was a trade: information for a hefty reward. The contact person was 'Braeden Runar.' I whispered the name aloud.

The date issued was in September, the day after the attack.

Suddenly, I felt like I knew what the "you-know-what" was.

"Do you know anything about this?" I demanded. "Can you take me to someone who knows anything about this?"

Jasper waived the flyer with my face on it and said, "Are you crazy? With a bounty this big on your head, you're lucky

I'm going to honour our deal and take you back to the Facility."

I bit my tongue, realizing I at least had some allies and supplies I could gather at the Facility. Besides… whoever this Blaise person was, he could probably afford to pay a lot more than I could. I swallowed and said, "Thank you for honouring the deal."

Jasper led the way back upstairs. I clutched the two bounties in my hands as I followed him.

Was Leo alive?

Jasper revved the engine as I slid onto the back of his bike. I felt the reassuring press of my pistols into my hips and Jasper's back into my stomach. I knew he wouldn't try anything.

The dead houses whipped past us. I closed my eyes to the freezing air that lashed at my face, wishing my helmet had a visor. The ride back went by slower than the ride there. As it was later in the night, the Rotters were now lurching around the darkened streets in full force.

It was only once we were back downtown that I finally relaxed. Jasper was true to his word. Within a few moments, we were back within walking distance of the Facility. Now, I just needed to work out two things: what was it about me that made me important enough for someone to raze an entire colony to the ground, and what did that have to do with Leo? I knew both of those answers were waiting for me at the Facility.

CHAPTER SEVENTEEN
The Archives

Jade sighed as I furiously paced around her office, ignoring the twitching in my injured leg. Her one eye slowly traced my agitated figure. The two stolen pistols sat on her table. Other than saying, "You could've asked me," she didn't comment on them.

I had the file in my hands. My cheeks were still flushed from the wind on the ride back, and my hair was chaos from the helmet. Jade ignored all of this as she let me try to get my thoughts in order.

"What does this mean?" I asked as I wrote down the words 'DoD(Est)' on a piece of paper for her to read. She took the paper from me and looked it over, her eyebrows furrowing as she peered at the little piece of paper.

"Department of Defence." Her voice was jocular.

"I'm serious."

She picked up the note and scrunched her face as she thought about it. "I know in genealogy it stands for Date of Death, so... Date of death, estimated, I presume." she said matter-of-factly.

I had a horrible thought. *The paper said September.* "Kaye was killed in September, right?" I asked her.

She looked at me in confusion. "What? Killed? Clara, Kaye got badly injured in September, but he died from the virus. He was a goner regardless of whatever Missy and Braeden failed to do."

I shook my head impatiently. *I was supposed to be killed in September, but now it said February. Roughly six months. That means if everything went well, I had less than four months to live. But why?*

"I need you to test my blood."

Jade looked at me quizzically. "Test it for what? You really should be speaking with Missy about this. Clara, she's your assigned physician."

There was a small surge of panic at the suggestion. I pressed on. "Typing. I need to know my blood type."

Jade's smile was bemused. "Oh, that's easy. You have the same blood type as Dr. Runar." She shrugged. "AB positive."

I felt a spike of frustration. "Is there anything else or just AB positive?" Jade shook her head.

"Okay, no, not just that. I mean a full blood mapping of my profile or whatever. Like the blood test in Leo's file!"

The smile melted off her face. Her scars pulled the surrounding skin uncomfortably tight as she squinted her one good eye at me. "Okay, first of all, I'm no hematologist, so I've got no understanding of how to do that. Secondly, why on Earth do you want to know that? What does that have to do with your family?" Her eye darted down to my stomach. "Oh my god, are you pregnant? Was it Braeden who asked you to do this? Because he's the resident expert here at the Facility. Do you want me to page him for you?" When she reached for her phone, I let out a strangled "no" as I knocked the phone out of her hands. Jade held up her empty hands. Her eyebrows disappeared up beneath her pale blonde hair.

She slowly stepped away from me and picked up her phone. I forced myself to stop biting the inside of my cheek. My eyes were locked on her hands to make sure she didn't alert Braeden. Her pose had slightly shifted into a defensive position and her back foot was planted firmly on the ground.

I realized my mistake.

She thinks I'm going feral.

I took two deep breaths to calm myself, and then I began to explain. I told her all my suspicions and what I'd discovered as calmly and as quickly as possible.

The more I spoke, the more her jaw began to go slack as she tried to process the barrage of information and accusations that I was sharing with her. She dropped her defensive pose and began to pace the room.

When I finished, her eye locked onto mine. Flashes of incredulity, horror, and understanding crossed her face at lightning speed. Finally, her face settled into a neutral mask. I felt a moment's worry.

When she spoke, her voice was quiet. "Is he aware that you know any of this?"

I shook my head, feeling a rising sense of dread creep up my chest. Every muscle was tense as I prayed that I'd told the right person. She sat down on the examination table; her thighs crumpled the neat paper covering the cushions.

"Okay, that's good."

Cautious relief replaced the dread. "I don't think he knows that I know," I added.

Jade nodded thoughtfully, "Let me just get this straight. You think your brother is alive, after all." I nodded. She said, "And you think that when the Resistance attacked the Facility, they breached wherever your brother was being kept and then freed him?" I nodded. She scratched her chin and continued, "And this Blaise person you heard mentioned.

You think that he is both part of the Resistance and leading a plan to assassinate you?"

"Yes."

"This all somehow ties into a weird link between you and Braeden from way before the pandemic started, where he knew you were a blood match. And this knowledge is why Oakville was destroyed?" I nodded. Jade shifted in her chair, "Okay… so… what exactly is your plan?" She asked.

"I'm leaving tonight. I need supplies, a Medi-kit, food, and weapons. I'm going to take one last look around the Facility, but by midnight, I'm out. I can't risk looking for any longer than that."

"What information are you after? Why not just get out right now?"

"Look, the Resistance has a bounty on my head, but they also might have my brother. I can't exactly stroll into their hideout if they're hostile. I think the information behind my bounty is hidden in the Facility, and if I can use it to keep both me and my brother safe, I want to do everything I can to find it."

"Where should we start?" Jade sat upright, giving me her full attention.

I took a moment to think and asked, "Were there any other patients in the hospital that went missing, ones who he's taken a special interest in?"

Jade's eyebrows knotted. After a moment, her face darkened, and she nodded. "Most of his family were recovered and lost to the virus… although that doesn't mean much. It's happened to so many of us at some point. And of course, he was close with them." She tapped her fingers on her lips. Her eye was unfocused. "Although… hold on a moment." She shot up so suddenly I took an involuntary step backwards. She ran over to the computer.

Feeling panicked, I jumped to stop her. "Hold on!"

Her gaze snapped back to me. "What?"

I forced myself to move towards her calmly, and I gently placed my hand over hers to stop her from typing. "Whatever you're about to do, or about to search, I need to know that there's no possible way Braeden can find out. He cannot know that I'm suspicious."

Jade's fingers stopped moving, and she pulled them away from the keyboard. "Okay. Good point." She erased what she had started typing and put the computer back into sleep mode. "There are physical files in the hospital archives. We can look for it down there, undetected." She gave me a light smile, "How good is your poker face?"

I furrowed my brow at her in confusion.

She shrugged. "Look, if we get caught, we need an excuse. I know we're friends, but I've got my own assistants to dig through that mess in the basement. Any ideas of what that excuse could be?"

I mulled the thought over in my head for a while. Finally, the answer that came to me was so obvious; I marvelled that it took me so long to come up with it.

"My father. If they catch us down there, we'll say you were trying to help me find any record of my father. Besides, if my theory is correct, Braeden ought to be just as interested in his whereabouts as I am. My mother and I don't have the same blood type."

"You've spoken to him about your father before?"

Suddenly, I had a sickening feeling in the pit of my stomach, as memories of us bonding over our lost loved ones came back. His heartfelt questions about my father, the now obvious obsession-like desire to know every detail that I had mistaken for caring, the task force he had set up to find him.

"Yes, I've spoken with Braeden about my father." My voice was icy. "He took a keen interest, in fact."

Jade turned back to the computer and switched it on.

"What are you doing?" I asked as she logged in and

began typing into the database.

"Covering our tracks in case they check our cover story." I leaned forward quickly and pulled the keyboard away from her.

"No!" I waited for my heart rate to slow down a bit, and when I spoke again, my voice was soft. "Look, I can act distressed and panicked. If there's even the slightest chance we can get away with this with zero detection, we need to do it that way. We *cannot* let him know."

Jade gave me an exasperated look. I tapped my hunting blade. I understood that I was acting panicked and let out a sigh.

"I think my life is in danger right now. The sooner he realizes what I know, the sooner he'll come after me. But I need to know what's going on first." *I need to find out if there's anything more here about Leo.*

Jade's face was resolute when we left her office. She gave me a brown leather satchel "just in case." It bumped against my thigh as we went.

The archives were in a windowless room in the subbasement. They reeked of mould and dust. My flashlight swept the large boxes, which loomed ominously in the dark. I was certain I heard a rat scurrying deeper into the darkness as we opened the door.

About half the lights dimly flickered to life when Jade flipped the switch. Jade's face mirrored my own look of disgust. The files were haphazardly labelled and disorganized from the many careless reshufflings and lazy placements.

"There's a reason I always send my assistants down here," Jade muttered, as her eye raked over the piles of paperwork. She inhaled deeply and strode into the canyon of boxes.

"What exactly are we looking for?" I whispered at her. Her voice was somewhat muffled when she replied, "The right year, of course." She began to pull out box after box before adding to me, "You look over there to see if you can find anything with your last name, or Braeden's." She gestured vaguely to a pile of over-stuffed files in a cabinet. "Or look for the last name Valyiff."

"Valyiff?"

"His sister married and took the guy's last name. She was here, briefly, when I first got here. So was her son."

"We're lucky that her husband's name wasn't Smith." I eyed at least five boxes labelled 'Smith' and was thankful that I didn't need to dig through those.

I heard Jade grunt as she shifted another few boxes around. "Well, we were bound to get lucky every now and then. Let's just hope that luck holds out. This place is a mess."

I pulled over a promising box labelled with a 'V' and began to look through the stacks of papers within. I didn't see anything, but I placed it into a special pile, just in case I'd missed something. I pulled forward another box and continued my search. As I pored through boxes and files, I became accustomed to reading the various cramped or loopy handwriting styles of medical personnel long since gone from the Facility. The handwriting began to blur before my eyes. I shook my head and squinted, trying to refocus.

Moisture had leaked through the cracked walls and turned many of the pages yellow. A few had vestiges of dead mould ringing the water stains. Most of the writing on the water-damaged pages had faded, and in some spots, been completely erased.

I pulled away from the files and glanced around the room, trying to get my brain to behave.

I was suddenly standing in front of an open shelf, lined with hundreds of files. Disoriented and angry with myself, I looked down the aisle and realized I only moved a few feet away from where I had been. The leg of my jeans was damp above my wound and the fabric was tight from swelling. I took a deep breath and headed back to where I remembered standing before the blank-out.

As I walked, my eyes landed on handwriting that I would've recognized anywhere.

"Hey, Jade," I called to her as I pulled the file towards me. Her head popped up from the other side of the boxes like a meerkat. "How many patients does Braeden personally take on?"

She shrugged, "Hardly any, personally, since he took over this place."

I smiled. "In that case, I think I've found something."

I was disappointed when I saw that it was not a patient file. Instead, it seemed to be a long list of names and addresses. Several of the names were crossed out. A few had new addresses written underneath them.

There was also a map of all the Horseshoe Colonies plotted with dozens of little red and black dots. A few arrows pointed to various points along the south side of Lake Ontario from Sugar Beach. Little black X's marked points in Burlington and Stoney Creek, flanking either side of the Burlington Bay Bridge.

I frowned at the map, trying to make sense of it. "Maybe not… I'm not actually sure what this is." I heard boxes being scraped across the floor as Jade battled her way through the files over to me. She emerged between two towering stacks of papers and pulled the list from my hands. I continued to study the map, trying to make sense of the dots. She scanned the list of names. "I recognize some of these. Some of these people were at the Facility."

"Do they have addresses next to them?"

"Yeah."

"Read me some," I demanded.

Jade rattled them off and flipped around the file quickly.

"What are you looking for?" I asked.

She smiled when she found it. "The date. Dates are

important, you know. This information is from… a year and a half ago."

A map plotting the homes of Facility members from a year and a half ago? One by one, the pieces began to fall into place. My fingers lightly traced over the Burlington Canal Bridge site—encircled in red. Only one thing was written on the map, along the bridge: 'Drop Day: 14 March.' My stolen shoulder tightened painfully as anger ran through my entire being. "When exactly?" *I hoped I was wrong.*

"February."

I wasn't.

I remembered the conversation with Braeden about hope. *"Two years ago, in the wintertime, the Facility was almost empty. It was a miracle the whole place didn't die out. We needed to press on, and we found a way. We're survivors, Clara. We'll make it through this virus, too. We can't lose hope."*

I was reeling as I sat back on my heels, unable to stop looking at the map.

I peered over at the Oakville camp. My jaw was set in anger as I saw one little red dot, right over the home I shared with my family. I studied it carefully. Unlike the others, it was circled, making an infinitesimal bullseye. Curiously, I glanced over to Milton and felt my blood run cold. There was another tiny bullseye, right over where my father used to live.

Curious about the bullseye, I scanned the dots that would have been close enough to go to the Burlington Bridge drop site. There were two small bullseyes next to each other. I looked at the street and the suburb, unsure of what the address would be.

"Jade. I need you to find this exact address." I pointed it out to her on the map. She shifted her gaze back to the list.

"This is going to take forever, Clara. It's organized by name, not location."

"Then I want you to look up the last name Valyiff and tell me if it's on there."

Jade confirmed. "Yeah, his sister and her son are both on here. The address was on Glow Avenue, in Parkview West." I looked back at the two little bullseyes beneath my fingertip. *The street read Glow Avenue.*

"Any mention of the husband?" I asked dully, already knowing the answer.

Jade shook her head. "Nope, I don't think he was interested in him. He might have known that her husband was already turned at that stage."

I put my hand to my forehead, shaking my head in disbelief. *I had been so, so stupid.*

Jade put her hand on my back. "What is it?" she asked me gently. Her touch was tentative. I smiled and wondered if she knew how right she was to be cautious.

My voice was soft and distant. "We've been hunting them. Or I mean, they hunted us before we were..." I looked up to see her face wearing a mask of confusion. "They didn't weaponize the Rotters first. We did."

"Clara, what are you talking about? We've never used the infected for anything besides research." Jade's voice was consoling.

I laughed bitterly. "Maybe you haven't, but they did," I said, thinking about the lines drawn on Kaye's head. I pointed to the map. "Burlington Bridge, Jade. Look at the Burlington Canal Bridge site. It's encircled, but there are no red dots. But look." I pointed to both sides of the bridge. Either side was littered with hundreds upon hundreds of red dots outside of the circle. "The Burlington Canal Bridge Massacre happened in the springtime of that year."

I stood up abruptly. My heart was racing. "All right, we've got the year and the names. We need to find Anita Valyiff's file. I need to know what I'm looking for when I go get mine from Braeden's office."

A surge of panic and anger flared in my chest. My whole body was shaking and surging with adrenaline as I fought to rein my brain in to focus on the task at hand. *I needed to do this.*

I slipped the map and the address list into my satchel.

I felt like I was fighting my body on two fronts now. The survivalist in me wanted to take action. The rotted part of me just wanted to slip back into that blissful nothingness. I gritted my teeth and forced myself to start looking for the right file.

We paused our frantic search only when a scream echoed down the hallway. Jade's amber eye went round as her gaze met mine.

CHAPTER EIGHTEEN
The Blood

"What was that?" I whispered towards her. Jade was mid-shrug when her mouth went slack, her eye rolled into her head and she inhaled deeply. Confused, I asked, "What's wrong?" when a richly tantalizing smell hit me. "What's that?" I asked dreamily.

Jade sniffed the air. "It smells like an uninfected human." I was already at the door before I knew what was happening. Jade collected the binder and followed me. Drool began pooling in my mouth as we peered out the crack to see two guards, drenched in peppermint.

They strode down the hallway, laughing. One clutched a cooler in his arms.

"Man, she was a screamer, wasn't she?" He joked. The woman next to him chuckled.

"They really should let us use some of that numbing stuff. I wonder if transplants work the same as steak. You know, the more tense the cow is when it's slaughtered, the tougher the meat." The two laughed.

"They must be coming from harvest," Jade said. She

glanced back to me and whispered, "I know they have some specialty transport coolers. We could make sure you have enough patches to avoid returning to the Facility for a long time."

We finally came to a heavy door. Jade pulled out her wallet and flipped through about fifteen different ID badges. I raised my eyebrows at her, and she shrugged. "Only one has a high enough clearance to get in here. I've never used it because the entry logs are always checked the next morning." She scanned the photo of a 'Dr. Renken' at the door. "And I never had a good enough reason to risk it before now." The heavy mechanical locks clanged as it unlocked itself. The thick door swung open and a cold blast of air hit us. It unnervingly reminded me of the nests.

"Is this what I think it is?" I asked, taking in the clinically clean, cool room for the first time. Bright fluorescent lights shone off the stainless steel in the room in halos, making it almost feel mythical.

Jade was a little breathless when she answered, "It is indeed. Here is the donor tissue cold storage system, but everyone calls 'em 'The Harvest Chambers.'" Jade spritzed disinfectant on a large table. Endless rows of shiny silver drawers lined the room. Jade opened one, it was filled to the brim with blood bags. Jade scoffed.

"How long can the organs stay good when they're outside the body?" I asked. Jade stopped her browsing, pulled a steel drawer from a chest, and placed it onto the table in the centre of the room. Cool mist billowed out from the opening of the chest.

She looked thoughtful as she poked through the packages in the drawer. "Organs? I mean it depends on the organ, but several hours. Now tissue, like we've got here, this stuff can last for years if we can keep it preserved properly." I looked around the room with new appreciation. I had always thought they'd harvested the tissue for the transplants straight from the Rotters. *"Man, she was a screamer, wasn't she?"* The man's words replayed in my head. He could have been talking about Rotters, but if my brother had been kept here secretly, how many others were there?

I felt another chill run up my spine. The thought of Kaye's peaceful face entered my mind. *And Braeden's.*

She moved around the room, collecting instruments and inspecting specimens as she went. I looked around, some of the refrigerators had glass doors revealing even more blood bags, sitting on the shelves. In one corner was a large refrigerator unit that said 'Human Organs.'

I was most intrigued by the door on the far side of the room. It was thick steel, with what looked like a vault wheel locking it.

Where do they get the donors if the organs are only good for a few hours?

I grabbed the vault wheel lock and strained trying to turn it. I licked my lips as I was nearly mesmerized by the promise behind that door. It gave way, and the deadbolt slid back with a clang.

"What are you doing? What if they catch us?" Jade hissed at me. "I don't know if anyone is gonna need an emergency patch tonight. We can't be in here long."

I gave her an apologetic look over my shoulder before I threw open the cold steel and entered the darkened room below. In front of me was a stone staircase. I followed the steps downwards. From the depths came the sound of low murmurs. Intrigued, I pressed farther into the darkness. My fingertips brushed my blade. At the bottom of the steps, lit by my flashlight, was another heavy metal door.

It opened with an ominous clank and the room fell quiet. The smell of unwashed bodies and feces hit me like a wall. The beam of my flashlight revealed drains in the floors that had trails of yellowish waste leading towards them. The ground was sticky. Pressing forward, I had desperately wished I brought along a vial of peppermint.

What I saw chilled me to the bone.

In the dim circle of light, I could make out hundreds of cages, some empty, others filled with people. There were almost fifty people from what I could tell. Some of them looked barely conscious, others were well-fed and robust. Bits of flesh were missing from all of them. A buzzing white noise filled my ears as my pulse thundered.

We hadn't been taking our transplants from only brain-dead donors. We'd been hacking up sentient humans.

The people were silent. My beam caught wide, terrified eyes. They shrunk away from the bars of their cages. With horror, I noticed another thing about these humans.

Though they were missing limbs and had burn marks from cauterized flesh all over their bodies, I didn't see a single marking. These humans weren't bitten and ready to rot. No, these were uninfected humans that were being chained down here like dogs.

My knuckles were white on the flashlight. I forced myself to remain calm, but the blood was rushing to my ears, calling for vengeance.

I looked down at my markings with disgust.

Jade stood there, with her arms hanging limply by her sides, shocked. Her eye wide, she looked at me as a flash of distrust settled on my face. "Clara, I swear, I never knew this was down here."

I nodded. "I know. I just…" I shook my head. *I needed some answers.* My brain began to buzz, overwhelmed by the sights, smells, and realizations.

I knelt in front of an empty cage, my hand pressed against the bars. *How many people had been held prisoner down here? Were they kept for long, like Leo, or were they only here shortly?* I glanced at a girl, crying silently, who recoiled as far away from me as she could within the cage.

I pressed my hands into my face, pushing as hard as I could until white spots danced around my closed eyelids. "We need to get them out of here."

Jade looked panicked, "Clara, these people are in no condition to run. Maybe a few of them, but everyone else that we leave behind will die. Remember, he wants you for some reason. You need to get out of here. You'll be no good to anyone dead."

I stood up from the cage and paced for a moment. Not knowing if I was being smart or choosing the coward's way out, I announced to the room in general, "I need to leave, but I will be back."

My blood thundered as I ran up the steps. *I found it.* The evidence that Leo could have been kept here this whole time. Live humans were being kept in the Facility.

Knowing how much Braeden wanted to find my dad, was he keeping tabs on Leo the same way, just in case?

The reek of human filth disappeared once the door closed tight in the sterile tissue room. In one of the shiny cabinets, I spotted a clipboard with a long list of names sitting on a silver tray. Wondering if my luck would come through again, I picked it up and read through the papers. As I scanned the list of names, some I recognized, some I didn't, I could feel the panic growing stronger. *Braeden wanted to kill me.*

I took several deep breaths to calm myself. "Come on, Clara, get a grip on yourself." I raked my hand through my hair, staring down at the papers trying to piece together what I was doing. *Why am I looking at these?*

I picked up the papers. They were covered in medical jargon. I shook my head, betrayed by my brain. Annoyed at myself, I began to rummage through them quickly. There had to be some clue as to why I thought these were important. *Was this what blank-outs were like at the start?*

"Clara!" Jade's whisper was harsh. I glanced up from

the papers. "They're coming back! We need to go."

"Hey, look at this." It was a long list of everyone in the Facility, with their blood type, and little notes next to their names. Beside my name, with numerous transplants, was an asterisked note. Jade frowned at the note in the file. "It says you're only allowed AB positive tissue for transplants." She peered closer at it.

There it was again. That thing about the blood. With my terror from the blank-outs still fresh in my mind, I was determined to leave this place with at least one piece of information.

Why was my blood important enough for him to want me?

Something told me the answers were in his office.

"Look, Clara, you need to get out of here. I've done what I can for you, but there's no telling what else they might do. I can't keep helping you, knowing they might catch us at any minute."

"I just need to go to his office," I said as I stuffed the papers into my satchel.

"Clara, don't be stupid. You need to get away. I'll find a Leuko to look after you."

"I don't even know where to run to!" I thought back to the desolate place I used to call home in Oakville. "But that folder in Braeden's office, it might have a clue about Leo."

Jade's expression was so frustrated; she looked like she was on the verge of tears. "God damn, you're a stubborn jackass." She wailed as she hugged me. "Come back to your room once you've finished looking through his office. I'm going to get you a ration bag for your trip: food, water… I'll even nick you a Medi-kit for patches." She gave me another hug before running off to get supplies. I sped the other direction, towards Braeden's office.

Braeden's office was bathed in a warm glow, reflecting from the rosy wood. His careworn books filled the shelves. I moved over to his cabinet and began my search.

My gaze settled on the one drawer in his desk that was always locked. I looked around until I managed to find a thin letter opener and a paperclip. Delicately, I began to wiggle both instruments into the elaborate brass lock, holding and tapping down, waiting to feel the release in the mechanism. It eventually gave way, and I could turn the lock. The drawer popped open.

Inside sat a pile of papers and a little lockbox. My heart beat wildly in my chest as I scooped out the lockbox. Picking up my makeshift lockpicking set, I worked the lock in the same rhythmic fashion, until it, too, opened. Inside was a small worn red diary. The pages dated back to August 31.

Braeden's handwriting was difficult to read at points. Every so often, a small entry would be made about me, a recording of some of my favourite foods or some memories that Leo and I had shared. These entries must have been from when Leo was held captive.

I felt sick, recalling the time Braeden just so happened to get me a bouquet of lilacs, marvelling at the coincidence he would pick my favourite flower. Written there, right beside the name of my first dog, were the words 'Lilacs—favourite.' Nothing was written about Leo.

I flipped through it to just after the attack, seeing if he had recorded any thoughts about Leo's escape. Every few pages or so, the handwriting itself drastically changed. It moved from Braeden's to something much more cramped and uneven.

The words written in the new hand were haunting. They were confused ramblings that were almost nonsensical. *Brain rot?*

Underneath this diary lay another notebook. I flipped it open to a random page and the handwriting was even and bubbly. I recalled the same writing style on Leo's folder, spelling out 'Belford.' I had a sickening realization that Braeden could not be conducting these operations alone.

Flipping through the notebook, which contained medical jargon about Missy's brain transplants, I found more information about her experiments with Meredith. I paused and scanned her notes. Next to the observations about her subject's rapid degeneration was Braeden's writing, which had only two words written: 'cytokine storm.'

I snapped it shut and placed both the notebook and the diary into my satchel. Lifting the box, I saw another map nearly identical to the one I found in the basement with Jade. This one, however, was dated for May of this year. Written on it was the date 'May 11,' the same day as the Oakville attack.

Encircled in dark red was the Oakville compound. Dozens of little red dots resided in the area. Over my house, I saw a little red bullseye.

I pulled the file over and flipped until I found my last name. 'Belford' was printed clearly on the page. A red strike was through my name and address. My hands were shaking so badly I could barely read the piece of paper in front of me. Scribbled underneath my name was the word 'Leo.'

My heart leapt into my throat.

Inside were hundreds of brain images I didn't recall being taken. I pulled the file out to take with me, then paused. Underneath my file was another one, one with only a few papers inside of it. The name 'Leonardo Belford' was written on it.

I placed my file down on the desk, gently picking up the other folder, my fingers pinched the smooth paper as though it might detonate.

I carefully opened the file and scanned the document in front of me. It read 'cross-match positive,' which caused my heart rate to pick up.

I was so lost in thought, it took me a moment to realize the door clicked shut behind me. I froze until I heard a gentle chuckle. The scent of his musky cologne sent a thrill of fear through me.

"Hello, Clara." Braeden's voice was soft.

Goosebumps erupted over my flesh. I slowly slid Leo's file into a nearby book before I turned to face him. My voice was steady despite my heart beating wildly in my chest. "Evening, Braeden."

"Doing some light reading?" His voice was quiet. He pulled the book from my hands, "Developed a sudden interest in hematology, have you?" His words dripped with condescension. He tossed the book onto the desk, where it spilled open. His eyes fell onto Leo's file. "I warned you about going to see them." His voice was still quiet as he made his way towards me. "Did you try to go find them and fail? Is that why you're in my office?"

I tried to keep my demeanour calm. "What do you mean?"

"How was Oakville?"

My mouth opened, but no words came out. I was like a deer in headlights. "I-I-I…" I stammered, unable to process. *How did he know I went to Oakville?*

I closed my eyes, unable to believe my overwhelming stupidity. Blaise probably could pay handsomely for a reward, but the man in charge of the Facility would pay even more.

Braeden quickly crossed the room towards me, and I flinched. His body went still. It was a moment too late that I realized he wanted to kiss me.

Fearfully, I looked up and met his gaze. Braeden's eyes suddenly looked soulless. "Are you frightened of me, Clar' bear?" His voice was low. An involuntary shiver ran down my spine when I heard him say Kaye's old nickname for me.

It wasn't a homage to his memory at all.

His eyes slid over to the notebook and diary, visible in my open bag. His face became frightening and unreadable.

"Did you see something you weren't supposed to, Clara?" Braeden's voice had turned mocking. My body and brain were frozen, trapped once more between fight or flight. He paused and picked up the book again. His eyes swept my body. "What do you want with me?" I asked finally." He chortled to himself and continued, "You know, the study of blood is a very complex branch of medicine."

I blinked and he continued, "It's a funny thing, blood. You know, everyone thought that it just boiled down to the usual: O, A, B, AB. Then we learned about the Rh antigens.

"Suddenly, rare blood types started cropping up. Extremely rare blood types. These were people who couldn't even accept O negative blood—the supposed universal donor. Of course, those blood types only really showed up because they couldn't accept other types of blood.

"There is a true universal donor. It's a blood type no one thought existed for the longest time, one void of all the Rh antigens entirely. Not until the '60s. It was even hypothesized that no one who had this blood type could survive. But lo and behold, it did. It came up in the strangest of places too, an aboriginal woman in Australia."

He walked closer to me. I backed up slowly, edging so that the table was between us.

"It's extremely rare, this blood. Less than fifty people in the world were known to have it… well, before the virus hit. I can't imagine there are any with it now." He laughed, but it was a humourless sound.

A lock of dark hair fell across his eyes, and a long-fingered hand brushed it away. "I'm AB positive," I said stupidly. Braeden's smile deepened. His laugh lines cut deeply and ghoulishly into his skin. His face became a mask in the dimmed lighting.

"Oh, you're not just AB positive. No, you're very special, Clara. Just like O negative isn't the true universal donor, AB positive blood isn't the true universal receiver. And the virus. The virus reacts to these antigens in a very special way."

"If you're a universal receiver, just use anyone. Why does it have to be me?" I bit my tongue, feeling ashamed of the deeply selfish thing I'd just said. My panic and rapid heartbeat were making it hard for me to focus on anything.

"Clara, you saw what happened with Missy's experiments. You know what happens if there's an improper match. Try to use your brain." He gave me a sardonic smile that made my blood boil. "Perfectly matched donor transplants slow the progress of this virus. A person with AB positive blood will always respond better to an AB positive donor than to any other type. My blood only truly matches yours. I need you. As I said, it's like we were made for each other."

I remembered him yelling at Missy after the raid. "You really weren't worried about my safety at all, were you?" Braeden looked at me almost pityingly, but his tone was filled with disdain when he said, "Well, I really couldn't let my golden girl go and get herself shot, now could I?"

"If your—our—blood type is so rare, then how did you manage to find so many other … candidates?"

"Blood types usually run in families. And I had a very big family." I couldn't keep the look of revulsion from my face, and he laughed. "I guess the cat's out of the bag."

I wanted to slap the smug smile off his face. Instead, I gathered my wits about me. He stood between me and the door. From the way he positioned himself, I could tell he had no intention of letting me through. I needed to coax him from the entryway. Backing up a few paces, placing the desk between us, my eyes swept the room. On his desk laid a long metal instrument, it was thin and sturdy and could be used as a weapon. Just beyond the desk, the old doorknob had been replaced with a large, elaborate handle. *Thank god he had ostentatious taste.*

"All the cats are out of the bag. I know about the

humans in the chambers," I said.

His handsome face was impassive. "Sometimes, we need others for the transplants. It's easier to keep healthy humans around and then infect them. Anything else we tried made it impossible to perform the transplants. It was a necessary evil."

"It's only a necessary evil because you chose yourself over everyone else," I hissed.

He sighed in exasperation. "You're not looking at the big picture, Clara. If I find the cure, then this will all be over. The world needs me. I have the most knowledge about the virus out of anyone. I have the training, the resistance, and intimate, detailed knowledge of the virus. Every one of these humans sacrificed for a noble cause."

"Why do you need the others? Why not just yourself? Why not share what you know with other humans?" For a moment, I thought he looked almost guilty. "It's because no human would work with you after knowing what you're doing, right? That's why you wanted to infect the doctors. The infected work more feverishly, right? Do they believe the propaganda you tell them about the greater good?" I spat at him.

Two spots of colour appeared on his cheeks at my accusations. Seeing my opportunity, I pressed him. "That's what happened at Burlington Bridge, isn't it? You were about to die out, so you went and collected a whole bunch of new people for the Facility, right?" His face grew redder. "I mean, your own sister. That's low. It's almost laughably low. You're pathetic." I taunted.

"That's enough!" He shouted at me.

I grinned at him. "What, you can't handle being told the truth? You're a loser. You're not helping anyone. You're just prolonging your own feeble life, aren't you?"

He glowered at me. "You know nothing."

I laughed.

This sent him over the edge. He rushed around the table to grab at me, and my fingers curled around the metal instrument. I swung it as hard as I could at him. It collided with the side of his head and sent him stumbling. I threw the leather strap of the satchel over my head. I scrambled over the desk, sending papers flying, and ran through the door. I yanked it tightly shut and slid the pole through the awkward handle, wedging it across the doorway. It wouldn't hold long, but it would slow him down. Sprinting down the hallway, the sound of the pole rattling faded as I headed towards the stairs.

In no time, I was on the fourteenth floor.

I approached my door and breathed a sigh of relief. I looked down to grab for the handle. A moment too late, I noticed there was light spilling from beneath my door. *Jade?*

I couldn't recall if I turned off the lights that morning.

CHAPTER NINETEEN
The Unravelling

I dimly registered a gurney beside my bed as I dropped my bag. The door shut behind me, and I whirled around.

"Missy!" I cried when I saw the redhead. Her eyes were wild.

"Clara." Her voice was hard. The hairs on the back of my neck stood up straight. In her hand, she held a pistol trained at my gut.

"Missy… put the gun down." I took a shaky step towards her but stopped when she raised the gun to my heart.

She shook her head violently, sending her red curls flying across her face. "As soon as you left, he called me, and I came here. And look, you were trying to steal from us. You were trying to abandon and rob us." She jerked the gun towards the bed where Jade's knapsack rested heavy with supplies.

"I need to go. You need to let me leave. Missy, he wants to kill me." As I spoke, I recalled her in Treatment Unit 4 with Kaye. My blood ran cold as I stared at her for a moment, the full truth hitting me. "But you don't care, do you? You never intended to help Kaye. You're going to butcher me, just like you butchered him."

I was sickened as I looked at her. Missy's eyes were welling up with tears. "Clara, don't you see? He's going to let me keep working on my experiments."

"All I know is that because of you, Kaye is dead." Another thought struck me. "That night, when you operated on Kaye... you stole his bone marrow."

Her cheeks turned red and blotchy. "Clara, please just sit down. He'll be here any moment. Braeden now knows how to save himself. To save all of us. And now that I know, he's going to help me too." She stood up straight and tilted her chin defiantly at me. Glowering, I towered over her. I didn't care about the gun anymore.

She flinched as I yelled, not bothering to keep the scorn from my voice, "Really? Is he going to help you? It's been two years. Two. Years. The first thing I was told when I got here was that we last only a year tops, more like six months. Are you honestly stupid enough to think that you're the first little doctor he's come to? That you're special? And where are all these miraculously cured doctors now, Missy?"

Missy bit her lip.

I pressed closer into her space, my mouth just an inch away from hers as I whispered in a low hiss, "You're not even on his radar, you moron. You're just the latest in a long line of assistants, just like I'm the latest donor." I felt another surge of rage as I watched her, "He doesn't know how to do this to anyone but a certain blood type, you idiot."

Missy glared at me, but to my shock, put the gun down behind her. She stepped forward, her huge eyes searching mine. I watched her mouth intently as her jaw set. She instead took a deep breath, and I felt something pierce into my leg. A thick needle was buried in my upper thigh.

I swatted the needle away and the empty syringe tumbled to the floor. I reached for my knife as Missy darted away from me.

I felt an odd, warm sensation near my thigh. I sneered at her. *I felt perfectly fine.*

I lunged across the room at her. She ducked, knocking over an array of equipment. The loud crash brought a guard into the room. Missy and I both froze.

The guard looked between the two of us, unsure who was attacking who. "Just a misunderstanding," Missy said airily. I hid my knife behind my back. This was the same guard Missy had watching Braeden's hospital room.

He looked around uncertainly. "No blank-outs happening?" He asked. Missy shook her head and waved him off. Somewhat reluctantly, he left the room.

Once the door clicked shut, I took my knife out from behind my back. "I'm not going to die here. Not for you, or anyone else."

She eyed my blade a little apprehensively in my hands. I lunged at her again and tripped, stumbling to my knees. My legs didn't seem to want to cooperate. Missy smiled triumphantly as I fought to regain my feet.

She moved closer to me. I clutched my knife and swiped it at her. It hit nothing but air. As I brought the knife back towards me for another slash, my fingers felt thick and clumsy. The blade flew free of my hands, clattering uselessly across the room.

I battled to stay upright, but it was futile. I collapsed.

Missy caught me. "You're lucky I need you alive. Because I've got a solution," her breath was hot in my ear as she growled, "and it's in your bones."

I sluggishly tried to throw her off me. Like swimming in molasses, I moved my hand to hit her in the chest, but I couldn't seem to raise my arms. She slipped a zip tie around my wrists.

Missy grunted as she hoisted me onto the gurney. There was a prick on my arm, and a familiar sensation as something else flooded my system. I started to gag a little bit, but in horror, I realized that I was having trouble breathing.

I lay on the hospital bed, gazing at the ceiling when Missy grabbed me by the throat and forced my head back.

I was choking. *Please let someone help me.*

Frozen in my own body, I felt her fingers probing at my throat while she held my mouth open. Something suctioned my tongue as she forced a large plastic apparatus in my mouth and down my throat.

My brain was screaming. My body was useless.

She was going to suffocate me.

Panic flooded my system with adrenaline, but nothing happened. After a few moments of Missy moving around me, I heard the familiar beeps of a machine to my left. An odd feeling hit my chest as it rose and fell, while Missy gently squeezed a balloon. She threw a blanket over my prone body and bound wrists, buzzing for one of the nurses to come assist her.

Shortly, I felt quite warm and drowsy. Fighting my own body was useless; I felt myself falling asleep. The last thing I saw was Missy's blue eyes sparkling from behind her mask as she placed drops into my unblinking eyes.

My own loud snore roused me from the light sleep that I had slipped into. I was being wheeled through the corridors; my tongue was fat and unhelpful in my mouth. Missy was still squeezing the balloon above my head, forcing my breath.

I had trouble recalling where I was.

Is this the virus? Or whatever Missy did to me?

I saw an unfamiliar man peering over me, wearing a Facility uniform. "She's sedated and heavily confused," Missy said. "Please fetch Dr. Runar for me. Tell him Dr. O'Donnell needs to see him in the O.R. immediately."

"Which operating room?" The Facility member asked.

Missy stroked my hair as I tried to gurgle out that I

needed help. "He'll know which room; it's already been prepped. Please hurry." The member looked at me sympathetically before rushing off to retrieve Braeden.

I was rolled into the darkened hallways of subbasement two. "Thank goodness." Braeden's voice was filled with such warmth that I almost forgot he wanted me dead. He bent down over my bed, examining my slouched face and paralyzed body.

"What did you give her?" he asked.

Missy shrugged. "A sedative and neuromuscular blockade… she didn't want to come willingly." She jostled my unresisting body. Braeden smiled with satisfaction as he stood up to his full height over me.

"How long ago was that?" He asked.

Missy glanced at the clock hanging on the wall. "I'd say about five minutes ago. We've got less than ten to get her ready."

Braeden sliced through the zip ties, and my hands flopped uselessly to my sides. I noticed that my fingers could twitch a little bit.

"Not so easy to run this time, is it?" he whispered into my ear. His breath sent a chill down my neck. I wanted to recoil in disgust, but my body refused to cooperate.

"You know, I got soft for you. I almost wanted to let you live. At the start, I had planned to drive you from the Facility in a rage, and then hunt you down and harvest your brain. You were so angry and unwilling to listen to orders. But then, Kaye and I were injured at the same time. And you came. Then, I didn't want to hunt you down like an animal. I was hoping I could find a way to prolong it, maybe find your father…to save you," he whispered against my temple and softly kissed my cheek. I wanted to cry, but my open eyes remained bone dry.

The two of them pushed my bed into the room, the old Treatment Unit 4. The cosmic irony made me almost want to laugh and cry at the same time. The same room in which I had spent so long trying to save my life, was going to be the room where I died.

Braeden and Missy both hoisted me up by the elbows and roughly tossed me onto the metal table. In a sloppily defiant act, I managed to roll off. The tube stayed in my mouth, but the balloon was ripped out of Missy's hands.

"The paralysis is wearing off."

"No shit."

I flopped around uselessly as they tried to force me back onto the table. "If you don't stop resisting, I'm going to sedate you again." Missy snarled at me and stabbed the needle into my arm, missing the vein. Braeden moved slowly and deliberately as he tightened down the straps on my body. A fiery hatred settled in me as I watched him.

"Clara, please don't look at me like that. I want you to have pleasant memories of me." It took me a moment, but a deep revulsion overcame me as the meaning of his words became clear.

He crouched down so that his face was level with mine. "Think about it this way. Think of how much your contribution is going to mean to the world. With your sacrifice, we'll be able to continue our research and find a cure. The information I have needed to live on. For the sake of humanity." He was murmuring this to me in a low soothing tone as he stroked my hair. My skin crawled at his touch.

Missy managed to hit the vein, and she gave a low, excited whistle as red swirled up into the syringe. "We're in. You can remove the breathing tube. She should breathe okay on her own."

"It's not even like you're really dying." He continued as though he hadn't heard her. "Consciousness is contained in the brain. You'll be living on. Parts of you will. And those parts will help heal the world. It's the noblest thing you can do."

His words were beginning to have their desired effect. I was relaxing as I prepared myself for the inevitable. Braeden gently dislodged the tube from my throat. Each muscle slowly released until I was completely calm. The only sign that betrayed my acceptance was the twitching of my right hand, reaching for my empty thigh holster.

My heart rate picked up as my fingers brushed against the neoprene and nothing else. *They took my blade when they subdued me. Or did I lose it?*

I looked into his shining eyes that mirrored the night sky. I wanted to believe him so badly. But there was one question I had that I couldn't let go.

"Who's next?" I rasped nearly unintelligibly. My voice scraped like I had swallowed sand.

Braeden's eyes squinted in momentary confusion. "I'm sorry. Who's next for what?"

"After you've taken my brain, if you can't find the cure in time, who's next?"

"Your father," Missy said in a heartless tone.

My muscles tensed. Braeden continued to stroke my hair. I strained to lift my head up. "What?" Panic rushed through me, washing away some of the effects of the sedative.

Braeden spoke quickly before Missy could reply. "No." He shot Missy a look. "No, not your father. We don't even know where your father is. How are we supposed to find him?"

Missy stopped fussing with my IV and stared at Braeden in confusion, "Then who are you planning to use?"

Braeden gave her a thoughtful look and said, "We just need to find new ways. And there are others. We'll find them." Missy clenched her jaw and nodded.

Braeden began prepping the massive machine before he interrupted Missy.

"Doctor? Can you please give me a hand? It's almost

time." He held up a syringe. Missy took the syringe and flicked it as she held it up to the light.

"Is this the anticoagulant for the heart-lung machine?" She asked, still flicking the syringe. He nodded.

Braeden rolled up his sleeve and held his arm out to Missy. She placed the needle down and wrapped a piece of rubber around Braeden's strong bicep. Soon, large veins bulged down his arm. Missy placed the line, picked up the syringe, and administered the dose.

I found myself a little fascinated by watching the play of his muscles as she undid the rubber around his arm. I shook my head to clear it. Involuntarily, my muscles spasmed, and I felt a little room being made against the restraint on my right arm.

Confused, I looked at my wrist. The underside of the restraint was still frayed and clumsily tied from my fight with the Rotter, Meredith. I tugged at the bond a little harder. It gave again. I rocked my wrist back and forth as the stitching became further undone. My eyes were trained on Braeden and Missy. They were too busy fussing over the images from my MRI decorating the room.

I went still when Missy turned around and approached me. She opened a little package and inserted something that looked like a plastic banana into the casing and tipped it with a razor.

I forced myself to stay still as she placed electric clippers to my forehead and ploughed them through my hair. I couldn't help the tears that streamed down my face as hair fell around my head. Missy was nonsensically hushing me as she bared my scalp.

Braeden stalked through the operating room, shirtless, like some demi-god. He languidly lined up the tubes to his veins. I held my breath as he aimed the needle, waiting for my chance.

Missy was still busy with my hair. I clenched and unclenched my toes. Whatever paralyzer she had given me was wearing off. When she turned away to grab some antiseptic foam, I yanked my hand free.

My fingers wrenched into her curls and I slammed her temple onto the metal table. She stumbled, and I slammed her head again. Her eyes showed nothing but white as she collapsed. Braeden swore and tried to leap forward, but the tubes connecting him to the machine held him back. I frantically undid my restraints and ran. In a rage, he threw the instrument tray at me. I ducked most of the flying metal, but a scalpel slashed my left side. I shrieked as blood began to pour from the wound. I leapt over Missy's body and left behind that damned Treatment Unit 4.

CHAPTER TWENTY
The Healing Garden

I tore through the hallways and heard his footsteps right behind me. I ran up the stairs towards the atrium, holding onto my bleeding side. *I needed to get my hands on the Medi-kit in my ration bag.*

At the main room in the subbasement leading to the stairwell, his footsteps stopped behind me. I glanced back to see he had punched in the access code for the Facility's P.A. system. Ignoring that, I continued to sprint up the stairs to the atrium.

The automated voice echoed throughout the stairwell as well as the rest of the Facility. "All able-bodied personnel, please report to the atrium for counting. Security detail for emergency wards on floors nine, twelve, and seventeen only. A member of the Resistance is within the building." I heard his footsteps behind me, but they were quickly drowned out from the mass rumbling that came from upstairs.

Braeden's voice was ominously close behind me. "Clara, get back here! You already need to be patched up again!"

He caught me on the stairs. His hand grasped my upper arm, while the other hand wrapped itself in my half-shaved hair. He jerked my head back so that I was looking directly into his eyes.

"I mean, really, Clara. Where are you expecting to go?" I slammed my elbow into his gut, winding him. He doubled over. I kicked him as hard as I could in the knee. His kneecap made a loud popping noise on impact, before he tumbled down the stairs.

Clutching my bloody side, I ran full tilt towards the elevators. Tears streamed down my face as I pushed myself to make an escape. I ignored Jade's warning about my leg, hoping the bandages and new patch would hold.

I made it inside the elevator and hit the doors closed. They moved glacially slow while they shut. Cursing loudly, Braeden hobbled across the atrium after me.

I held the buttons down as the elevator zipped straight to the fourteenth floor. *I just needed to get the Medi-kit to heal my side, and then I was off. No sense in running away just to die.* The words echoed in my head like a mantra, until the doors dinged open.

The Healing Garden was sparkling and quiet in the moonlight. I darted across the room to the corridor, hugging close to the shadows along the wall. The lights were out, and the darkness took on a menacing shape. The only illumination came from the ghostly silver streaks of moonlight that reflected off the snow. Pain spasmed up my side. I pressed my hand over my shirt, and it pulled away red.

Hobbling and clutching my side, I tried to tiptoe as I ran, but in the utter silence, my footsteps rang throughout the halls. I cursed and decided that it was necessary in order to move quickly. The elevator doors opened, and I threw my hand over my mouth to muffle the whimpering that came from my throat as I pressed onward.

I got to my room and shut the door quietly, locking it.

I leaned against the door, squeezing my eyes shut tightly to clear away the tears that were pooling. My breathing was ragged and gasping. Steeling my nerves, I looked for something to barricade the door. Heavy footsteps echoed loudly down the hallway. I grabbed a thin metal chair and wedged it underneath the door handle. Not feeling secure enough, I also slid my nightstand against the door, kicking aside the brown leather satchel containing the diary and notebook.

I leapt from the door as the knob began to rattle violently. My barricade, by some miracle, held strong.

The rattling stopped.

"Open the door, Clara." His voice sounded calm, almost pleading. My heart crashed against my ribcage, like a trapped bird. He cajoled and pleaded through the door. When his words were met with silence, he realized I was not going to open it for him. Suddenly, his sweet promises turned into shouts of rage and a litany of insults. Shaking, I looked around the room. The ration bag Jade left for me was gone. I tried not to panic and pressed my hand to my side, tighter. Before I left the Facility, I needed to either get patched or cauterized... or at least find a lighter. The memory of burning my torn flesh was still fresh in my mind. I began to tremble violently.

I shook my head to clear it.

This was not the time for a panic attack.

I was desperate, trying to work out how to escape the room. The walls were too thick for me to get through, and the windows didn't open. Sparkling behind the glass, shone the Healing Garden, looking calm and inviting as the snow drifted upon it. I eyed the window.

I bet that glass will shatter easily enough.

A loud bang from the door made me jump.

I pushed my other chair over by the window and clambered up. I grappled with the curtain rod for a few moments before I removed the long metal pole from its holdings. Suddenly, the banging stopped, and all was quiet outside the door.

I felt a renewed sense of urgency, certain he was getting the key to my room. I smashed the iron rod again and again into the thick window. Finally, the tip of the pole pierced through; a fine sprinkle of shards hit the snow outside. Cracks darted away from the hole as the wind whistled through it.

The first icy blast of wind hit my face, and I felt myself break out into a huge smile. *You're not going to kill me tonight.*

I smashed around the edges of the hole. Shards rained into the thick snow as it slowly got big enough for me. Once I could fit through without skinning myself, I grabbed a thick comforter from the bed. It covered up the remaining glass edges that lined the window frame. I threw the curtain rod out of the hole, and the movement caused me to double over momentarily, hands pressed painfully into my side. Both of my palms were smeared with bright red.

I stood in front of the mirror in the bathroom.

I blinked in confusion before I realized what had happened. Shaking my head, I quickly washed my hands, blood swirled down the drain.

I went back into the main room, pulled on my heavy winter coat, grabbed my knife and satchel, and jumped through the window. My boots crunched in the snow. I stood amongst the glass flowers.

My breath ghosted in front of me as I reached down for the curtain rod. My damp hands froze to the pole. It stung like fire, and I swore loudly as the cold fused my skin to the metal.

I let out a small hiss, clutching my hands and the rod close to my chest, I ran across the courtyard.

The sparkling snow was white and unbroken. The glass

orbs seemed alien underneath their dusting of powder in the moonlight.

I arrived at the opposite side of the garden. The small door was locked, so I turned to the great windows facing the sitting room and smashed the pole into the glass. It barely made an impact. I pulled back to strike again when I heard a crash from behind. I glanced back to see furniture askew in my room as Braeden's silhouette was clambering through the hole in the window.

I turned to the one in front of me. Hairline cracks ran away from the impact points in the glass. I bit the inside of my cheek hard enough to draw blood. Tears froze on my eyelashes and down my cheeks. The coppery taste exploded over my tongue. My vision focused, and suddenly I felt superhuman. I slashed one last time, and the glass shattered.

I almost cried with relief as I began to climb through the window, but suddenly there was a sharp tug on my hood, and I stumbled backwards.

"Gotcha," Braeden growled. I threw myself onto him, using the momentum to catch him off balance. He tripped over the plastic hedging that swirled around the garden, and the two of us smashed into the flowers. The glass bulbs shattered like fireworks into hundreds of sharp spikes. One purple bulb gashed deep into my arm and another tore through his hand. The white of my coat quickly turned sodden and red from the outpouring of blood.

I scrambled away from Braeden as he tried to regain his footing. His bloodied hand grabbed onto the metal stem of a flower. The ice-burn distracted him, but his blood poured so fresh and hot that his hand quickly unsealed from the metal.

I picked up the curtain rod and swung it at his head as hard as I could. He ducked, and in the time it had taken me to right myself, he tackled me to the ground.

I shrieked in pain as my injured side collided with cement. He was on top of me, and his bloodied hand clamped down over my mouth. I bit down hard into the warm flesh of his palm. Another flood of copper hit my tongue, and I felt almost drunk at the taste.

"You bitch!" He snarled.

He jerked his hand back automatically, but I didn't relinquish my hold. A small bit of his skin tore away into my mouth as he wrapped both his arms around my shoulders, his body pressed into my back.

I popped the button from my coat and wriggled free of his grasp. Spinning around, I slammed the palm of my hand as hard as could into his nose. His head flew back, but he managed to grab my left wrist.

I twisted away from him; my right hand reached for my thigh. His eyes widened at the sound of singing metal as I unsheathed my blade. I pulled my hand back to deal a fatal blow when he slammed his fist into my gut.

Gasping for air, I stumbled backwards and fell from the hit. He stomped his boot on my right wrist, atop the first patch he did on me. My fingers spasmed, and the blade sunk into the snow. He kicked hard, and I lost sight of my knife.

Rolling onto my stomach, I tried to get some distance between us. Braeden reached down to grab my leg, and I kicked him as hard as I could. My boot connected with his injured knee. He howled and sunk to the ground. I flung snow to the left and right, trying to feel the cold metal of my only weapon.

The snow turned red as I searched for my blade. Dozens of slices covered my hands from the broken glass. Purple shards from the flowers glinted innocently in the fresh snowfall. Suddenly, I found a thin shard of glass. Braeden's hand wrapped around my leg and I struck. I slashed frantically at his arms and face. He wailed and recoiled as blood began to pour from his forehead and down into his eyes. My own palm bled freely and dripped down my arm.

The cuts were shallow but bled heavily. As I retreated, my knee knocked something solid.

Relief, so intense I almost moaned, flooded my veins. My heart pounded stronger as I retrieved my cold knife from the snow.

Pulling myself to my feet, I ignored the bleeding man next to me. The slashes I'd made against his arms did not slow in bleeding like mine had. Feeling stronger than I should have, I waded through the snow towards my room, leaving him to live or die.

My only goal was to get away from this place.

I shrieked as Braeden slashed the tendons behind my knee, and I fell into the snow. The blood smeared down his scowling face like war paint.

He stood and hobbled towards me. My fist was still clutching my knife, buried in the snow, hidden from view. I shifted my fingers along the blade until I felt the grip of the handle. Leaning onto my left hip, I tensed my arm, willing him to get close enough.

I tapped into a flood of adrenaline in my chest and felt an instantaneous rush as my heart began to thrum wildly. I became razor focused as he drew closer... and closer....

He snarled as he grabbed me by the hair. I didn't bother blocking it. He wanted me alive and that gave me an advantage.

I punched his knee again, causing him to sink to the ground. I pushed away, favouring my non-injured left leg. With a fistful of inky hair, I jerked his head back and sank my knife through his throat, thrusting it as hard as I could sideways. His eyes went wide, and he gurgled, choking on his own blood.

I pulled the knife free and plunged it into his chest. Three, four, five times... losing count in my frenzy.

My arm became tired, and the knife slipped from my fingers as his body fell into the snow. The cold suddenly hit me as the adrenaline faded. I collapsed into the snow next to him.

The stab wounds only trickled now. The blood ran thick around us, steaming as it began to pool.

Finally, there was stillness.

CHAPTER TWENTY-ONE
The Snowfall

My breathing was ragged and raw, as a sob wrenched from my throat. Exhaustion and cold settled over me like a heavy quilt. I curled up next to his cooling body as tears began to pour down my face. My whole being shook, though I was not sure if it was from the cold or adrenaline. Snowflakes against the black sky looked like infinite stars.

The air fell out of me as my breathing began to slow. My tears stopped, and a feeling of calm acceptance overcame me. My side spasmed from the injury, and I pulled myself upright, trying to gather my wits about me.

I was going to die unless I got moving.

I tried to tap into my adrenaline, which was usually heightened by the virus, but instead, I just felt cold and empty.

Slowly, I pushed myself into a sitting position. The exertion caused my breathing to come in sharp, little gasps. My arms shook as I tried to pull myself to my feet and fell again.

It was no use. I couldn't get out of here alone. My eyes closed as I started to slip away into darkness.

With a final burst of energy, I lifted my eyes and screamed one long unbroken cry.

Fat snowflakes fell over me as I lost my breath and the will to keep trying. My hair was dusted completely white. Braeden's skin looked waxy underneath the pure snow. Preparing to fall asleep one last time, I searched for the moon. Instead, my eyes landed on something else.

Aidan's face was pale behind the glass. His eyes darted between me, hunched over and bloodied, and Braeden's prone body, my dagger buried to the hilt in his chest.

Aidan disappeared like a phantom.

Maybe he was never really there anyway. I had lost a lot of blood.

I fell silent in the snow beside Braeden's body.

No more tears came. Braeden's blood froze my skin to the cement. His lifeless eyes stared up at the midnight sky. A thousand stolen kisses ran through my mind.

"He attacked me," I whispered this to myself repeatedly.

He didn't love me. He was going to kill me.

The marks on my shoulder peeked through my torn jacket. My gut twisted. The patch was perfect. Braeden was nothing short of a perfectionist.

All that knowledge was gone now.

The snow blanketed both of us in gentle flakes. In the cold, I felt deep exhaustion creep over me again. My breathing slowed. *Maybe sleep wasn't so bad.* My eyes fluttered shut again.

As I began to fade, I heard a crash in the distance.

Aidan and Jade were framed by the shards of the window. Aidan tried to widen the hole, but Jade impatiently pushed him off to the side and clambered through. She waded her way through the snow, tripping a little as it deepened. I heard him frantically shouting to her through the window, "I saw the fight from the seventeenth floor where I was patrolling. When I saw who it was…" he trailed off.

Her one eye went wide when she saw Braeden's motionless body; my dagger still plunged into his heart. "Jesus, Clara. What happened?" Her breath escaped in a mist before her. Thick flakes sparkled in her white hair. Her eye darted between my partially buzzed head to Braeden's. The lines Missy had drawn on his scalp were still visible, and Jade frowned.

I opened my mouth a few times, trying to explain. "It's in the blood," I said. I closed my mouth. "The blood, he said my blood was special. And family. His family had the blood too. But now he doesn't have any family."

Jade's eyebrows knitted into a frown. She didn't understand me, and I let out a frustrated noise.

"It's my blood!"

"No, Clara. That's Braeden's blood." She spoke slowly, shaking her head. I closed my eyes tightly; I could see the bruises spreading and darkening. *I was going to lose my damn mind before anyone understood this.* I looked at Braeden's hands. The edges of his fingernails had the same bruising.

In response, I lurched my way over to my forgotten satchel. She flinched as I trudged towards her. I stopped dead in my tracks and tossed the notebook cataloguing Missy's operations. Jade caught it sloppily, her eye focused on my distraught figure. Not looking away from me, she slowly bent down and collected the papers, saving them from the growing puddle of blood. I sat on the ground beside Braeden's prone body as she picked them up, apparently in shock.

Jade only broke her stare when she flipped open the notebook and began to read. She glanced at me occasionally, but I could see that the more she read, the more absorbed she became. "Jesus..."

She put down Missy's notebook and stared at me and the corpse.

"How long has he been dead?"
"What?"
"How long has he been dead?"
"Not long."
"How long!" She shouted, and I jumped.
"Five minutes? I'm not sure." My thoughts were jumbled in my head. Her face shifted from a look of panic to a blank mask.
"Good. Come with me." Jade's voice was cold and distant. Her demeanour had changed from one of panic to an eerie calm. Her previous fear forgotten, she offered herself as a crutch for me to hold onto as I hobbled my way out of the garden.

Aidan moved over to help us. "Here, I can take her to the medical ward." he said. Panic rose in my chest. Jade glared daggers at him, as she hugged me a little closer to her body protectively.

"No, go fetch my assistants, Dave and Kristin." She paused and looked down at me. "What room did he and O'Donnell have you in?"

"Subbasement two. They converted the old treatment units." My voice was weak.

"The one where they bricked off the stairwell at subbasement one?" She asked, and I nodded.

She faced Aidan again, "Find a sledgehammer and break down the wall in the stairwell of subbasement one to get to subbasement two. Send Dave down to subbasement two, tell him to do a base-prep of the O.R. Tell Kristin to come up here with a stretcher. Go!" I had never heard Jade sound so fierce before. Aidan only had a moment to look puzzled about subbasement two before he scurried to fetch Jade's assistants.

She pulled me through the window, and I fell to the stone floor. I was no longer shaking, but I couldn't feel anything other than how heavy my body was.

I closed my eyes.

CHAPTER TWENTY-TWO
Post-Op

Darkness.

I didn't want to open my eyes just yet. The sheets smelled funny, like antiseptic. A faint smell of mint permeated the air. *The Facility.* Blinking open my eyes, I saw that I was in the recovery ward on the sixteenth floor.

They brought the girl here when they first found her. Why was I here, though?

Whispered voices rose from behind pulled curtains. The room warped, and I squeezed my eyes shut as a pounding had started in my head. I pressed my palms to my eyes until white spots appeared. When I opened them, I was shocked. My hands, instead of being long-fingered and elegant, were short and stubby, with grubby fingernails. Two of the fingers were a different colour than the rest.

These weren't my hands.

A wave of pain hit behind my eyes. I groaned and then looked at my hands again. They looked like they should, grubby nails and all.

Was I hallucinating now?

Uncertain, I swung my legs out of bed. The shiny scar on my thin leg had been partially redone with a new patch. I ran my finger along the knotted mass of scar tissue. I reached down to my calf and lifted it, surprised to see the clean patch that Braeden had done.

I dropped my pant leg and rubbed it absentmindedly.

Where did Jade go?

I felt a simultaneous flash of worry and annoyance. Unsure what to make of these emotions, I supressed them both down.

I was probably just confused. Jade had sedated me. I must have been freaking out because of Braeden.

Braeden.

My throat constricted, and tears formed in my eyes. His smiling face almost resurfaced in my mind when blinding pain gripped my skull. I moaned and stumbled my way to the bathroom. The pain was nausea-inducing.

The reflection in the mirror made me gasp. My hair was completely shaved. The top of my skull was a patchwork of nasty markings. I turned my head. The strip of flesh that kept my skin together was almost the same shade as mine. *I wondered if the person whose scalp I was wearing had the same colour hair as I did?* I reached up to touch it.

"Careful. It'll take a bit for the bones to knit back together." Jade's voice rose from the doorway. She held a cup of coffee in her hands. Her eye was bloodshot, with a dark purple bruise underneath. I paused before my fingertips touched my scalp.

"The bones?"

She took a sip of coffee and eyed me sideways. "I'm not a brain surgeon, and my staff aren't surgical assistants, but I think we managed it."

I turned to face her. Strange memories flitted through my head.

A bone saw cutting open a skull.

I shook my head, trying to clear it.

"How do you feel?" Jade looked at me a little apprehensively. I took a moment to take stock of myself. Physically, I felt fine but a little bit groggy. However, the war of emotions and thoughts inside my head was a different story.

"I feel like there's more than one person in my head." Jade bit her lips and nodded. She had expected this. "Jade. What did you do to me?"

She swallowed hard and brushed several wisps of hair from her face. "They had already done all of the legwork, Clara." Her voice was soft as she searched my eyes, a quiet note of a plea filled her words. I already knew what she was going to say, but I needed her to say it. "All I needed to do was switch the recipient and donor. I know it was selfish. Terribly selfish. You were having blank-outs... and I couldn't stand the thought of you going like all the others, not when I knew I could try and stop it." She took a deep breath and continued, "I also knew the Facility couldn't cope with the loss of Braeden's knowledge. He was a monster, but he knew more about this disease than anyone else. Clara, I had a way to preserve that information through you. I know I used you, but we needed to do it, and fast, before the oxygen deprivation caused further damage."

I closed my eyes. *A map of my brain and her brain. There was enough overlap. We'd have to move quickly.* I felt a brief surge of anger at Piper. *She was supposed to last for a few more months, at least until Kaye's transplants had started to go.*

The memories gave me a headache.

"Where's Missy?"

"She's down in the cells where the humans were being kept." This information tumbled through my brain in a chaotic jumble. I felt a quick flash of arousal at the thought of Missy in a cage and decided to push that particular reaction way down in my mental recesses.

Braeden dead. Missy imprisoned. The enslaved humans

freed. My feeling of relief was punctuated with occasional flashes of panic. I was quite certain the panic didn't belong to me. This notion didn't sit well, so I pushed that thought down too.

"*Were* being kept?" I raised my eyes thoughtfully.

Jade nodded. "Were. They're being looked after by some of the doctors with... stronger constitutions than the others."

Thoughts began whirring through my mind, and a splitting headache developed along both sides of my skull, curling just behind my ears. I tried to brush my hair behind my ears, tracing along the path of the pain.

Instead, my fingers just met bald skin.

The surgery. Right.

I shook my head a little bit and looked into Jade's worried eye. I could tell she had slept very little, but I was unsure of how long the surgery had taken. "Also, you should know, Missy helped with the transplant. She's probably the reason you're alive right now." Her voice was quiet.

"Did she ask for anything in return?" I asked, wondering exactly what Jade had bargained with Missy.

Jade grimaced and replied, "She wants his... uh... corpse—the cadaver." A thrill of curiosity rushed over me, followed just as quickly by confusion. I wasn't sure what to make of that.

I gently pinched the bridge of my nose. "Did you ask why?"

Jade made a face again. "She said the only person she would want to speak with about that is you." My curiosity was piqued.

"How soon until I'm ready to meet her?"

Jade shrugged as she looked me over. "I've got no idea, Clara. This is brand new to me."

"I need to talk to her."

Jade nodded and then paused. "If you feel like you can talk to Missy, you should know, there are some mercenaries next door who refuse to leave until they speak to you." She sighed. "I would have them wait until you're more healed, but one is human."

We decided to meet the mercs first. The room reeked of peppermint.

The Leuko merc and his human companion sat in the corner. The human spun his knife. I felt the familiar urge to rip the human's throat out before I calmed myself. The Leuko glanced up at me and smiled. "Hey there. Glad to see you've made a full recovery."

"I thought you worked for Braeden." My voice was cold.

The Leuko grinned and stood upright. He sauntered over to me. "I've been helping Runar long before I was bitten, Miss. I know how this goes. So you can tell the bits of Braeden that are rattling around in your skull that I've upheld my end of the bargain. I want you to uphold yours."

Unfamiliar memories flickered for a moment in my mind before pain shot across my skull, making my brain feel like it was cleaved in two. I was on my knees, clutching at the sides of my newly sutured head. White-hot pain curled up around my skull as tears formed in my eyes. My mouth was open in an unending scream. I became light-headed from a lack of oxygen. My screams were cut off by shallow gasps.

A gun. Somebody get me a gun. I tried to form the words, but I couldn't get enough air. I squeezed my eyes shut, unable to move. *God, I hoped someone would shoot me.*

I felt hands on me, and someone kneeled next to me.

The pain slowly subsided. I saw Jade's scarred hands on my arm and shoulder as she tried to get me to focus on anything besides the pain. A mask was pressed over my mouth. I moved to jerk away, unwilling to be put under again.

"Hey, hey, calm yourself, Clara." Jade soothed me as one of her hands rubbed my back, the other holding the mask to my nose and mouth. "It's just a bit of oxygen to help you breathe." I closed my eyes and began to gulp down the air. Involuntary screams came with each surge of pain. Eventually, it completely died down, and I could see again.

Jade's face was worried as she examined me.

"What's happening?" She asked as I shook my head, unable to answer her. Her mouth set into a thin line. "I think we need to go talk to Missy." After a few moments when my breathing returned to normal, and the pain subsided just shy of incapacitating, she removed the mask.

I shakily got to my feet with her help. The merc looked at me and shook his head, "I'll talk to you once you've pulled yourself together a bit more. I am coming back, though." He gestured to his uninfected companion.

"Wait," I called out, my fingers outstretched. "A man named Blaise, he had a plan, something to do with me," I said, fumbling over my words as my memories clicked together like a faulty filmstrip. The Leuko turned around with his arms crossed over his chest.

"Are you asking if I know anything about Blaise? Or his plan?" He taunted. He lifted one finger and wagged it condescendingly at me. "You know the deal, give me what we bargained for first, then you and I can discuss a new bargain for information. Sound good, girlie?"

Before I could say I didn't even know what bargain he was talking about, the two of them exited the room. Jade gave them angry glances before returning her attention to me. My head was still throbbing unpleasantly, and I decided that I would ponder the Leuko and his strange bargain later.

Jade moved me to the bed and laid me down. Moments later, she reappeared with a wheelchair. As soon as she shifted me over and made sure that I was comfortable, we made our way down into the subbasement.

Sitting in one of the prison cells, recently vacated by the humans, was Missy. She looked surprisingly small and frail inside the cage.

Missy smirked when she saw me. I felt both aroused and repulsed when I saw her shiny red hair and finely boned face.

"I'm glad to see you survived." she said. I felt a moment of anger.

I did not survive. Followed by another feeling of anger. *You never intended for me to survive.*

Feeling two unique forms of rage at once shocked the emotions out of me. Light confusion and a small headache took their place. She laughed, a little tinkling sound. "I've seen that look before. How bad does your head hurt?"

My voice became lower than normal when I spoke, "Knives. It feels like knives, doctor."

She nodded like she had been expecting this. More words came to my lips, but they were not my own. "I take it from your request, you've determined a suitable method of ablation?" Missy, with her stolen blue eyes, nodded again. "Very well. I will assist with the procedure if you are confident and wish to proceed. We can begin negative eight tomorrow."

"Thank you, Dr. Runar."

ABOUT THE AUTHOR

Nora Ashe has a love of adventure and has explored sunken ships in the Great Barrier Reef, gone dog sledding in Canada, visited enchanted faerie wells in Ireland, and climbed to the peaks of the Rocky Mountains in Colorado, where she lives with her partner and dog.

Nora's helped write everything from TV scripts to case briefs, but her true passion has always been writing books. So, after a decade of travels, she packed up her things and headed home to Colorado to release her debut novel Blood and Bone.

Nora has had a love of writing dark, dystopian stories ever since she completed her first vampire novella at age eight. She majored in Creative Writing at the University of Melbourne and has published numerous short stories. This is her first novel.